GAVIN LYALL

has long been admired on both sides of
the Atlantic as a master fashioner of
sleek, tense, high-speed thrillers. Now,
after five years, he climbs to a higher
altitude.

THE SECRET SERVANT

charts a new course through the sinister
terrain of international espionage, creating a rich novel of depth, mystery, and
menace that binds one to every page and
goes on echoing long after the last one is
turned.

THE
Secret
Servant

Gavin Lyall

BALLANTINE BOOKS • NEW YORK

To the late Mrs F. Foot

Library of Congress Catalog Card Number: 80-14712

ISBN 0-345-29744-X

This edition published by arrangement with The Viking Press

Manufactured in the United States of America

First Ballantine Books Edition: November 1981

◉ 1

To Harry Maxim it seemed as if his wife died twice. He was watching the boxy little Skyvan climbing slowly away up the white-hot desert sky when it suddenly shuddered. A puff of smoke flicked out behind and immediately dissolved. Then one wing twisted gently off and fluttered away and the aeroplane was just a thing tumbling down towards the plain.

And all the time he could hear the distant whine of the Skyvan when it was still flying smoothly and Jennifer was still living. It was seconds later that he heard the thud of the explosion and the scream of an engine which had shed its propeller. He afterwards wished he hadn't listened to that.

Beside him, Sergeant Caswell muttered: "Oh Christ. Oh Christ. No. No."

The Skyvan hit the ground and exploded into a cloud of flame-filled black smoke and dust. Oddly, that seemed to make almost no sound at all. Maxim turned away back towards the Land-Rover. Some part of his mind was carefully sorting and filing his impressions for the court of inquiry, or whatever they might call it. Another part wanted to get out and drive and shoot—particularly shoot.

Caswell hurried after him. "Harry, *Harry*. Major!"

At four o'clock it was already dusk in the tangled garden beyond the french windows. Gerald Jackaman was a neat man and he'd wanted to get the garden straightened out, but he had absolutely no touch as a gardener, and together with the pressure of work, the time he'd had to spend in Brussels . . . It was a pity, all the same.

He collected the cleanly typed pages—he was a good typist and not ashamed of it—and skimmed quickly through them. He had written in French, because he was writing to his wife, but also because it made the pages less likely to be read out in court. His French was very good, good enough for him to know it wasn't perfect. He'd like to have worked on that, too. The trouble with dying was that you had to leave so many things unfinished. It was untidy.

He clipped the pages together with the letter and laid them on top of the typewriter, then took down a decanter of port from the cupboard below the guns. How often, he wondered, have I had a drink— alone—at four in the afternoon? Well, it won't become a habit. He drank a glass quite quickly and considered a second.

I don't need it, he thought, but I can have it if I want it. I'm a free agent. I can even tear up those pages and start again in the morning as if they'd never been written. I am free.

But he knew he wasn't free. He was a civil servant and, in the end, a servant is not free. His freedom was his choice to become a servant. Young people coming into the service didn't understand that nowadays. Never complain, never explain.

Am I being too complicated? he thought. Dressing for dinner in the jungle and over-dressing? The weak joke cheered him a little.

He lifted down one of the Purdey 12-bores that were a little short in the stock for him because they'd been built for his father. He could never have afforded them for himself; a single gun would mop up most of a year's salary. Purdey must be building just for Arabs and property speculators now.

Automatically he put in two cartridges, then economically took one out again.

Bless me, Father, for I have sinned. The long-unspoken words seeped back into his loneliness. *Peccavi*— no, that should be *peccabo*, I shall sin. Or better still, *peccavero*, I shall have sinned. That puts it precisely. At least I got that right.

Quietly, so as not to alert his wife, he opened the french windows and stepped out into the November sunset.

"In the early 1960s," said Professor John White Tyler, "American policy became one of Assured Destruction, or Mutual Assured Destruction. M-A-D." Nobody laughed. "The American assumption was that they could, in any foreseeable circumstances, knock out twenty to twenty-five per cent of the Russian population, and from fifty to seventy-five per cent of its industry."

Tyler had a deep slow voice which became extra deep when he was lecturing, perhaps to give extra authority to his words. Eight undergraduates huddled on stiff folding chairs and watched him unemotionally. They all still wore their outdoor clothes, and the fact that they were there at all was a tribute to Tyler, since the room was heated only by a paraffin stove that did little but smell like a wet dog. Everyone on the college council agreed that something had to be done about That Room, but nobody could agree on what. So it stayed a part of the attic above the Victorian Library, draughty and uncleaned, floorboards grey and gritty, the only furniture the folding chairs, a broken ping-pong table, and a blackboard. Chalked on it was EUROPE AND NUCLEAR STRATEGY.

"Of course we don't know," Tyler continued, "just what estimates the Russians were making of what damage they could inflict on the US. But let's take the twenty per cent figure on casualties."

He put on a pair of heavy-rimmed glasses and stared at a piece of paper whose figures he knew by heart. Some figures deserved a little showmanship.

"Now . . . a twenty per cent immediate casualty figure in the Soviet Union would be about fifty-two million. In the US it would be around forty-four million. That doesn't count long-term deaths from radiation-linked diseases, of course."

He stood up, stretching carefully because the damp cold made his back feel brittle. He was past sixty now, with a small pot belly growing on what was a tall and commanding figure. His hair was neat and full and still almost black except over the ears; he had a long face and nose, rather big teeth, and a small gallic moustache. He wore a dark, rumpled tweed suit, as he

3

did on almost every occasion. Nobody minded, because they knew he was Professor John White Tyler.

"But do fifty-two million casualties really matter?" He took the glasses off and pushed them into his breast pocket. "They sound a lot, but if we stick to percentage terms, the London plague in 1665 killed nearly that many, and the Malta one in 1675 probably killed more."

One of the civilian undergraduates said: "Nobody chose to have the plague, though. I mean, they couldn't do anything but try and survive."

Tyler nodded gravely. "I agree. But the people to die in a nuclear war won't be the ones who decide to have it, either. Once any disaster has happened, the choices are simply to fold up or try and survive—and on that I think you could say the human race hasn't done too badly, so far."

"How would anybody know they'd taken fifty-two million casualties, sir?" That was one of the Army students. Usually they kept stolidly quiet in Tyler's seminars, knowing that nuclear warfare was really nothing to do with the military.

"A good point. If twenty per cent of your population has become casualties, it could be in one day, even in a couple of hours, then your communications are bound to be so disrupted that nobody can tell what the situation is for a long, long time. But what we're really talking about is the *threat* to creat those casualties, the deterrent factor, the damage the Soviet Union believes the West can inflict and which it would find insupportable."

They stared back at him, the civilians indistinguishable from the service students even by hair length. Almost all wore the same rally jackets over open-necked shirt, jersey and blue jeans. Who washes those shirts? Tyler wondered.

"Come on, gentlemen," he cajoled them. "We've already bid twenty per cent. Do I hear any advance on fifty-two million deaths? Will someone take us to sixty—that's a nice round figure. In 1968 Robert McNamara was bidding thirty per cent, over seventy-five million casualties. Can anyone do better than *that?*"

4

They chuckled nervously but said nothing. He let them think about it, making a show of easing his stiff back and walking over to peer out of the window. For once, 'peer' was the right word: the window, a Victorian imitation of a leaded Tudor oriel, was covered with a sticky brown film from years of tobacco smoke. The grass in the court below glittered in the lamplight, already covered with a fine dusting of frost.

In the far cloister a dark bulky figure moved. Just restlessly. There was no sense of menace, but Tyler would have liked the movement to have a purpose. Suddenly uneasy, he turned back to the room.

"So . . . so, have we come to any conclusions?"

Martin, a military historian, gave him his cue. "But British and French nuclear forces couldn't create anything like those levels of damage, could they?"

"It seems very unlikely. McNamara was talking about using up to 3,400 nuclear warheads, 170,000 kilotons total yield. I don't think we can foresee a scenario that gives Europe any such force. And if we assume a counter-city targetting policy, and assume further that we could knock out the sixteen biggest Russian cities west of the Volga, then . . ." he took out the useless paper again; ". . . then the maximum immediate casualties we could inflict are in the region of twenty-six million. After that, the law of diminishing returns sets in because we'd be targetting in smaller and smaller towns, so a few more warheads don't help much."

"Are you including Leningrad and Moscow?" Martin asked.

"Yes. And ignoring Moscow's anti-ballistic missile defences for the moment, too. But in the Great Patriotic War—" they chuckled at the phrase but he had them with him; "—the Russians suffered, well, the figures aren't certain, but they usually claim up to twenty million. By contrast, Britain lost under half a million dead and the United States less than 300,000—almost none of those civilians, of course. That may throw a new light on deterrence. Perhaps Europe can threaten the Soviet Union with really no more casualties than they know they can absorb fairly comfortably. After all, they did win that war.

5

"So where does that leave us, gentlemen?"

They became very quiet and thoughtful. It was important that one of them suggested the answer, so he waited. He wanted to see if the dark figure was still in the cloister, but was afraid it still would be. There had been others loitering recently, he believed.

Surprisingly, it was another of the service undergraduates who spoke up. "Then we either leave nuclear affairs to the Americans, don't we, sir?—which is just about what we're doing at the moment anyway, I think—or we try to find some unacceptable damage we can inflict on Russia that isn't just measured in terms of casualties."

It was the right answer, but he waited a little longer. Another Army student gave a murmur of agreement, out of trade union solidarity.

Tyler said: "If we can't afford to cause damage in quantity, then we should try to cause damage of quality."

"That's what I meant, sir."

"It seems like a good idea."

Carefully briefed, the porter turned them out at twenty to eight. Tyler could have held the seminar in his rooms—his set was quite big enough—but then the keenest undergraduates stayed on to argue and he had either to throw them out rudely or be late into hall. This way, he had time for a leisurely drink first. A whisky mac, he thought, on an evening like this; he was getting old for the Cambridge winters. There was nothing romantic and Dickensian about winter here, just a cancerous dampness rising from the old stonework and a wind that swept in unhindered by any hill more than a thousand feet high from well beyond Moscow itself. The traditional invasion route of Northern Europe had been plotted by the east wind long before the first Mongol horde.

He took a detour to pass through the cloister opposite the Library, but it was empty. His first thought as he reached his rooms was that he shouldn't have left so many lights on, then he saw the black figure in front of the gas fire. For a moment he just stared.

6

"Cher Maître," George Harbinger said, holding out his hand; "You do keep such a *bloody* cold university here. But say, is that a bottle of spirituous liquor I see in the corner, its cap towards your hand?"

The darkness was a thick expensive overcoat, now unbuttoned and its effect rather spoiled by a soft hat that should have fishing flies in it. Tyler went quickly to the corner and poured two whiskies, skipping the plan of a whisky mac.

"Will you come into hall?" he asked.

"No thank you, no insult intended, but I think we'd do best not to advertise your connection with the seat of the almighty." George was one of the Prime Minister's private secretaries, particularly concerned with defence and security. He was in his early forties, but his Hanoverian figure and thinning fair hair made him look older.

He took a big gulp of his drink. "Sorry to intrude like this, but had you heard about Jerry Jackaman?"

Tyler felt a sudden lurch in his bowels. "No, I don't think so . . ."

"Well, he went and *shot* himself this afternoon." George sounded more irritated than anything. "I don't know why, except that Box 500 seems to have been investigating him about something, and now the Headmaster's climbing the walls at Number 10 . . . and I'm here."

"So you are," Tyler said, very calmly. "Is there any particular reason?"

George sighed. "You did know he was very much against your appointment?"

"I had that impression."

"Was there any special reason for it, do you know?"

"I rather assumed that he didn't go along with my theories." In conversation, Tyler often ended a remark with a little chuckle, almost a grunt, as if to soften the seriousness of his deep voice.

"You don't think there was anything personal in it?"

"I never made a pass at his wife, anyway. No, I can't think of anything."

"You're quite sure?" George made his third and last try. "This is absolutely vital, I'm sure you appreciate.

7

We really must know if there are any landmines we might step on."

"I really can't think of any. But did he leave a suicide note?"

"Why does everybody call it a suicide *note?* Why not a letter or even an essay? No, nothing that's been found yet. I talked to the Kent police super myself, on the phone . . . Oh well." George finished the rest of his drink. "We're planning to announce your appointment some time after the end of term, if that's all right with you. Then you can be out of touch if you don't want the media chasing you."

"That's very kind of you, George, but I don't really mind."

"Good. We'd rather not give an *impression* of secrecy. May I use your phone?—I'd like to reassure Number 10."

"Of course. Help yourself."

George dialled the familiar number and got an immediate answer. "It's gorgeous George here, me darling, can you find me the Headmaster? And see if the office wants me for anything: I'll be on the road for the next two hours . . . I'll hold." He turned back to Tyler. "When did you first meet Jackaman?"

"I can't remember . . . soon after he went over to Defence, and that would be a dozen years ago, wouldn't it? He was just one of those people who kept cropping up around the circuit, at defence seminars and Brussels and so on."

George grunted. "The moment we make the announcement—and it could leak before—you'll probably get the cads and rotters from Greyfriars prowling around. If you notice anything, let me know, will you?"

"Of course."

George suddenly lifted the handpiece to his mouth. "Yes, it's me. I'm in Cambridge and I'm assured there's absolutely no connection at this end . . ."

Putting on his gown for hall, Tyler wondered why George, with his impeccable background of a landed family in the west country, Marlborough and Christ Church, always talked of the Soviet Bloc secret services in the language of the old lower middle-class schoolboy comics. Perhaps the answer was in the question: to

George, the KGB, GRU, the Czech STB and all the others *were* lower middle-class cads and rotters.

But that didn't explain why schoolboys had ever wanted to read comics about schools. This time, he locked the door as he went out.

◙ 2

Maxim came to Number 10 in the second week of January.

The Prime Minister had five private secretaries, but only two were in the house that Monday morning and only one of them had a hangover. It had to be George Harbinger. He was sitting at his desk and trying to remember what he had said to—or about—his brother-in-law that had caused Annette to drive him back to London in total silence for the whole hour and a half.

He had no intention of regretting whatever he had said. He just wished he could remember it.

In the corner, the duty clerk shuffled the morning post as quietly as he could and answered the telephone quickly, in a hoarse whisper. With luck, it should be an easy day. Everybody knew the PM was in Scotland, getting photographed with some aspect of North Sea oil, so the flow of calls and callers should be reasonably light. There was just the paperwork. The paperwork always ye have with you. George took a sip of coffee, which had got cool and very nasty.

Now that's odd, he thought. You can drink hot coffee and cold coffee but never cool coffee. Yet you can drink hot tea and cool tea but never cold tea—except for tea without milk, which is a whole new ball game, as our Big Brothers would say. A fairly philosophical thought for the way I feel now, he decided, and began to feel better. Then Sir Anthony Sladen came in.

"George," he said, with exaggerated politeness, "you are looking particularly terrible this morning." He went over and laid the key to the Cabinet Office door on the duty clerk's desk, as security demanded. It was a pompous affair and Sir Anthony deliberately made it more so.

"Do you think," he asked the clerk, "that you could rustle me up a cup of the same? Our girls seem to have hit on a cheap offer of charred sawdust. What time's the PM due back?"

"About six," George said.

"I must say—" Sladen sat down: "that Aberdeen is becoming the political spa of our time. Our masters go there to take the oil as they might once have gone to Baden-Baden to take the waters."

George forced a smile. The joke had a well-polished sound, particularly in Sladen's high Church of England voice. Perhaps ten years older than George, he was a tall thin man with a tall thin face and slightly curly dark hair going grey in just the right places. He was one of two deputy secretaries to the Secretary of the Cabinet and very nearly a very powerful man. From here, his career could go on up to the topmost bananas, or just out along the branch to drift off with the dead leaves, though in neither case would he die poor.

Sometimes, George thought, he could smell fear in Sir Anthony Sladen.

A messenger brought in Sladen's coffee and they chatted meaninglessly for a while. Then Sladen said: "Am I right in thinking that we are about to have a new face in our midst? And that he's a military gentleman?"

"He's an officer so I assume he's a gentleman."

"I don't quite understand why *military*."

"Why not? Maybe the Headmaster's looking for the old virtues—clean in thought, word and deed."

"It's all rather a long time ago, but aren't you mixing him up with the Boy Scouts?"

George shrugged. "Maybe the Headmaster is, too. Our chap's done two tours in the Special Air Service and you know how prime ministers are about that."

"I do indeed," Sladen said gloomily. His own view of the SAS was that it simply trained up, expensively, soldiers who promptly went off and became over-paid mercenaries in African troubles. But for politicians, the Regiment's semi-secret image—you couldn't tell from the Army List just who was serving in it at any one time—had all the thrill of election night, victory-

11

snatched-from-the-jaws-of-defeat. Send in the SAS and all will be well. Politicians loved Secret Weapons.

"I would have thought," he said, "that somebody with—say—a security background might be more . . . well . . ."

"If you mean somebody from Box 500, then you can disabuse yourself—not that I imagine you abuse yourself, either. After the Jackaman business, I spent half the night talking the Headmaster out of setting up a select committee on security. They deserve it, but we can't stand that sort of thing, with the security service splattered all over the front pages."

"Indeed, no." Sladen—in fact the whole Cabinet Office—hadn't known how close the PM had come to an open row with M15. That titbit alone justified his visit. "But if not that, then why not someone fairly harmless, like a retired policeman. With a Special Branch background, of course."

"This is not a job creation scheme," George said testily, speaking through the jungle drums of his headache. "It's . . . just call it an experiment. We can unattach an Army man at any time. If we got some retired copper, we'd be stuck with him until he dropped dead."

"Yes, I do see that. But what is your . . . Major Maxim, is it?—what is he actually going to *do?*"

"Yes. Well. There you may have hit on the one weakness in the whole affair. *I* don't know what he's going to do. I'll try and find him something, but he's never worked in Whitehall before . . . If he just keeps the Headmaster happy, then let's just be thankful for large mercies. The one thing he *won't* do is hound deputy under secretaries into committing suicide."

"I'm sure he won't."

George looked into his own coffee and decided not. "If we can only get through the next two months or so, if the bloody French would only set a date . . ."

Sladen frowned politely and leant his head towards the young duty clerk, who wasn't supposed to hear Certain Things.

George grunted. "Oh yes, and did you hear that Box 500's appointed Agnes Algar as liaison with us? You must know her?"

The phone rang. George listened, then said clearly: "Ah, you've got Major Maxim, have you? Hold him for just *three* minutes and then shunt him along."

Sladen knew he'd been meant to hear that *three*. Dealing with George could be tricky at times. Everybody knew—or said they knew—that he would inherit a large piece of Gloucestershire the moment his father died, which couldn't be long now, as everybody had been saying for a long time. Trying to lean on a man who may have no long-term ambitions in the service is like leaning on a ghost. Of course, that might be why the PM had snatched George away from Defence to become a private secretary.

"Have you met this galloping major?" he asked.

"Not yet. Sir Bruce gave us a choice of three—on paper. You know the Army: tell them who to appoint where and they scream like a trade union. We just have to take what's the special offer of the week."

"Ah yes," Sladen said sympathetically. "I assume he's properly house-trained and so on . . . Do you want us to find him a little niche?"

If George hadn't had such a hangover, he would have seen this coming: Sladen was head-hunting. The Cabinet Office, very much bigger than Number 10, could always find room for a new face, or even a whole unit, particularly if it might mean increased influence. But the Cabinet Office was a ministry without a minister, a citadel of pure civil service power, with not a voter in sight. The locking of the door between the two buildings had a ritual significance beyond mere security.

"That's very kind," George said, "but we've already got him a little cubby-hole up on the second floor, near the Political Office. We did think of putting him downstairs, but the Garden Room girls would eat him alive, him being unwed as you might say . . ."

"D'you mean he isn't *married*?"

"Oh, don't worry, Anthony, our Major is not One Of Those. His wife got killed in an air crash—I think somebody put a bomb on board; this was out in the Gulf when he was attached to one of the local armies—anyway, I think they must have been rather much in love still. He apparently did his best to get

13

himself killed, along with whoever he could find on the other side. Well, it's a pity to waste that sort of attitude on the desert air, isn't it? There's far too many people here who spend their time looking over their shoulders at the future—don't you think?"

"Oh quite," Sladen said, suspecting that remark was aimed at himself. "D'you think that's why the PM chose him?"

"It could be, could be. I tell you what . . ." George lifted a buff folder with a red SECRET sticker on it; "This is a run-down on him that Sir Bruce sent us. Why don't you pop next door and bother Michael while you read it?"

As consolation prizes go, it was the only one going. Sladen took the folder and stood up. "To whom will he be working?"

"The Private Office. Normally that'll mean me." George was still polite but quite firm. Sladen stood up and went through the tall door into the Principal Private Secretary's room just as a messenger knocked on the passageway door.

At first glance, Maxim looked like any Whitehall civil servant. He was trying to. He wore a new blue suit, finely striped shirt, innocuous tie, carried a car-coat length raincoat over his arm and—the only individual touch—a worn soft-leather briefcase bought in a Beirut *souk*. He was just under six feet, and his mousey-blonde hair was of properly average length.

But as he came forward from the door, George saw something else: the relaxed movement of a man who is totally at home in his own body, something you find in the best ball players, in fighting men. Being overweight and not wanting even to find out how much by, George felt a pang of jealousy, then got up as fast as he could and they shook hands.

"I'm George Harbinger, we spoke on the phone. Sit down, sit down . . ."

Maxim sat on an elegant but hard dining chair, presumably chosen to discourage long-term visits. It was surprisingly warm: somebody had just spent some time there.

"This is the Private Secretaries' room," George went

on. "It's usually a good deal busier than this, but the House isn't back from the hols yet and the Headmaster's up subduing the Picts and Scots . . ." He rambled on while he watched Maxim and Maxim looked around. It was a tall, well-proportioned room with delicate mouldings, all recently repainted in golden yellow and white. Two deep sash windows looked out onto the handsome backside of the Cabinet Office and the gloomy morning beyond. The four desks gave it the look of a drawing-room which had unfortunately, but only temporarily, been turned into a place where work had to be done.

In the corner by the far window, the duty clerk was staring openly at him. Maxim smiled back. He had a thin, slightly concave face with lines beside the nose that made him look older than thirty-five, and a quick reflexive smile which sometimes got there ahead of the punch line of a joke, which was disconcerting.

George wound up. "We've found you a little nook a couple of floors up. Not so grand, but a lot quieter. Are you all ready to move in?"

"Yes, sir."

"No, no. Don't call anybody 'sir' around here. Except back-bench MPs, it makes them feel loved and wanted, but we don't usually let them into Number 10 until after dark. You call the Headmaster 'Prime Minister', that shouldn't be too difficult to remember, and you call ministers 'Ministers,' I'm George, you're Harold, is it, or Harry?"

"Harry, usually."

"Cry God for Harry, England and Saint George, with particular attention to poor George." He tried to rub the hot feeling out of his eyes and stood up at his normal speed. "I'll lead the way."

From the corner, the duty clerk said softly: "Don't let him lead too far. He's a bad man. He drinks at lunch-time."

"Lies, all lies," George said calmly. "I just happen to lunch at drinks-time." He took Maxim back into the corridor, past a modernistic agency tape machine and up the main staircase, tapping a fingernail on the silvery silk wallpaper. "The taxpayer's done a good job, don't you think?"

Sir Anthony Sladen sat at the Principal Private Secretary's desk—he was away with the PM in Scotland—and read carefully through Sir Bruce's letter about Maxim.

Malaya, Borneo, Oman," he counted. "Germany of course, Northern Ireland of course, the Gulf again . . . at least he's got his knees brown."

At the second desk—the room was rather smaller than the one next door—Michael Gale looked up from his paperwork. "Who *are* you talking about?"

"Major Harold Maxim. Your new club member."

"Oh, the soldier." Gale went back to work. He dealt with foreign affairs, which didn't include defence since George had been brought in.

Maxim, Sladen saw, had even managed to get himself wounded—quite badly, though recovery was supposed to be complete. But it had been an expensive wound, losing him six months at a vital stage in his career. For a man who hadn't come in through Sandhurst, it might be decisive. He had made it to major but not to staff college, and that was when you found the up staircase bricked off. Maxim could stay a major for the next twenty years, until the Army had fulfilled its bargain of giving him a career until age fifty-five.

And a very old fifty-five he would be by then, Sladen thought. It was an odd choice for Number 10, where the best was supposed to be barely good enough.

Then he said: "Good God."

Gale sighed without looking up. "What do we have now?"

"He's got a boy, a son."

"They're usually much the same thing."

"But George said he was trying to get himself killed, after his wife died . . ."

Still without looking up, Gale slapped down his pen. "Are we to understand that, on top of all else, he has a personal problem? That is approximately all that we need. I shall never understand why we did this. Security is Five's job."

"Well, as George was saying, after that Jackaman business—"

"Exactly. After that, we'd got them so agitated that they'd have promised us anything. For once, we'd got

16

security under control. Now they'll just sulk and start plots . . ." He sighed again and picked up his pen. "Has he got here yet?"

"George is meshing him into the machine now."

It might once have been a box-room or a servant's bedroom. "Not so wide as a well nor so deep as a church door," George commented, "and about as friendly as Death Row, but 'twill serve. Or if it doesn't, there's nothing we can do about it, though if you scream loud enough the Housekeeper's Office might change the furniture."

At the moment, the furniture was a roll-top desk straight out of Pickwick, a mahogany desk chair, a second and completely plain chair, a hatstand, a small bookcase and a standard Government issue filing cabinet with a lock that Maxim could bypass in five seconds. It all filled the room quite thoroughly.

He hung his raincoat on the stand—a flag-raising ceremony, perhaps—and sat in the desk chair. It creaked wearily.

George picked up the phone and told the switchboard: "Major Harry Maxim is operational at this extension as of now. All right, me lovely? Splendid." He put down the phone. "They say we've got the best switchboard in the country, they can find you anybody anywhere. But always let them know where *you* are, will you? It's slightly vital."

He lowered himself carefully onto the second chair. He was wearing a well-cut suit in a light check, a Dragoon Guards tie and well-polished but well-worn brown brogues. George, Maxim came to learn, always dressed as if he were just about to leave for Goodwood.

Maxim opened his briefcase and took out what looked like a bundle of leather and elastic straps. "Do you think I could get a small safe up here?"

"A safe? If you're handling any classified material you give it in to the Confidential Registry at night. I suppose you could always bring the family heirlooms in— Oh I *see*." He had suddenly realized that the bundle was a shoulder holster, complete with revolver.

"Have you been carrying that all over. . . ? Well, of

course. They wouldn't search your case, you being family now. Was this Sir Bruce's idea?"

"He thought I might need to get at a weapon sometime without having to run round to the Horse Guards and fill in a lot of forms," Maxim said evenly. "I don't imagine it's the only one in the building."

"It certainly isn't, though in Whitehall the paperwork is generally regarded as being mightier than the pistol." George chuckled. "It does seem a bit silly to bring in a soldier and tell him to leave his gun behind. May I?" He lifted the pistol from the spring clip holster. It was an unfamiliar American make, in the usual .38 Special calibre, but surprisingly light, despite having a reasonable three-inch barrel. "Is this what the SAS sports, these days?"

"You get quite a choice."

George put the gun back carefully and waited, fascinated to see what else Maxim had in the briefcase. A sawn-off pump-action shotgun such as the SAS were rumoured to favour? A framed portrait of the dead wife? Like most good managers, George had the curiosity of a village gossip. But all Maxim brought out was *Whitaker's Almanack*, the *Statesman's Yearbook* and a pad of paper.

He's been swotting, Goerge thought. "You're all fixed up with a place to live?—yes, you told me on the phone. And you're a Londoner anyway, am I right?"

"Mill Hill."

"That'll help. And about your little boy, he's what age now?"

"Christopher, he's ten. He's down with my parents in Littlehampton. They retired there a couple of years ago, and they've found him a school locally." His voice was quite calm.

"Good. I suppose you'll be down there most weekends. You'll always let the switchboard know where . . . no, I said that already, didn't I?"

I need a drink, George thought.

"What am I going to be doing here?" Maxim asked.

"Yes. Well. Roughly speaking . . . at the Headmaster's discretion, you get first crack at any security problem we think is likely to, or might . . . cause embarrassment in the area of defence, as you might say . . ."

Sir Bruce had told Maxim: "I can't find out what the hell they want you for, but they've had a bad case of wet knickers since before Christmas so maybe they want somebody to piss on when the pot's full. You've been in the Army quite long enough to be used to that."

When George had finished, Maxim said:"I'm not a detective."

"No, we don't expect that. But you've done the Ashford course, haven't you? You can organise a surveillance and so on?"

"I've got more theory than practice."

"Well then . . . I tell you what—" George looked at his watch; "—why don't you and I slide over to Boodle's and continue the briefing there?" He looked at Maxim hopefully. Thirstily.

Maxim gave a quick smile, but wondered if this was going to become a regular invitation. George picked up the phone and told the switchboard where they'd be. At least nobody could accuse George of being a *secret* drinker.

"And one thing you won't be doing," George added, "is hounding deputy under secretaries . . . damn it, I'm sounding like a bloody Quaker. Whenever you ask them what they believe in, they start listing the things they *don't* believe in, beginning with the Scarlet Woman. But now I suppose it'll turn out you're a Quaker . . . no, I suppose not, in your job."

"My sister married a Friend. I know what you mean." And maybe, Maxim thought, I'm as close to Quakerism as to anything. Jenny would have had something to say about that, but we never got around to it. Oh, Jenny, the things we never got around to.

George led the way out.

◉ 3

Maxim had run a company office in a wrecked armoured personnel carrier and the broom cupboard of a Belfast school, so a whole box-room to himself was pure luxury, and like an alley cat he stretched out and enjoyed this temporary treat. He also learned that 'room' was the right word. In Number 10 an 'office' was the Private Office, the Political Office, Press Office, and so on, sometimes whole suites of rooms.

But for all that, it went on being a house. There was an air of quiet busyness, a polite official scurrying behind every wainscot, yet in its decor, the pictures on the walls (nothing so crude as maps or charts of organisation), the whole style, it was still the town house of a duke who had occasionally to pop up to town to govern the nation instead of the partridges. The Housekeeper's Office, afraid that Maxim might forget he was a soldier, offered him a selection of solely military pictures for his own room. He chose a lively watercolour of the Mahratta Army at Seringapatam and put up maps of London and Europe on the other walls. The Housekeeper's Office expressed Unvoiced Disapproval.

"Lunch," George had warned him, "is not one of the great thrills of Whitehall. Just thank your choice of career that you aren't entitled to eat in most of the civil service canteens. All fried fish and spotted dick, just as nanny used to make. But I suppose if you've spent twenty years eating in the nursery, prep school, public school and some Oxbridge hall, your taste buds must look like the Dutch elm disease."

Whitehall was, Maxim soon saw, two Whitehalls, living in the frigid intimacy of an unconsummated marriage. In between the ponderous ministry buildings, the Abbey, the Palace of Westminster itself, there had developed an undergrowth of worn-out pubs, greasy ham-

20

burger bars and small shops selling overpriced models of London buses and Big Ben.

Only the tourists bridged the gap between the two Whitehalls, standing in the January rain to photograph anybody coming out of the multi-million-times photographed doorway, then dodging across the road to buy a fresh film, a stale sandwich and an ashtray shaped like the Imperial State Crown.

Not lunchtime country.

Maxim met the Prime Minister on the third day. It was a disappointing meeting but doomed to be, because Army officers have an exaggerated respect for politicians. It can take at least ten years to design, develop, test, redesign, re-test, produce and issue a new rifle. It can take a politician ten minutes in Cabinet to argue that it's the wrong rifle and get it cancelled. The Headmaster—George called him that to his face and he seemed to like it—was shorter than he looked on television, his Scottish accent was stronger, and he spent most of the time talking about his experiences with the 51st Highland Division just before St. Valery in 1940. Maxim was used to people learning he was an Army officer and then recalling their own military careers, however brief. He was intrigued to find that it applied to Prime Ministers as well.

The PM didn't tell Maxim any more about what he was supposed to do, so for ten days he did nothing except re-arrange his room, try to work out the command structure in the house, and read some innocuous files that George sent up. Then came what was later known as the Day of the Grenade.

The first Maxim knew of it was one of the girls from the Political Office put her head round the door and said breathlessly: "You're not to go downstairs. I mean not to the hall, it's a bomb, I think they said." At the same time, the phone rang. Maxim smiled quickly at the girl, who smiled back and studied him a few seconds longer—it was the first chance she'd had—and then rushed off without closing the door.

It was George on the phone. "Not to panic, old boy,

but someody's thrown a grenade in through the front door."

"A grenade? I didn't hear anything."

"It didn't go off, not yet anyway. If you do hear anything, it'll be the Security Officer committing hari-kiri. They've sent for the bomb squad, so all you have to do is nothing."

"What sort of grenade?" Maxim asked.

"How the *hell* do I know what sort? I haven't gone and interviewed the bloody thing!" George slammed the phone down.

Maxim thought for a moment, then walked out and downstairs. At the end of the corridor leading to the entrance hall, a security guard stopped him. "There's an unexploded grenade down there, sir . . ."

"Yes. I know a bit about grenades. I just wanted to see it."

"The bomb squad's on its way, sir . . ."

"It's all right, I'm not going to practice penalty kicks with it." He stepped around the guard, who grabbed his elbow and then found his own arm almost twisted from its socket. Maxim's reaction had been quite instinctive.

"I'm sorry." He smiled at the guard and went on down the corridor.

The entrance hall was deserted, the front door slightly open. Then a uniformed policeman leaned in from the hats-and-coats lobby and said in a hoarse whisper: "Get back, sir. There's a grenade in there."

Why on earth do people always whisper in the presence of explosives? "Where?" Maxim asked.

The policeman pointed to Chippendale's huge black leather hooded chair. An olive green egg the size of a fist had rolled up on the tiles beside it. Maxim squatted down and peered at it.

"*Sir!*" the policeman squawked in what was still really a whisper. Maxim bowed down to the grenade. Telling the story afterwards, most people said he was listening to it. In fact he was smelling it. Then he got up and walked across the lobby.

The policeman had a phone in one hand; several of the messengers were peering out from behind the rack of visitors' coats.

"You can cancel the bomb boys," Maxim said. "It's a drill. A dummy." The policeman just stared at him. Maxim went back and met George coming down the corridor, very much more likely to blow up than any grenade.

"Harry, what the *hell* did I just tell you? You aren't the bloody—"

"It's a dud, a drill. But if you want a nice big news story, let the Ordnance come screaming round and put mattresses on it . . ."

The PM was out of town again, so the story lacked something already. Maybe it could be played down as just a bit of hooliganism, whatever it really was . . .

"How can you be sure?"

"Oh balls," Maxim said, and went back and picked up the grenade and held it under George's nose. "Smell it. There's no fuse been burning. Just fresh paint. You don't paint a grenade before you throw it. But the drill comes in light blue; somebody's tried to make this look live."

George pushed the grenade gently away. "Harry, if that thing were now to explode, I would *never* forgive you." He went to find the Security Officer. Maxim walked back upstairs.

George rang him just after lunch. "You are the hero of the hour. You, with your hands, nay, your own bare teeth, personally defused several time bombs within split seconds of doom and destruction . . . you haven't heard any of these rumours? Never mind, in Number 10 the hero of the hour lasts just that long. They've got the chap that did it over at the Cannon Row fuzzery and I think we ought to have a word."

"Is it all right with the police?"

"That's fine, all squared away. I'll see you downstairs in five minutes."

On the way out they passed the Security Officer. He had disliked Maxim from the very beginning; now he gave him a smile of pure hatred.

Just across Whitehall and down a side street, the police station was a shapeless grimy-black Victorian mass in the shadow of the old Scotland Yard building. They sat in the Chief Inspector's office while a sergeant took Maxim's finger-prints, since he'd handled the grenade without due care and attention.

"Our friend's name is Charles Farthing," the Chief Inspector read from his notes. "Aged fifty-one, unemployed, there's an address in Barnes that we're having checked out. He's either divorced or getting divorced, but he didn't want to say much about that."

"Did he put up a fight?" George asked.

The Chief had a skull face with curly grey hair and pale blue eyes. He obviously knew George well, but still took a cautious time before answering. "No, he came quite quietly, as I understand it. He just threw the . . . the object in through the front door, and I believe he shouted 'Grenade!' or something along those lines. Then he let himself be arrested by the constable on duty at the door."

He had, it seemed or was alleged or was held, got the door opened by saying he wanted to present a petition against some motorway scheme.

"Has he been charged?" George asked.

"Only with creating a disturbance. We're holding him so that a doctor can have a look at him, but I wouldn't say he was drunk."

"Has he asked for a lawyer?"

"No, sir. He seems just to want to get into court and say his piece."

"About what?"

"That's why I called you, sir."

George stared at his fingernails. "Is it all right if Harry here goes and has a word with him?"

"It's perfectly all right with us, sir, although the accused doesn't have to answer." He gave Maxim a warning look.

At the far end of the narrow cells corridor there was a deep washbasin where Maxim got most of the fingerprint ink off. Only one of the cell doors was shut, and on the little blackboard fixed to it was chalked

FARTHING
DISTURB

"Just so that we don't get them mixed up when the van comes for them in the morning," the Chief explained. Maxim thought of saying they'd missed out a DO NOT, but neither the dim corridor nor the occasion encouraged jokes.

A uniformed policeman peered in through the Judas window, then unlocked the door. It shut behind Maxim with the whirr and snap of an automatic lock.

The cell looked as if it should smell, but it didn't. It was long and high, lined to head height in glazed white brick and with a wide wooden shelf running right down one side. At the near end it was a bed, at the far end it became a lavatory seat. But there was no cistern or chain, from which you might hang yourself. You pressed a buzzer and sooner or later somebody came and pulled a chain in the corridor. Even the single light bulb was actually in the corridor, shining in through the thick porthole, so that you couldn't electrocute yourself or slash your wrists either.

In the gloomy light, Charles Farthing sat on the mattress puffing quickly at a cigarette. He didn't look up. Maxim walked past him and sat further down the bench.

After a time, he said: "Nice place you've got here."

"I don't come here often." The voice shook a little. He had a puffy face with sunken eyes, a big nose and thin dry hair. He wore a suit that was some years out of date and greasy suede shoes—though perhaps you didn't put on your best clothes to get arrested in.

"And who are you?" Farthing asked.

"Harry Maxim. From the Ministry of Defence."

"Oh *yes*." Farthing threw his cigarette against the wall and sparks spattered in the dimness. "The dear old Mine of Dung. They're all honourable men, there. So they sent you down here to shut me up, have they? Well, you can go and tell that I'm going to let it all hang out, as the Americans put it so charmingly. All, everything." His voice had a flatness within the anger, as if a regional accent had been carefully polished out.

"All what?"

"I'll tell the court, don't you worry. They can't stop you there."

25

"They don't let you make irrelevant speeches, either."

For a while neither of them said anything, then Maxim asked politely: "What work do you do?"

"I don't do any, do I? I was twenty years in the arms business, until you people started buying everything from Washington or the Germans. Do you know what we were doing at Warrington before I was made *redundant?* Sub-contract work on grenades—and even those were really the Yank M26."

So at least we know where the drill grenade had come from.

"And you wait and see with these anti-tank mortar trials," Farthing went on. "It'll be the same again there. You wait and see."

"Is that what you're going to say?"

"It gets worse than that, doesn't it?" Farthing looked craftily sideways.

"I've never known it when people weren't saying the country's defences were going to the dogs."

"Yes, but you people weren't always killing people and suppressing evidence to hush it up, were you?"

"Who got killed?"

"You know bloody well who!"

"Sorry, I'm new in Whitehall."

Farthing's look turned to distrust. Then he lit another cigarette, using both hands to keep the match steady. "Most people think the government makes the decisions, don't they? Or you people. But governments come and go—even you people get transferred every now and then. And you can have three different prime ministers in the time it takes to develop a new tank or field gun. But there's one man who's always there, one man who makes the real decisions and he's not the right man to do it. He'll see us all destroyed, ruined. And I'm going to say it, to tell them. Even if it gets me killed, too." He ended on an almost triumphant note.

"Who are you *really* working for?"

The questioned knocked Farthing off balance. "What . . . what d'you mean?"

"You throw a grenade in the door of Number 10—that isn't exactly a patriotic thing, is it? You say our defence is being loused up, but not how or by whom. Just whose side are you on?"

"D'you have to ask that?"

"With you, obviously yes."

"Jesus! Well, you go back and tell your bosses that the professor isn't going to . . . oh no. You slimy rotten sod. Just tell them . . . I'll say it all. I'll say it."

He threw down the cigarette and stamped on it. The floor around his feet was a mess of ash and crushed butts. Others had made their mute protests by scratching names and rude words on the paint of the door.

Maxim waited, but it was over. He pressed the buzzer by the lavatory.

"He means Professor John White Tyler, of course," George said. "It's quite ridiculous. He's probably our best theorist on defence since the war—have you read any of his books?"

Maxim nodded.

"Well . . . but he's never had any direct influence until he joined the policy review committee a few weeks ago. Ridiculous."

"What about somebody getting killed?"

"He didn't say any names?" But George had hesitated just a moment and Maxim knew he was dodging something. They were sitting in the bleak neon-lit charge room just before the cells corridor. The Chief Inspector had instinctively placed himself behind the desk, leaving Maxim and George in front about to be warned that anything they said would be taken down in writing . . .

"No names," Maxim said. Was George a little relieved?

"Well, I don't see how we can follow that up until he *does* say something. D'you think he's barmy?"

Maxim glanced at the Chief, who left the question to him. "I think that's the word I'd use. He's been out of work some time, his marriage is on the rocks, he's about broke . . . I don't know what it adds up to medically, but if he were in my company I'd make sure he stayed back and loaded blankets into trucks rather than let him near a weapon."

The Chief smiled his skull smile. "He's not too bad with a hand grenade."

"So now," George said, "he's going to stand up in court and spout a lot of rubbish with absolute privilege, no libel suits, and muddy the water properly. How long can you delay the case?"

The Chief thought carefully. "Do you think we ought to hit him with something more than just creating a disturbance?"

"What have you got on the menu?"

The Chief opened a file on the desk. "This is something fairly new, from the Criminal Justice Act 1977. 'A person who places any article in any place whatsoever, with the intention of inducing in another a belief that it is likely to explode . . .'" He looked up. "Fits him like a glove, doesn't it, sir? Up to three months on summary conviction."

"Well, how long can you wait?"

"He'll get bail, of course, even if we opposed it. After that, the magistrates won't be in any rush. I'd say five weeks, give or take."

"It's the best we can do, I suppose."

"There's just one thing," the Chief said. "The suit our friend is wearing. He was properly searched when we got him in—the suit was made in Canada. Montreal. I don't know if that means anything, sir."

They dodged through the Grand Prix of Whitehall traffic and into the backwater of Downing Street. George walked with his shoulders hunched against the wind, a petulant frown on his face. The inevitable little group of tourists goggled at them as the policeman nodded to George and had the door opened immediately. The stares still embarrassed Maxim: he always felt a fraud for not being somebody important.

Once inside, George muttered: "We are going to turn that bastard inside out. I want a witness to every breath he ever drew." He glanced at Maxim.

"I told you I'm not a detective."

"I know. This isn't a one-man job, anyway. It isn't a police job, if we've got to back-track him to Canada . . . You haven't met Agnes Algar, have you? I'll get her over."

28

◘ 4

The ladies' annex of that particular club was being re-decorated, so for a few weeks women were allowed into what was called the Library, although there was no sign that anybody ever dared touch the leather-bound books lining the walls.

George introduced them. "Major Harry Maxim—you probably know more about him than I do anyway. Miss Agnes Algar from Box 500, Five, whatever you care to call it."

"It's nice to meet a real professional," Maxim said tactfully.

"Thank you, kind sir." Agnes was about Maxim's own age, with an oval face that could be called 'friendly' and looked as if it should have freckles. She had blue eyes, a snub nose and light ginger hair cut straight but in no definable style. She wore a skirt, blouse and jacket in light brown and oatmeal shades, which most women were wearing that season. Being friendly and unmemorable was an important part of her work.

They sat on huge studded leather chairs in a corner of the room, which was long and tall enough for them to speak normally without being overheard. Agnes kept a hopeful smile on her face as she studied the man whom the Intelligence community was already calling the Unknown Soldier. She had foolishly believed that, after fourteen years of security work, she knew every stupidity that Downing Street could get up to in that field. She had been wrong. They had brought in a soldier, an *infantryman*, no matter what he might have learned in the SAS and the Ashford course. Presumably he was a crack shot and a born leader who could crawl invisibly across a thousand miles of desert, if that was any help in Whitehall traffic, but probably he knew as much about real security work as she did about the mating habits of the giant squid.

But he will pass, all things pass, particularly soldiers when their brief postings are up. Until then, she could live with it. Agnes had that most valuable of all talents in the intelligence world, something the M15 head-hunter at Oxford had hoped for but could only guess at all those years ago: loyalty that lasted beyond disillusionment.

"Does this meeting mean that we have found favour again in the eyes of the All Highest?" she asked. She had a gentle, controlled voice, more Oxford than shire.

"You have most certainly not. There are standing orders to set the dogs on any of your calling who sets foot within a quarter mile of Number 10."

Agnes could live with that, too. Prime Ministers also passed, even if each new one was just as paranoid about the security service as the last.

"All we want—" then George caught the eye of an elderly steward. "What will you drink?"

"Ow, a small tonic wiv a large gin, pleeze, duckie." Around George, Agnes often slumped into a stage cockney accent, originally intended to embarrass him, now just a habit. Maxim and George had asked for whisky and water. The steward crumbled away towards the service door.

"All we want," George went on, "is for your mob to dig up everything they can about this Farthing person *without* triggering off any nuclear disasters or Questions in the House."

Agnes kept her friendly smile and fumbled in a shoulder bag shaped like a pony express pouch until she found a notebook. "I looked up his file at the Registry."

"Was he positively vetted?"

"No, just the standard procedures when he got into armaments, and topped up from time to time. He never got above junior management and he wasn't in anything real sensitive. He was . . . born in York. No university, just Sheffield Polytechnic. Engineering, he did quite well. National Service in the Royal Tank Regiment—" George, ex-cavalry, gave a small grunt, just as Maxim had expected. Agnes ploughed on; "—became a corporal, then he was a management trainee at BSA, he got married in . . ." It was a drab, dull list of facts that got fewer and less important as Farthing grew older, until, with a cutback in defence spending, his last employer dumped him on the street.

"It sounds," George said, "as if today was the high point in his life."

"How far have we got?" Maxim asked.

"Four years ago. There's nothing after he left the arms business. Despite what some people think, we don't keep files on everybody in the country."

George asked: "What about Canada? If he was there long enough to buy a suit he must have had a job. They wouldn't let him stay, otherwise."

"He wasn't working in any defence industry. The Mounties would have vetted him and asked us what we knew."

"Unless your people lost the letter."

"Unless our people lost the letter," Agnes agreed calmly.

George made a noise that could have been apologetic. "And no connection with Professor Tyler?"

"There's no hint of it. Farthing seems to have spent his working life in the north, and Tyler's always lived in the south, hasn't he? Cambridge and London?"

"Yes. Where the *bloody* hell are our drinks?" George leant round sharply and almost butted the steward in the stomach. With dreadful precision, the old man put down the glasses in the wrong places, flooded George's whisky with too much water and went away.

"Just ain't yer night, is it, me ole china?" Agnes said. "Cheers."

George took a vast mouthful of his drink. "I want those four years filled in."

"There's two ends to the business," Agnes said.

"I know. Harry's taking the other one."

Maxim looked up. "Am I?"

"He mentioned the anti-tank mortar trials, didn't you say?"

"Yes, he said that—"

"I know. They aren't secret, but they aren't news either. There hasn't been anything in the papers."

31

"He'd still have friends in the arms business."

"That's probably it. Tyler's going to watch a demonstration by the development unit at Warminster on Monday. You'd better go, too. Get onto Sir Bruce and have yourself fixed up as Tyler's temporary ADC. And when you're with him, *listen.*"

"That's all?"

"I don't know." George looked uneasy. "And guard his back. Where there's a drill grenade there might be a real one . . ."

▣ 5

Just past Andover, they overtook a convoy of Bedfords and Land-Rovers. From the back seat of their own chauffeur-driven car, Maxim watched the dull black-and-green vehicles, feeling an unexpected pang of pleasure. Absurd, but it was partly a sense of coming home: Salisbury Plain, ringed with Army camps, covered in ranges, and with Stonehenge seemingly shunted off into one corner, was home to any infantryman.

Professor Tyler commented: "Familiar country, I imagine."

"I'd take a penny for every pace I've marched across Wiltshire. Were you here in the war?" Maxim wasn't sure whether to call Tyler 'sir' or 'professor' or just 'John', as Tyler himself had suggested. So for most the journey he hadn't called him anything.

"Only for a few weeks," Tyler said. "When we were winding up for D-Day. I did most of my training in Cumberland, before I went to Africa."

"I remember."

Tyler turned to look at him and asked in his serious deep voice: "Have you really read *The Gates?*"

"I read it when I was at school. Only in paperback, I'm afraid, sir. It might even have been one of the reasons I joined the Army." The 'sir' had slipped out naturally: now he was talking to a famous soldier. And not flattering him, either. *The Gates of the Grave,* in particular its chapters on Tyler's adventures with the bearded land-pirates of the Long Range Desert Group working deep behind Rommel's lines, had hit young Harry Maxim like a star shell. This was war as every schoolboy wanted it to be. But unlike most other schoolboys, Maxim had gone on to re-live Tyler's experiences. Now he too had driven armed trucks across hostile deserts, had lifted land-mines with his own hands, had shot his way out of ambush.

For that very reason, he had never dared re-read the book. He was frightened that he might find giveaway hints that showed Tyler had faked or exaggerated parts of it. You don't always want to meet your first love twenty years later.

"Do you know why I wrote that book?" Tyler gave one of his little grunt-chuckles. "To finance my first divorce.. Well, at least it did that. But if you're thinking of an academic career, don't ever write anything that sells well. That book kept me out of any Cambridge job for years. Hell hath no fury like a Senior Common Room seeing somebody actually make some money by publishing." He chuckled again and hunched himself down into a shabby-expensive plaid overcoat. "Are those pullovers as warm as they're supposed to be?"

Maxim was wearing the everyday Army dress of a green 'woolie-pullie'—it was the first time he'd been in uniform for weeks—and carrying a combat jacket of Disruptive Pattern Material (the Army's abbreviation of 'camouflage') which had a pistol in the side pocket. He didn't know if Tyler knew about that.

"They're pretty good. I think they're very closely knit."

"I suppose I'm growing old, but all these pullovers and combat kit jackets—you call it DPM, don't you? —it makes the Army seem rather casual."

"I hadn't thought that 8th Army set any very high standards of dress in its time, sir?"

"Good Lord, no. All those córduroy bags and suede brothel-creepers, and Monty with two badges in a Tank Regiment beret he wasn't entitled to wear . . . This country's always had a tradition of making the word 'uniform' quite meaningless when applied to military clothing. But as least there was a pretence of trying. Twenty-five years ago you couldn't go through a mainline station without seeing dozens of soldiers and airmen, all in their walking-out uniforms or whatever it was called."

"I remember."

"Now we forbid people to wear uniform when travelling, or after tea, or . . . I suppose defence was still popular in those days . . ."

"But it's a thin DPM line of heroes when the guns begin to shoot."

Tyler didn't answer and perhaps hadn't heard. He had turned away to watch the damp plain drifting past outside. Or perhaps something far further away.

Like most Army camps, Warminster barracks is a collection of unnaturally clean buildings of all ages and sizes laid out at random: a model railway village set up by a child too young for model railways. The commandant of the School of Infantry gave them a drink and chatted to Tyler throughout lunch, then passed them on to the lieutenant-colonel in command of the development unit itself.

So far, Maxim had met nobody he knew personally, but the Army grapevine had made sure everybody knew about him, once they'd heard that he would be shepherding Professor Tyler. Several officers who had never met Jenny said they were sorry to hear of her death. Maxim was growing a mental scar tissue, finding phrases to fend off commiserations that nobody really wanted to make. But suddenly, when they were drinking coffee in the ante-room, he felt a flush of anger.

God damn it, is having my wife killed the only memorable thing I've done in this Army?

It was a relief to get out into the damp cold air again.

The firing point was up on the edge of the plateau, a bleak exposed area where no commander would ever set up his mortars for real. But it gave a view of the target area, and visitors liked to see two bangs for the price of one. There was a small but permanent plank grandstand for them, already nearly filled with senior officers, including the RAF and Navy.

Maxim and Tyler chose gumboots from neat rows laid out for spectators, and clumped across the grey winter grass that looked dry and brittle even when it was squishy-wet under foot. Two of the senior officers came down to shake Tyler's hand and a sergeant appeared with an expensive camera and started taking pictures.

At that, Maxim decided that Tyler couldn't have

35

been safer locked up in the Bank of England, and faded back to talk to one of the organising officers, a Gunner major called Tom Shelford, and the first one Maxim could really say he knew. They'd worked together in Germany.

Shelford had the outdoors face of a farmer, ruddy, chubby and cheerful. "What are you doing with the mad professors, Harry? I thought you were something don't-touch-me-there in Whitehall these days?" He tapped the side of his nose conspiratorially.

"I'm just standing in as Tyler's ADC for the moment." Maxim hoped that sounded good enough.

"Nice work if you can get it. A bugger about Jenny, wasn't it?" He chattered on before Maxim could reply. "I don't know why everybody seems to think that when the cavalry gave up horses it took to *tanks*. It simply traded down to *dogs*." A small group of cavalry officers was squelching across to the grandstand, each with a perfectly groomed and disciplined golden retriever or red setter at his heels.

"At least," Shelford said, "they used to have their brains in their arses; now they're somewhere down around their *knees*. D'you want to know what you're going to see this afternoon? A load of balls, that's what. You need a point-target weapon for anti-tank work, not a barrage . . ."

His running commentary ran on as two teams from the demonstration battalion charged out from a ring of vehicles parked in the background and started assembling the competing mortars—one American, one French. The field telephone jabbered and sergeants called out fire orders—quite unnecessarily, since both teams could see their target and had known what it would be for days past.

The mortars began to fire with deep metallic *chunks*, setting up puffs of blue or orange smoke around a battered old Centurion tank, lopsided and half sunk in the turf 1500 metres away. The RAF and Navy spectators lifted their binoculars to watch the fall of shot; the Army looked blasé. Tyler seemed to be making polite small talk, but turning his head to watch each smokeburst with a perfect sense of timing.

"The trouble is," Shelford said, "that tanks don't just sit there, they *move*. How can you correct fire?"

"It could have a tactical influence." Maxim slipped comfortably back into the argument about weapons and tactics that is as basic to army life as brown Windsor soup. "If they know that tanks *could* be knocked out by . . ."

"You've got to have terminal guidance, infra-red, laser, even magnetic . . ."

"But if you could just frighten off the armoured personnel carriers . . ."

"Mind, infra-red would only home onto a burning vehicle, a complete waste . . ."

"You have to choose between fragmentation and penetration . . ."

"Dropping mines ahead of a tank, now *there* . . ."

A large man with cropped grey hair and wearing a short coat in a lumberjack tartan came up behind them. He had vivid blue eyes, a very coarse grainy skin and a bald eagle on his shoulder couldn't have made him more American. The eyes flickered from Maxim's cap badge to the crown on his shoulder to the parachute wings just below, taking in all the information going in one sweep.

He stuck out a hand. "Good afternoon, Major. I'm David Brock, Seddon Arms." Back among the parked vehicles was a heavy, unlabelled, American camper truck.

"Harry Maxim." They shook hands and Brock waved at Shelford, who said: "Hi, David."

"Anything I can tell you about our wonder weapon?"

"I'm not buying, just browsing."

"Sure, but you could be shooting, one of these days." Brock had the easy manner of a man who is always selling but always in low gear. "Tell me, was that Professor John White Tyler who came up with you?"

"That's him."

"I heard his lectures at Princeton when I was doing a graduate year. He married a girl there . . . I don't think it lasted. Are you baby-sitting him?"

"Just temporarily." It had been a jolt to realise that

Brock, who looked a fit fifty-five year-old, must really be some ten years younger.

"Is it all right with you if I go and say hello?" Brock asked.

"Of course."

"Once the war's over, I'll try and get him to take a cup of coffee with us in the caravan. Would you join us?"

"Where he goes, I'm supposed to."

Brock smiled and tramped off to the grandstand.

"Nice guy, that," Shelford said. "But he's on a hiding to nothing here."

"What's going to happen, then?"

Shelford looked at him curiously. "I thought you'd have known already. Politics."

"Nobody tells me anything."

"I'd assumed Tyler was here just for a laying-on of hands . . . well, for what you're about to receive, be truly thankful. The buzz is that you're going to get the French mortar stuffed down your throat, base-plate and all."

"Is it all that much better?"

"No," Shelford said. "I just imagine this is Be-Nice-To-The-French year. But I don't know why."

Seddon Arms' camper truck was fitted out like a stateroom on a millionaire's yacht. The furniture and wall panelling were a gentle golden beech with a matt finish, the chairs and sofa covered in a baggy cream leather, the carpeting went from wall to wall. The only hint of merchandising death was in the tinted prints of early ironclads along the walls. Even with eight or nine people aboard, it didn't seem crowded.

Maxim found himself cornered by Brock's aide-de-camp, a bright young man whose glance was always wandering, looking for a glass he could refill.

"You don't seem to have the company's name on this caravan," Maxim said.

"We prefer to keep a low profile. It comes cheaper in trucks. When we put the company logo on side, we got anti-war nuts slashing the tyres and scratching up the paintwork." He grinned. "No kidding. It really happens. What are you drinking?"

"Just the coffee, thanks." It was only half past four, but Tyler and some of the others were sipping champagne from tulip glasses. The only other soldier was the lieutenant-colonel from the development unit, and he was on coffee, too.

Tyler was saying: "We just don't have your tradition of easy interchange between the academic and government worlds, that's all. In Whitehall you're still either an insider or an outsider . . . but at least the military look on me more as a hawk than a dove—am I right, Colonel?"

The lieutenant-colonel smiled. "They know you've been up at the sharp end, sir."

Brock had waited patiently. "But just what are you doing in your new job, Professor?"

"I'm just chairing a policy review committee." Tyler gave his deep little chuckle. "It's one of those little Whitehall cactuses that only flowers every ten years or so. The chiefs of staff don't like it, but it keeps them guessing."

"I thought," Brock said, "that you were mostly involved with nuclear strategy these days—sir."

"That's more or less true, David—" Tyler obviously remembered his one-time student; "—but one of the main functions of the review committee is to look at the whole spectrum of defence, as one and indivisible. We've always been too compartmentalised in Europe. Our military—I'm sure you'll forgive me, Colonel—" he chuckled politely at the lieutenant-colonel; "—they tend to see nuclear warfare as a civilian affair, a matter of politics and diplomacy, nothing to do with them. What I feel we have to do is just what Herman Kahn was preaching when we were at Princeton: find the spinal cord that links your anti-tank mortar to the intercontinental missile, and all the vertebrae in between . . ."

Tyler wasn't speech-making, Maxim realised. It was quite natural for him to talk like this, and just as natural for his audience to stand quiet and listen.

When he had finished, Brock took a breath to ask a well-prepared question, but the young aide beat him to it: "What was your view on our mortar then, sir?"

Brock lifted his head and flashed the boy a look as

fast and sharp as a slap in the face. The aide wilted, but Tyler talked his way slowly and gently around the social blunder. The Colonel's experts would, he was sure, provide the expertise since he himself was really incompetent to judge. And in any case, it wasn't his job. The review committee was to review policy, then break it down into tasks, perhaps, and then we'd have to see . . . Anyway, his own experience with mortars had only been with the old Stokes-Brandt types—which showed the aide he had known about such things before some people were even born.

The poor lad's in for a royal bollicking after parade, Maxim thought. Over-selling in the face of the customer. Bad show, or its American equivalent.

The talk decentralised again, and he was looking for a place to put down his cup when Brock touched his shoulder. "The Professor's agreed to join us in a little end-of-trials dinner party at an inn just over the hill. We've got rooms booked there, so he'll probably stay the night, but maybe you'll be looking up old friends in Warminster?"

Perhaps there was no politer way of putting it, but Maxim had his orders. "I have to stay with the Professor, I'm afraid. Obviously not at the dinner, but if he's spending the night there, I'll have to as well."

"You just have to, do you?" Brock's temper wasn't quite restored.

"That's right."

Brock suddenly grinned. "Okay, Harry. Don't worry, we'll fix you a room."

"Next door to the Professor, please."

▣ 6

The hotel was an old coaching inn—most were, in that area—north of Warminster under the steep escarpment of the Plain. With its creaking corridors, low oak beams and the horse-brasses and hunting horns in the bar, it looked very English, particularly to those who weren't. Maxim changed quickly into plain clothes and went down to ring George from the phone at the desk.

"The trouble is," he explained, "I feel I'm embarrassing him without really sticking close enough to do the job properly."

"Well, that's hard bloody luck on both of you. You'll just have to get used to playing gooseberry and so will he. He's a national asset, now. Stick as close as you can and think of England."

As advice, it didn't help, but Maxim felt slightly cheered. He prowled around the hotel inside and out, then found a seat in the bar from which he could cover the front door. He had the shoulder holster on under his jacket.

By dinnertime, the Seddon party had grown: Brock's wife, a lean blonde with a Texan accent, together with another husband-and-wife from the London office and the elderly defence correspondent of a national newspaper. Three very good-looking girls who obviously didn't belong to the hotel helped pass around drinks in the dining-room annex.

Maxim ate almost alone in the dining-room itself and dawdled over the meal as long as he could, although it was nasty even by the standards of famous old coaching inns. Then he went back to the bar and sipped a pint of beer until the party broke up in a burst of laughter and cigar smoke just before midnight.

"Ah, my faithful watchdog!" Tyler was a little drunk. "It's all right, Harry, you can go to bed now."

But: "A last Drambuie, Professor?" Brock suggest-

41

ed, so they all had a final liqueur at the bar. The landlord, doing the barman's job to save overtime by now, was happy to stay open as long as Seddon Arms wanted to drink. Maxim was beginning to guess at the scale of 'hospitality' which the arms business could afford.

They got to bed at about half past. Another snag about old coaching inns is that the old coaching lines they once served have become main-line lorry routes. But it wasn't a lorry that shook Maxim awake, just the double bang of a gun.

He was on his feet, revolver in hand, before he had worked out what gun and where. Probably a double-barrelled shotgun, and close. As close as the next room?

He lunged at Tyler's door. It was locked. He yelled: "Professor!" and got no answer but heard something move and there was a small mat of light at his feet, coming from the ill-fitting door. There was a heavy conical fire-extinguisher hanging on the opposite wall. He tore it free and smashed it into the door-handle in one sweep.

Tyler peered at him, bright-eyed and unsleepy, from the rumpled big bed. "Harry, what *is* going on here? What are you——"

But Maxim had slipped into old ingrained habits: looking for an armed man you either moved very slowly or very fast, and he was already moving fast. He threw a chair at the curtains and hit nothing, barged open the bathroom door, opened the wardrobe——

If she had been chosen for looking decorative, Seddon Arms had proved themselves good choosers, assuming they hadn't seen her stark naked, as Maxim now did. Well, not really stark, since somebody had been drawing interesting patterns on her in lipstick. She looked at Maxim with a small, cold smile.

He said: "Do you want to come out, or shall I close the door?" It sounded silly, but it was the only polite remark he could think of. She walked regally past him and shut herself in the bathroom.

He glanced back at Tyler, who was clutching the

42

sheets up to his chin, but knew he was in the wrong place. There was no smell of gunfire.

In the doorway he bounced off Brock, also wearing just pyjamas. Behind was the young aide, who had shyly waited long enough to get on a dressing-gown.

"Nothing wrong in there," Maxim said, pushing past.

"I guess outside, then . . ."

Maxim grabbed his shoes and combat jacket from his room and met the landlord at the top of the stairs, twittering like a lost starling chick. Maxim shoved him back down. "Get that back door open."

"But there's somebody outside, he's just waiting to——"

"Or I'll throw a chair through the bloody window. Now *move!*"

The landlord had spent years catering for Army celebrations and arms company parties, but Maxim was actually holding *a gun*. He unlocked the door with shaking hands.

The night was far darker and quieter than a London night and in his pyjamas Maxim felt both vulnerable and ridiculous. *But I know more than he does. Whoever it is out there isn't as good as I am.* You believed that or you looked for a job selling encyclopedias. He began to circle the building anti-clockwise, wanting to come up on whoever from the right. For a right-handed man it is more difficult to swing a long gun to the right than to the left.

Unless he's standing facing the hotel, of course, which puts you on his left. Or he may be left-handed anyway. Maxim shivered.

A lorry rumbled past, shaking the ground, and he moved ten yards before the noise had faded. There was a stone wall about the height of a desk just ahead, he recalled. But there's a bush that breaks the sharp line of it. Get behind that . . .

Somebody moved on the porch. Maxim carefully brought the gun up, cupping it in both hands. The figure stepped back, just a black silhouette against the near-blackness of the sky, but carrying something long.

Maxim took a slow breath. "Drop the gun or I shoot."

43

The figure turned, not fast, but not dropping the long thing. "Are you the police?"

"I said drop it!"

Suddenly Maxim got tired of playing a TV detective. He lifted the revolver, remembering to shut his eyes against the flash, and squeezed off a shot towards the sky.

There was a moment of silence, then the night tore apart in light and thunder. The bush above Maxim shattered, sprinkling him with twigs, and for a moment he had to try and think if he were hit or not. But it had been another double bang, certainly a shotgun and almost certainly empty now, so then he was over the wall and rolling up with the pistol pointed . . .

Maxim said, very calmly: "Put the gun down."

Farthing put it down. It was a double-barrelled shotgun, all right.

Maxim walked quietly up and put his pistol against Farthing's forehead. For a long moment they stood there, and perhaps it was Farthing's trembling that made the gun shake in Maxim's hand.

"Don't ever shoot at a soldier," Maxim said softly. "It gives him funny ideas about wanting to shoot back."

"Oh, I didn't mean to . . . I thought you were from MoD."

"Where else do soldiers come from? Spread yourself against the wall. Just like on the telly."

Farthing leant against the wall while Maxim searched him. There were three unfired 12-bore cartridges in one pocket.

"You've done it now, haven't you?" Maxim said.

Farthing straightened up painfully. "I said I didn't *mean* to shoot you. I was just trying to get arrested."

"Last time it was something like football hooliganism. This time it has to be attempted murder. There's a big difference. You committed it while out on bail so you won't get bailed for this one. And you won't get any suspended sentence, either. In about twenty minutes you will be in a cell in Warminster and you will stay in cells for just about all you could call your life. You've probably had your last drink and by the time you get out you won't even remember what

44

women are for. Oh, you may get buggered in jail, if you look clean enough, but Charles Farthing, that was your life."

"I didn't mean to shoot you," Farthing whimpered. "I didn't *try* to shoot you."

"Don't tell me, I'm not the jury. I'm only giving evidence."

A light glowed from the first floor, a window creaked up and a voice—standing well back, it sounded—called: "Are you all right? I've rung the police."

"Fine," Maxim answered. "Everything's under control." Except the temperature. It must be only just above freezing and he was in pyjamas and the combat jacket. His breath steamed in the dim light, but he had to stay. In maybe five minutes Farthing would become public property; for those minutes he wanted him private.

Farthing said: "I just wanted to . . . to get into court again."

"It's funny you should say that. When I felt the shot going through my hair, I thought: 'This bloke just wants to get into court, he isn't trying to hurt me or anything.'"

"It was an *accident*. I didn't want to harm anybody."

"Tell them why you didn't bother to take the shot out of the cartridges." Maxim clunked the three shells in his hand.

Farthing was quiet for a while. Then: "I was going to. I meant to, but it didn't seem to matter that much . . ."

"You've no idea how much it matters to me."

"Can you . . . I mean, if I was just firing that gun to get arrested, and . . . I mean, if I told you what I was going to say, and you know I wasn't really trying to hurt you."

"I'll listen until the cops get here."

Farthing sat on the low stone wall of the porch. "After Warrington dropped me, I went abroad. To Canada. It wasn't a very certain job, they just wanted somebody to advise them on export markets, Elizabeth didn't come with me, and that was about the end of the marriage. After I'd been there nine months, something like that, I got hepatitis, you know, liver trouble. They thought it might have been cirrhosis—well, I had been drinking a lot. And I was in the same ward as this Bob Bruckshaw."

He took out a packet of cigarettes and then asked: "Is it all right if . . ."

"Ask your doctor."

Farthing lit a cigarette. "But this chap Bob, he really did have it. The way he was swelling up, I mean . . . it was splitting his pyjamas. He'd come from Yorkshire, too, so we were talking. He wasn't very bright by then, but . . . he said about this Professor Tyler. He'd been with him in the war, he said, and he knew something about him that he said had spoiled his whole life. That was why he'd left England. He gave me this letter."

"What letter?"

"The one he gave me. He said it wasn't fair that Tyler had gone on and become a professor and written famous books and all that. He wanted me to get this letter to somebody back in England."

"And did you?"

"Yes. When I came out of hospital I'd lost my job, so I came back to England. I found out where this man was and I posted it to him."

"What happened to the man in hospital?—Bruckshaw."

"Bob died just two days after he gave me the letter."

"Did he tell you what was in it?" Maxim's voice was beginning to shiver as much as the rest of himself.

"No. He said he was too ashamed. He'd have to explain it to God soon enough. He became a Catholic in hospital, at the end."

"Did you read the letter?"

"*No.* No I didn't."

Far down the empty road, the police car sounded its pointless hee-haw.

"Who was the letter to?"

"D'you mean you don't know?" Farthing's voice came alive. "After you people had him framed and he killed himself and then what happened to the letter? You tell me!"

"I don't know who the hell you're talking about."

"Your Mr Jackaman at the Mine of Dung."

"Never heard of him."

The outburst had drained Farthing's aggression. He began to cry silently, his wet face glinting in the thin light from the windows above. Up there, the murmur of voices blended in the growing hum of the police car.

"And so," Maxim said, "you are going to stand up in court and say that somebody now dead knew something you don't know about Professor Tyler and it's in a letter to another man who's dead and you don't know where the letter is? Have I got that right?"

"I promised Bob," Farthing said sulkily. "And I said I'd make sure Mr Jackaman had got the letter . . . and I didn't. I didn't make sure. He couldn't write back because I hadn't given him an address, but I could have rung him up. I promised Bob."

"Get yourself together." The headlights glowed very close down the road.

"What are you going to tell the police?" Farthing asked.

"What are you going to say when you get into court?"

After a moment, Farthing muttered: "Nothing."

"All right. You fired in the air. And I'll do what I can to look into this letter and Jackaman—do you believe me?"

Farthing grunted.

"And do you also believe that if you speak up in court I will one way or another make the rest of your life very unpleasant indeed for you?"

"Yes." He sounded convinced of that, at any rate.

"Good." Maxim sat down on the opposite wall, still holding the pistol and still watching Farthing instead of the sudden blaze of light from the police car as it dashed onto the gravel drive.

"Oh God," Farthing began, muttering the old soldier's bitter and blasphemous prayer, "if there is a God, save my soul, if I have a soul."

"*Shut up.*" It was still going to be a long night, but at least Maxim could now put some clothes on. In all his life, he had never been so cold.

◙ 7

It was a very long night indeed—or a very short one, depending on which way you looked at it. Maxim flatly refused to leave Tyler and go back to Warminster with the police, or to hand over his revolver for some vague forensic reason. George had to be rung up. Tyler had to be moved to a new room because of the broken lock, and the landlord had to be assured that somebody would pay for it. Brock quickly offered to. Statements had to be taken, and the police—who were now far from certain that the world was a better and a brighter place for having a Major Harry Maxim in it—had to be persuaded not to take one from Tyler, since his version of 'on hearing what sounded to me like gunshots' wouldn't really be better than anybody else's rendering.

Behind the scenes, the lady with the lipstick decor vanished like (and probably with) the morning mist, never even getting a mention. At last, Maxim flopped back into bed, setting his alarm clock for eight-thirty.

George and Agnes woke him at eight.

"We fort as ow yer might like brekfuss in bed for a chiange," Agnes said, putting down a loaded tray on Maxim's feet. She started to pour coffee for all three.

Maxim tore his eyelids open; it was at such times that he wished he still smoked. Only a cigarette could bridge that interstellar gap between unfinished sleep and the feeling that you might live. It was a small consolation that George looked even worse than Maxim felt.

"What got you up at this time, George?"

"Following up the gunfight at the Warminster corral. And it isn't *this* time: I haven't been back to bed since you rang me. Oh God. What have they done with friend Farthing?"

"He's in the Warminster nick and I suppose he goes to court today. They were talking about creating a disturbance and illegal possession, but it might go further than that."

"Coppers," Agnes said brightly, "are a bit like wine connoisseurs, once they start talking about a charge. Shouldn't we have a drop of Section 17 in the '68 Act? Certainly, old boy, and then a sip of Section One, Prevention of Crime 1953. Dash it, why didn't I think of that, me dear feller? Black?" She gave Maxim his coffee and as he sat up to take it, saw the holstered gun under his pillow. "I say, I say, Harry, what *do* your girl friends think? Or do you fire it off at the magic moment?" She leant back against the foot of the bed and it rocked with her laughter.

George grumped: "It's lucky he had it with him last night, anyway."

"Lucky?" Maxim looked at him, then passed his cup back to Agnes. "More sugar, please."

"What's he going to say when he gets into court?" George asked.

"Nothing."

"Are you sure?"

"I think I persuaded him."

Agnes had gone thoughtful. "Firing off guns at three in the morning when he's already on bail for some other rumpus-making . . . he's going to get a remand in custody for medical reports. Will a week in jail change his mind?"

"I don't think so."

She looked at him dubiously.

"All right," George said. "So now what's this about a letter?"

Maxim told them. Agnes buttered and marmaladed toast and passed slices around. There weren't enough plates, and George had to make sudden pecking movements to stop crumbs and drips of marmalade falling on his tie.

He listened quietly and then looked at Agnes. "Do you believe in this letter?"

She thought, then nodded rather tentatively. "I think so. It's an odd thing to make up—and it does account

49

for something in Jackaman. Also I tend to believe a man who's trying so hard to go to jail."

"He could be just spreading alarm and despondency for Greyfriars."

"I'm hired to see reds under beds and I can't see any under his. But I could get one of our mob to chat him up. We could be a lawyer from Civil Liberties or something like that."

"You will do nothing of that sort whatsobloodyever. Oh blast. So now there is, or may be, a letter saying that over thirty years ago Tyler and a party of the second part did something Unspeakably UnBritish together. Or Unspeakably British, even. In wartime, in the Army . . . Who is, or was, brother Bruckshaw?"

Neither of them knew. Maxim asked: "Who was Jackaman?"

There was a sudden stillness. Then Agnes said: "Come on, duckie. If you expect Harry to act like he's twenty-one, you'll have to give him the key to the door."

Slowly and reluctantly, George said: "In a way, Jackaman's why you're at Number 10. Yes, he killed himself. The inquest heard a lot about the problems of overwork at Defence. It was in the papers but you were probably still out in the Gulf. Last November. He was a deputy under secretary and he wasn't going any higher. A good committee man, just rather stiff and old-fashioned. Then when it got around that Tyler was going to chair the policy review, he came rushing out of his hutch spitting fire and lettuce and saying Tyler was *unsound*."

"And you can't say worse than that in Whitehall," Agnes put in.

"None of this in public, of course. But it was embarrassing enough all the same. So Box 500 decided to help out, *without* directives from anyone, and put the dogs on him, sniffing around trying to find some dirt to roll in. And they came back with the idea of him having an illegal bank account in France. They put this to him, with what degree of tact we can only imagine, and he went home and shot himself. With a Purdey 12-bore."

"Full-length barrel?" Maxim asked before he could stop himself.

"Yes. It *can* be done, particularly if you've got the dogs yapping close behind you."

"Not this bitch," Agnes said. "I knew nothing about it."

"You would not be here if you had. Anyway, that's why the Headmaster wanted a . . . a new opening batsman against any more fast balls. Is there any coffee left?"

"What about the French bank account?" Maxim asked.

"We don't know if there *was* one. The Headmaster was so angry that a good man had been hounded to death—without anybody even finding out if he knew anything useful—that he ordered the whole operation closed, dead and buried."

"In Pandora's box," Agnes said softly.

Maxim said: "Farthing believed the whole thing was a frame-up, to keep Jackaman quiet, one way or another."

"Who told him that?"

"He didn't say. Was there a suicide note?"

"The police didn't find one. Thank God. But why write to Jackaman, for heaven's sake? He wasn't involved in security."

"When am I going to be allowed to get up?" Maxim asked politely.

Agnes grinned. "Oh, you won't impress me, love." But she turned her back while Maxim put on pants and trousers—uniform, since he was going to have to say an official farewell to their host the development unit.

When she turned back she asked George: "Jealous, duckie?"

George made a grumping sound. "Do you know when Farthing came back to this country and sent the letter to Jackaman?"

"No. Sorry, I should have asked. I get the impression that it wasn't in the last year . . ."

"We can easily find out. So Jackaman sat on the letter until Tyler's appointment came up." It was the Right Thing To Do, of course. You didn't attack a man's career lightly, but when the fate of the nation came into the picture . . . That was certainly the Jackaman that George had known, briefly, at MoD.

"Was Jackaman in the Army during the war?" Maxim asked.

"He was the right age, and I've a feeling there was something . . . but I'm pretty sure he was at the Foreign Office most of the war. He switched to Defence about twelve years ago, he wasn't going any higher in the Diplomatic."

"I could look him up," Maxim offered. "I'd better go over to Army Records to dig up Bob Bruckshaw anyway."

"Harry, I told you what the Headmaster ordered. Jackaman is *dead*."

"He doesn't seem very good at it."

George glowered into his fresh coffee, obviously suffering a clash of loyalties as well as an early dawn. Privately, Maxim had decided to look up Jackaman, no matter what George said.

Agnes came to life. "There woz this Greek bird Pandora, yer know? And she got this box and when she opened it, Lawd luv yer, wot kime out yer couldn't shoot wiv a Purdey 12-bore."

"I thought," George said tightly, "that the moral of that legend was not to open things that don't concern you."

"Or clean out your boxes before somebody else opens them."

George took a deep breath. "Very well. Harry can move on this. But step by step and never getting out of mummy's sight. All right? And Agnes, your mob can slow down on Farthing and switch to Bruckshaw. Did somebody of that name, right age, die in Montreal whenever—you know the sort of thing."

"We've heard of it."

Professor Tyler was sitting up in bed, alone, drinking a cup of tea, so Maxim left George to chat with him and went looking for Brock. He found him in the Seddon Arms camper truck parked behind the hotel. Overnight, somebody had cleaned up the remains of the evening party; the truck smelt faintly of polish and strongly of the coffee Brock was heating in a glass pot.

He was alone, wearing an open-necked shirt under a leather waistcoat, his face relaxed and untired. "Coffee, Harry?" He poured a breakfast-size cup without getting up. "Cream? Milk? Sugar? You did a good job with that nut last night."

"He wasn't dangerous." Maxim helped himself to sugar.

"When you fire a gun the shot's got to go somewhere. Something stronger?"

"I'm sorry?"

Silently, Brock opened the cupboard beside him to show bottles of Irish whisky, a single malt and Remy Martin. "Some people like it. Maybe not at your age. So what can I do for you this morning?"

Maxim found it difficult to begin. "I haven't mentioned it to anyone else . . . There was a girl in Professor Tyler's room . . ."

"From what I hear tell, there's usually a girl in Professor Tyler's room. There certainly was at Princeton."

"You provided this one."

Brock narrowed his eyes. "Sure."

"And there was a newspaper reporter staying here."

"That's right. He got one of the other girls. Were you thinking I was setting up Professor Tyler for a nice dirty story?"

"I was just asking."

For a moment, Brock was about to get angry. Then he shook his head and said gently: "Harry, it's a long time since I told anybody about the birds and the bees, but I'll try . . . Fact one: we aren't going to get any British contract for the mortar. We never were; I could smell that the moment we got here. I assume there's a political reason, but I don't know why.

"But so what?" He took a gulp of coffee. "There's no winning in being a bad loser. Next year maybe we'll sell you the biodegradable anti-personnel mine, or something new in rifle grenades. I could talk your ass off about what we've got coming up there.

"I believe I will have something stronger." He filled up his coffee with Irish whiskey. "Fact two: if you think I was setting up your Professor for a little blackmail, you've blown your tiny Neanderthal mind. For one thing, I really do admire him as a military thinker.

53

Sure, knowing him could be good for trade—or it could be no good at all, particularly if your prime minister loses the next election. Then the Professor would be back in the wilds of Cambridge, England, without any say in policy.

"But—" he stood up and made slow mark-time movements, stretching the stiffness out of his legs. He must have been sitting there a long time, Maxim realised; "—but let me tell you something that would be very bad for trade indeed: any whisper that we went in for blackmail. Giving big commissions, sweeteners, call it bribery if you like—yes, that happens all the time. In most of the countries we do it, there isn't even a word for it: it's just a way of life. And it hasn't hurt Lockheed or Dassault or all the others that there's a rumour they give away free money. They get it all back in the final purchase price anyhow.

"But blackmail . . . never. Last night I brought along those girls just the same as I made sure the hotel had the Professor's favourite brand of whiskey, that they wouldn't serve us shellfish, that I had some good cigars to offer him. Harry, this is just *routine*. If it had been boys instead of girls, I could organise that, too. And when you send me somebody who just wants to talk business, I'll be very happy to talk business and get to bed early. Until then . . ."

He sat down again. "Major Harry Maxim, takes coffee black with plenty of sugar, doesn't drink much but is particular about beer, doesn't smoke—except maybe a cigar? How'm I doing?"

Maxim smiled quickly. "Pretty well."

"And it would be girls not boys, if anything. Sheet, you should hear some of what we have to organise in the Middle East or Latin America. Europe's supposed to be easy territory."

"All it does is make you look ten years older."

"I'm sorry."

"That's okay. Sometimes you have to ask. But I'll tell you: if you're going to be baby-sitting Professor John White Tyler, you'd best get used to some help from the girls."

"Thanks."

Maxim stepped down into the frosty car-park.

8

Maxim, Tyler and George clattered back to London in
a helicopter; the night's excitement had startled the
Army into realising that while they couldn't guarantee
Tyler's life, they could at least make sure he didn't get
killed while technically their guest. Maxim's wasn't the
only gun on that helicopter.

Agnes drove back; she and George had come down
in her car.

An MoD car rushed them from Battersea to Liver-
pool Street station for Tyler to catch the next Cambridge train. "All very British," George said. "Up until
now you've been chairman of the review committee
and thus in imminent danger of your life. But when
you step on that train, you revert to being a mere academic whom nobody would wish to harm. Have you
ever thought about changing clothes in a telephone
box, like Superman?"

He was feeling better.

"George, I'm sure you never read those terrible
American comics. And there are far more old students
of mine who'd like to put a bullet in me than anybody
connected with national defence." Tyler chuckled.
"Anyway, thank you for your very present help, Major. I hope we'll meet again soon."

They shook hands, Tyler giving Maxim a nice open
smile with his big, wide-spaced teeth. Neither of them
had mentioned the lipsticked lady. Tyler climbed into a
first-class carriage and George and Maxim walked
away before the train left.

"Where away now?" George asked.

"Unless you want me, I'll drive out to Hayes."

"Where?"

"Army Records."

"Ah yes. Hadn't you better change first? You can't
go running around dressed like a soldier or people will

think you're part of a film and ask for your autograph. Shall I drop you off at your place?"

"Unless you know a good telephone box."

Maxim got home from Hayes at half past five, with the short night beginning to catch up on him. He rang George and found he needn't go into Number 10, put on a kettle and collapsed—carefully—into an old armchair.

He rented a first-floor flat in a gloomy Victorian terrace that was either in Camden Town or Primrose Hill, depending on whether you were buying or selling. He could have found a place just as cheap and far closer to Downing Street by going south, across the river. The idea had barely occurred to him. Born a north Londoner, he headed instinctively for the tribal lands between the Northern and Bakerloo lines. The house belonged to a musty arthritic widow who had taken to Maxim—as much as she took to anyone—because he was neither black nor Irish, and as an Army officer daren't bounce cheques.

"Structurally, it's about as insecure as you can get," Maxim had told George. "Somebody's just sealed off the first floor with composition board and frosted glass and a home-made door. I'll change the lock, but anyone could blow the whole thing down with a strong sneeze.

"But in practice, it might not be too bad. It's a quiet road and whenever you walk down it, there's about five old biddies sitting in their bay windows watching who goes past. I'd hate to try and mount a surveillance there. I don't know if that matters."

"It might," George had said. "Greyfriars has certainly opened a file on you by now—assuming," he added politely, "that they didn't have one already."

The kettle boiled. He got up, made a mug of coffee and went to rout in the tea-chests in the corner. Mrs. Talbot hadn't reckoned on her tenants needing much in the way of book-cases, and Maxim had only just begun to look for second-hand ones in Camden Town. Meanwhile, his books lived stacked against the wall or still in the chests. The one he wanted was, of course, at the bottom of the last chest he searched. The pages were yellowed and fragile, and the fly-leaf had the immature signature of Harold R. Maxim, but it was still this copy of *The Gates of the Grave* that perhaps had changed his life.

He put Duke Ellington's 'Far East Suite' on the record player and went back to the armchair. Later, he'd go down the road for some cans of beer. If he drank coffee for the next three hours he'd end up dancing on the ceiling.

On most afternoons there is a small, almost ceremonial, tea-party in the Private Secretaries' room. Visitors from other offices drop in and a few quiet words can often bypass a lot of paperwork and save trouble—if bypassing paperwork and saving trouble is your objective. Two days later, Maxim, Agnes and Sir Anthony Sladen were informally invited.

"I hear strange tales about goings-on in wildest Wiltshire," Sladen said. "Are you going to find yourselves all over the front page of the *Express?*"

"I don't think so." George sounded confident. "All that happened was that somebody fired off a shotgun in front of a hotel at some Godawful hour of the night and has been charged with this and that. That's not exactly stop-the-presses, and they can't comment on a case that's sub judice anyway."

"But our Professor Tyler was inside at the time, was he not?"

George shrugged. "What's secret about that? We've asked all three services to publicise his visits wherever he goes. That way, we keep the spotlight on conventional warfare."

Sladen frowned warningly, and drew them away from the crowd with delicate gestures of his cup and saucer.

"And," Agnes chipped in, "we now know we've got the fastest gun in Whitehall." She and Maxim exchanged rather false smiles.

"Nobody got killed," George said. "And Harry can also look up records. Would you like to hear what he found, or would you prefer to go on criticising?"

Agnes made a little curtsy.

Maxim put his cup down on the edge of a desk and took out a notebook.

"Gerald Jackaman. He was at Oxford when the war started. He tried to join up then, but they had too many people trying to get in so they told him to go back and do his last year. Anyway, the whole thing was going to be over by Christmas."

"I'm quite sure," George said, "that Odysseus's last words to Penelope, as he went off to Troy, were: 'Don't worry, old girl, I'll be home by Christmas'."

Sladen said: "Since it was to be approximately thirteen hundred years to the first Christmas, he was giving himself a fair margin of error. I *do* apologise, Major."

Maxim was wearing a small patient smile. "He joined up in June 1940. He was commissioned into the Rifle Brigade in October. In December he smashed up a knee playing rugger."

"A bit bloody silly," Agnes suggested.

George said: "Good for morale, to let the troops tear an officer to pieces occasionally."

"Reading between the lines," Maxim went on. "I gather he wasn't seen as any ball of fire, so when his knee didn't look like repairing properly, they gave him a medical discharge. He took the civil service exam and was accepted by the Foreign Office. He spoke French very well, so he was doing liaison work with the Free French. Then, in January 1943 he went to Algiers with Harold Macmillan. Churchill sent out a small Foreign Office mission to look after our political interests in North Africa, and Jackaman was part of it—"

"You didn't get that from Army records, did you?" Sladen said.

George said: "No, the FO. I squared it. Good practice, for Harry to find his way around."

"So where could he have met Tyler?" Sladen asked.

"They were both in North Africa at that time, but Tyler was with 8th Army, down in Libya and Tunisia. He was evacuated home a month or so after Jackaman got to Algiers. After that, they were both in Britain in early '44, but Jackaman went to Washington in May and stayed until after the war."

Sladen grunted.

"And what about Bob Bruckshaw?" Agnes asked.

"There was no Robert Bruckshaw in the Army at that time."

Isolated in a corner, the four of them were getting curious glances from the rest of what was, after all, supposed to be a General Exchange of Views. A couple of teacups were rattled, but George ignored them.

"And now let's hear the news summary from Liza Doolittle."

Agnes smiled and recited from memory. "Robert Bruckshaw died in Montreal General Hospital, cirrhosis all right, in December two years ago. He gave his age as fifty-eight and birthplace as Yorkshire, no next of kin. The only visitors anybody can remember were a couple of workmates—he'd been driving a truck on a building site. And yes, Charles Farthing was also a patient there at the time."

Maxim said: "There's no Bruckshaw mentioned in *The Gates of the Grave*, either. Nor a Jackaman."

There was a pause. Then George said: "Bruckshaw must have changed his name. God knows, so would I if I had to go to Canada."

Agnes nodded. "I've asked the Mounties to check it. They're good when they get their snow-shoes on. But it seems that name changes are registered province by province, not nationally, so they could have to try right across the country and going back thirty years. And that's assuming he changed it legally *and* in Canada. If not . . ."

"So where," Sladen asked, "does that leave us?"

"Just thankful that nobody's been killed," George said. "Shall we re-join the Mad Hatters?"

◉ 9

The PM owned a cat, a fat multi-coloured ex-female, who had taken a liking to Maxim's office—perhaps, he thought ruefully, because it was one of the least busy in the house. She would scratch on the door until he opened it, and rushed in staring around suspiciously, like a wife expecting to see Another Woman diving out of the window. Then she curled up on whatever papers Maxim was trying to read and went to sleep.

She was there that morning when George rang through to say that if Maxim wasn't too busy—he was trying to read as much of the *RUSI Journal* as the cat allowed—he wanted to pop up and see him.

He arrived a minute later, shutting the door firmly behind himself. The cat looked at him balefully.

"Do you like cats?" George asked.

"This one doesn't give you a choice."

"She's giving me one. However . . . this just might be as important as the old air-dog thinks it is, or it may be sheer bull." He gave Maxim the Kensington address of Wing-Commander Neale, RAF (Retired) and now MP for a West Country constituency. "He's a bit of a pain except when he's talking about tourism or defence, but he's one of the few MPs who still think this country's worth defending, so we toss him a bottle of rum from time to time. He wants to see you, or at least 'that new Army chap I hear you've got at Number 10'. Try not to knock any of his tail feathers off and call me if it's anything vital."

Maxim was already putting on his coat. "Should I take a gun?" He nodded at the squat little safe the Housekeeper's Office had found for him.

George gave it a moment's thought and shook his head. "It shouldn't come to anything like that." He turned out to be wrong.

Neale lived in one of a row of what estate agents call 'bijou mews cottages'. It had a neat doll's-house look to it, everything slightly smaller than life and brightly painted. Apricot walls, white woodwork, a blue front door with bits of black ironwork. All rather wasted, since it looked across the humpy cobblestones to nothing more than a drab line of lock-up garages.

Neale himself opened the door and held it on the chain.

"I'm Major Maxim from Downing Street."

Sharp blue eyes looked him up and down. "Can I see your ID, please, Major?"

The Wing-Commander was in his late fifties, a solid but fit-looking man with a good head of very clean white hair. His face was square and covered with deep creases, as if made from expensive leather. He wore a polo-necked cashmere sweater and checked slacks.

He looked carefully at Maxim's identity card and let him into the little dark hallway, double-locked the door, then led the way through to a living-room made from two small rooms opened right through.

"Sit down, Major." Neale indicated just which chair. "Would you like a cup of coffee?"

"If it's going, sir." A silly answer since it was already waiting: plain white bone china pot, two cups, two colours of sugar. It belonged with the fresh paint outside, the precisely arranged little seascapes and brass ornaments around him now. A whisper of money, but money carefully spent. The Wing-Commander was divorced, and there would be a home in his constituency to keep up, and with no grace and favour directorships in the city, there might not be all that much to spend.

"What did Harbinger tell you?" Neale asked briskly.

"Just that you wanted to see me and that it was confidential."

Neale grunted. "That's about all I said to him but I expect he dressed it up a bit. He comes of a good family, but I sometimes wonder if he takes his job seriously enough. Well . . ." he passed Maxim a cup; ". . . as you may know, one of my interests is tourism. I'm on the Authority board and I chair the House

61

committee on tourism. A couple of years ago I was with a delegation to Prague, promoting Britain, you understand, and I met . . . a young lady." A slight hesitation, a careful choosing of words.

"She worked for Cedok, their tourist bureau," Neale went on. "Usually she was stationed in London, but she'd come back especially for our visit, partly as an interpreter."

"Yes," Maxim said, in a voice so flat and dull that Neale looked at him sharply.

"I'm not entirely a bloody fool, you know, Major. All Czechs abroad are working for their government, even if they're not actually members of the STB. I assumed that from the start."

Start of *what*? Oh God, has a British MP been leaping into bed with a Czech agent, in Prague itself, with full sound and camera coverage, *son et lumière* as the professionals say?

"Her name is Zuzana Kindl." Neale folded his face into a cool smile. "And I was quite right: she *was* working for the STB itself. But now she wants to come over, to defect, to us." He took a large mouthful of coffee and watched Maxim carefully.

There was something he hadn't said, yet. An ace up the sleeve.

"When did she get in touch with you?" Maxim asked.

"This morning. At about nine o'clock."

"Has she actually jumped off? Committed herself?"

"Yes, Major."

"Do you know where she is?" Then suddenly he realised. "She's here?"

"Yes."

Maxim sat back in the dainty little chair. "Well . . . thank you for telling us. I'll ring George and he'll pass it on to Security, and they'll—"

"No." A simple word of command. "One thing Miss Kindl told me was that the Soviets, not her people but the KGB itself, have got a line into our own security service. That was why I called you in." He looked satisfied; he had played his ace and won.

Maxim took his time thinking it out. Then:

"Did you learn what sort of work she was doing for the Czechs?"

"Well, I don't think she was exactly a top-level agent. I'd say she worked mostly on research, background research."

No mention of any bed-and-breakfast work, setting up ex-military members of parliament for possible backmail. But maybe this time a fairy godmother had got her spell right. Victim recruits agent. Love makes the world go backwards.

"Would you mind if I had a word with Miss Kindl before I ring Number 10?"

"I'll ask her to come down."

Zuzana Kindl was around thirty years old, on the short side and with a full cottage-loaf figure and a perky, pleasant face. There was something immediately sexy about her, but it was country sex, not city. Her dark hair was cut short and straight and she wore very simple clothes: a blouse with a shirt neck, full calf-length skirt, a single gold chain around her neck.

They shook hands formally. "I have heard of you," she said. "The major who goes to advise the Prime Minister. We wondered what it was about."

"If you ever find out, let me know as well, will you?"

She smiled briefly. Her face looked as if it should have more colour in it; her big dark eyes were restless and one hand plucked and twisted at the folds of her skirt.

They sat down, and Neale went to get more coffee.

Keeping his voice low in that tiny house, Maxim asked: "Will your service know you've gone by now?"

"Yes. Yes, they must believe it."

"When would they have known?"

"Oh . . . I think—" she looked at a large plain wrist watch; "—I think at perhaps nine-thirty."

About two hours ago. There would be a standard procedure for defections, but how much of it could swing into operation in two hours? For all that, the gallant Wing-Commander had given them those hours and denied them to his own side.

"Does your service know about Wing-Commander Neale?"

She blinked and hesitated, not looking at him.

"I have to know. You must tell me the truth."

"Yes. Yes, they know."

"And do you keep any tame baboons in this country?"

"What baboons?"

"Tough guys, thugs, hit men—"

"Oh yes. No. For such affairs they would bring in a team."

That was certainly standard procedure. Then if a baboon got caught with a dripping knife, there was no traceable connection with the resident service in this country.

"Will they bring them in?"

"I do not . . . they would not usually, but now—yes, I think." She shivered.

"Why this time?"

"Because they are worried about Mother Bear."

"About who? Ah, I see." The Czech secret service had long experience and a high reputation, but there were strings attached—and Moscow Centre held the far end of those strings.

"Is there any special reason why the bears should be angry about you?"

"I will tell you everything, everything I know!" she suddenly burst out. "But please, are you going to let me stay and be safe?"

"Stay where? Here?" Maxim was puzzled.

"In England."

"Good God, yes. Of course." It hadn't occurred to him that she might believe they could send her back, to a certain and imaginative death.

Hearing her raised voice, Neale came back and stood behind her chair, looking sternly at Maxim.

He got up. "Can I use your phone, sir?"

"The bloody woman could just be spreading alarm and despondency," George said viciously; "we've had phoney defections before. Or they might have told her they'd penetrated us specifically to dissuade her from Seeing The Light. Oh blast it. But we'll have to take her seriously, we don't have a choice. Can you get her away from there?"

"If she agrees to come. I rather think the Wing-Commander's idea is for her to stay on while I play watchdog."

"No bloody fear!" George erupted. "Get her out. And you'd better tell him to get away, too. He can go down to the House and spend a day thinking he's governing the country. Damn it all, if he Had His Way with her in Prague, his is the first place they'll come looking."

"What about the police?"

"I don't want them. They'll need to know why they can't turn her over to Box 500, and that'll leak and then we'll have a security scandal even if there isn't one. The Headmaster is *not* going to enjoy this. You just get her away, take her to an afternoon at the movies, a drive in the country, anything, while I whisper in a few well-bred ears."

"She's pretty frightened. She's expecting rough stuff."

"If they've only had two hours, I wouldn't expect anything too uncouth just yet. Their first reaction is usually to run around counting the spoons. By the by, did she bring any paperwork or photographs?"

"I haven't asked her."

"Well . . . are you armed?"

"It was you who said I wouldn't need it."

"Let's hope I was right."

"The Prime Minister is being told about Miss Kindl at this moment, sir. George is sure he'll be delighted with the way you've handled things." Maxim was choosing his words with the dishonest care of a man hand-picking his ammunition for a Bisley shoot. "*But* he does think she ought to be got to somewhere more secure. You did exactly the right thing in calling me in, that's just why the Prime Minister appointed me, so now . . ."

I've mentioned the PM twice and *you* didn't call me in, George *sent* me. You pompous old nirk, anybody would think you were retired as an Air Marshal instead of just a . . . No, that's why you never made Air Marshal.

Mollified, Neale went to try and phone a taxi.

65

Maxim examined the mews from behind the nylon net curtains. It was narrow, too narrow to do a U-turn, and ended at a tall blank wall about a hundred yards to the left. The only way out was through an ornate arch onto the main road, a hundred yards up to the right. A single watcher beyond the arch could see everybody who went in and out of the mews, and if he were watching for Zuzana Kindl, he'd already know which house she'd gone to.

Anybody wanting to invent a better mousetrap could beat a path to this mews for a start.

Neale came back. "Sorry, there doesn't seem to be anybody answering at this time of day, but you should get a cab on the road."

"Do you have a gun in the house?"

The Wing-Commander looked startled. "No. No, not here."

"A knife, then. Anything serious, or just a kitchen knife."

A little worried, Neale showed him into the dolls'-house kitchen. Maxim selected a five-inch vegetable knife and plugged its tip with a champagne cork. There was an empty bottle standing on top of the refrigerator.

Zuzana was waiting for them in the hallway, now wearing a dark tartan coat with a wrap-over belt and furry collar. She carried a plastic airline bag without any insignia on it.

"Is that all you've got?" Maxim asked.

"I could not bring more. You know we have to share apartments, I have two other girls, so we can watch each other. If I had walked out with a suitcase ... I would not have walked out, that is how it is."

"It'll all be different now," Neale said soothingly. Zuzana suddenly wrapped her arms around him and kissed him thoroughly. The Wing-Commander went pink. Maxim led the way out.

The mews was empty of anybody and everything except dustbins. Not even a single illegally parked car. Maxim stayed on the girl's right, his hand holding the knife in his pocket. He was worried, and worried that he couldn't work out why he was worried. Perhaps he was just catching it off Zuzana, but perhaps there was a better reason . . .

The main road, lined with fat Victorian houses that were now mostly residential hotels, was wide but not wide enough for its rows of parked cars and the busy two-way traffic. There were perhaps fifty people in sight, and any one of them could be a watcher, and of course there were no empty taxies.

South or north? North, Maxim decided. He grabbed the girl's arm, and her muscles were locked solid as stone. She was scared, all right. *Why?*

They hurried, making themselves conspicuous but making anybody who was following conspicuous as well. Maxim kept looking back; he knew all about the theory of tailing and shaking tails in a city, but had almost no real experience. Born a townee, as a soldier he was a professional countryman by now. But an unarmed soldier, except for that piddling little knife.

That cork, that champagne bottle. Had they been celebrating her defection at ten in the morning? *Or at midnight? Oh God, she hadn't jumped off this morning, she'd got there last night, and the other side had had twelve hours to blow the baboon whistle, not just two.*

Then a sweet chariot, a taxi with its FOR HIRE light on, coming up behind them. Maxim waved it down, yanked open the door and pushed Zuzana in, turned to shout an address at the driver—

It happened very fast. A blue car swerved in to block the taxi, somebody pulled Maxim aside and he saw a hand with a pistol reach at the taxi's open door. As he went down, he grabbed the arm that was pulling him, and the man came over with him, the gun banging into the air.

Maxim rolled free, kicked at the man's head and missed, then tore the knife from his pocket. As the gun hand came up towards him he just swiped at it. The knife skidded off bone and the hand loosened. The man grunted and Maxim snatched away the gun, left-handed.

On the far side of the taxi, another man was standing calmly pumping shots through the window, now opaque with cracks and starred holes. Zuzana was lying flat on the floor, a bullet ricochetted out past Maxim and clanged into a shop front.

He fired twice through the blind window, and couldn't tell if he'd hit anybody, but the shooting stopped. He dropped the knife and dragged Zuzana out, pushed her behind him, kneeling in wait for the next attack.

An engine yowled above the traffic noise and the blue car screeched away, trailing blue smoke. Maxim ducked to look under the taxi and there was no one on the other side.

"Did you get hit?" He turned to Zuzana and she was already ten yards up the street and accelerating. For a moment the good citizen and the soldier in Maxim clashed, then he was back on the streets of Belfast and moving, too. Let the police pick up the pieces.

If she'd been wounded, it wasn't anywhere vital. Despite her shoes and shape, Zuzana could run, the way only a trained sportswoman or dancer can run. She weaved between pedestrians who were trying not to know about gunshots and that side of life, except for one old lady who swung her umbrella at Maxim and screamed. He realised he still had the gun in his hand and the chase could be misconstrued. Just as he caught up with Zuzana, she swerved left into a one-way street, running against the flow of traffic. It was a quieter, residential street. Then she turned right; Maxim said nothing, just keeping up with her. Nobody seemed to be chasing them.

Around the next corner she slowed abruptly to a walk, gasping.

"Are you hurt?" Maxim asked.

"I do not think so." She rubbed her left shoulder. There was a long rip in her coat, but no blood on her fingers when she looked.

Maxim was still holding the pistol. He glanced at it—a Heckler & Koch such as West German police forces use—and shoved it into his ripped coat pocket. That cork hadn't done much good. He should never have let go of the knife to open the taxi door.

"Where are we going now?" he asked.

"I thought you were organising me."

"You might have told me you went to the Wing-Commander last night, not this morning."

She said nothing.

"All right," Maxim said. "I'm organising you." And at least he now had a gun.

◘ 10

Even on a dull, chill day there were still a number of resolute outdoor lunchers and duck-feeders sitting around St. James's Park lake. George and Agnes met at the Cake House, bought packets of sandwiches, and started to walk.

"I don't know," Agnes said, "whether I shouldn't be seen with you or you shouldn't be seen with me."

"God knows," George munched gloomily. "I just can't tell where we go from here."

"Do we know where they are?"

"We don't even know if they're alive."

"Oh, come on, now."

George gave her his sandwiches to hold while he fumbled in an inside pocket and found a crumpled piece of Press Association tape, torn from the machine just outside his room.

She read:

GUN BATTLE IN KENSINGTON
POLICE ARE SEARCHING FOR FOUR MEN AND A WOMAN, TWO OF WHOM MAY BE SERIOUSLY INJURED, AFTER SHOTS WERE FIRED IN STANFORD STREET, KENSINGTON, THIS MORNING. SCOTLAND YARD'S ANTI-TERRORIST SQUAD HAS BEEN ALERTED AND A HUNT HAS STARTED FOR A BLUE SALOON CAR BELIEVED TO BE A DATSUN.
WITNESSES FROM AMONG THE SHOPPING CROWD SAID THAT AT LEAST TWO MEN EXCHANGED GUNSHOTS WHEN THE CAR FORCED A TAXI TO STOP.
THE DRIVER OF THE TAXI IS BEING TREATED IN HOSPITAL FOR SHOCK BUT IS REPORTED TO BE UNINJURED.
1231

"And that," George said, "was less than a quarter of a mile from Wing-Commander Neale's mews."

"Well, it certainly sounds like our Harry." Agnes sounded quite happy.

"He was unarmed. I told him he needn't take a gun."

"Oh." She looked back at the tape. "They didn't find any bodies."

"They could have been kidnapped, dead *or* alive. I blame myself. I should have . . . I don't know."

Agnes took the lettuce from her sandwich and tossed it to a passing goose. "If this really was the cads and rotters, they've moved very fast and acted very blatantly. Usually they'd wait for months to set it up, then go for something like the cyanide gun or those—"

"I *know* all that. And it's just the point: if they're that desperate, then the girl must have something that really worries them. But now what can we do? We can't tell the police to start looking for Harry, think where that would land us. And we can't call your service in because of what the girl said. Not even if you'd got the resources. Get out of the *bloody* way." He lunged his umbrella at a duck which was demanding a sandwich with menaces. It fluttered aside, quacking furiously.

"George, you know how compartmentalised we are. You aren't suggesting all the service goes into neutral just because some little bint—who was a sworn enemy yesterday—says we've got one bad 'un in our mob?"

"I don't give directives to your service. That's the Headmaster's job."

"Security," Agnes said doggedly, "is perfection. It's a picture that never gets finished. You keep putting on a dab of paint here, a dab of paint there and you know it'll never be perfect but it's the only picture you're ever going to get to paint. That's security work."

"You've said that before," George said rudely.

"I've said it to every bright young thing who joins us from Oxford and Cambridge and expects to make the world safe for democracy by tapping a couple of phones and getting screwed by some lovely big Russians. And none of them listens, either."

George grunted and they walked in silence for a

while. Somebody had thrown a deck chair into the lake and a duck was perched on it, as on the topmast of a sunken ship. He pitched the last of his sandwiches at it. "We just have to wait until Harry rings in, if he's still alive."

"He's not going to reach you in the middle of here."

They turned back towards the modest towers and flagpoles of Whitehall, showing above the skeletal trees.

"One thing you might do," Agnes said, "is get a police guard on the Wing-Commander. They could think she talked to him."

"I'll do that."

Maxim rang in soon after two o'clock. "We're in a pub just off the A41."

"How did you get there?" George demanded.

"Hired a car."

"Harry, you do know the police are looking for you?"

"I assumed they were. But I also assumed they'd think we'd steal a car rather than hire one. They haven't got my name, have they?"

"Not from us. All they've put out so far is some vague descriptions." Maxim knew that those things take time: he had spent hours carefully probing at witnesses, trying to work out who was exaggerating, who was really observant, and blending the results to get a likely picture of who had done what. And knowing that the *who* was using every minute of that time to advantage. Well, now it was his turn.

George said: "They must have a hit team already in this country to get onto you so fast."

"Not necessarily." Maxim told him about Zuzana jumping off the night before.

George swore luridly. "And we're supposed to believe that little bitch when she says that Box 500's been soured? Don't stop the next one who tries to bump her off, it could be me."

"I think she was trying to protect the Wing-Commander's good name. I don't imagine they spent the night playing chess."

"*Good name?* What did that man *do* in the Riff-

RAF?—command a latrine squadron? He rapes a Bloc agent in Prague, and then . . ." Maxim held the phone away from his ear while George wound down. A customer on his way to the lavatory gave an odd glance at him and the squawking receiver.

"Anyway, you just stay out of sight and keep in touch," George finished. "And try and find out all she knows about Box 500. We've got our fingers firmly sub judice until then."

They drove on north-westwards, going nowhere in particular. Maxim's first instinct had been to head for the nearest London barracks, show his ID and demand sanctuary. There they'd certainly have been safe from any stray baboons, but the duty officer would have been risking his career if he hadn't reported them to the police the moment there was any suspicion that they were wanted. The Army had to tread very delicately on the toes of the civil power.

For the moment, they really were on their own.

The hired Avenger didn't have a radio, so he stopped and bought a cheap transistor. As nobody had been killed, they only made fifth place on the three o'clock hit parade, and that only because there had been gunfire. Police were still looking for four men and a woman, two of the men believed to be injured . . .

So I did hit that second bastard, Maxim thought happily. It had been an awkward shot, left-handed, since the Heckler & Koch comes with a thumb-rest for a right-handed shooter.

Oh blast. He should have locked himself in the pub lavatory and checked to see how many cartridges he'd got left.

"Did you recognise any of the baboons?" he asked.

"I did not properly see them."

"D'you think they were yours or Mother Bear's?"

"I do not know. Where are we going?"

"Just staying out of London. If I can find a motel, I thought we'd book in there. Is that all right?" He didn't much like the idea, for more than one reason, but it was the only solution he could think of. They had to get off the road, and they had to start talking—privately.

Zuzana didn't seem to mind, but: "We have no luggage." In the scuffle, she'd lost even her airline bag.

"We'll buy something." George had suggested that he always carry a wad of cash—at least £50—and now he was glad he'd taken the advice.

The evidence lay spread out across a scrubbed table in a blank back room decorated only with road safety posters. There was a row of little plastic sachets, each holding a single spent cartridge case or used bullet, and tagged to relate it to a point on the sketch maps and photographs of the 'scene'. Then a larger sachet holding a five-inch kitchen knife smeared with sticky blood. All these were waiting for the afternoon bagman to collect for the Lambeth laboratories.

There was also an airline bag with a shoulder strap, without any name or logo on it. Odd, that. The textured plastic fabric probably wouldn't take much in the way of fingerprints, but the young detective constable still unzipped the bag very carefully. At the far end of the table, another d.c. waited to list whatever was inside.

"One packet woman's tights, medium size, unopened. One woman's night-dress, St. Michael's brand, cream polyester . . ." he held it against himself to judge the length.

"It's definitely *you*," the other said.

"Say knee length. Worn since washed. One pair green panties, clean, no maker's label. One bra, size 36A, clean. One blouse, embroidered." It was very much embroidered, obviously by hand, and looked old and valuable. "Is this silk? Oh, skip it, we'll get one of the girls to do this stuff." He felt carefully past the rest of the clothes. "One furry animal toy, not much fur on it now, looks as if the ears have been chewed off."

"Should I write all that down?"

"And one file holder of typed papers." He lifted it clear. "In . . . do you know what language this is?"

The other got up to look. Across the front of the file was stamped, in red:

TAJNY

Then a heading written in ink:

VEVERKA

and the usual dates and initials that files accumulate.

"I dunno. I'd say Czech or Polish. But I'll bet that red word means SECRET or something like it."

Up till then, both of them had assumed that the shooting had been some Arab terrorist affair or a barney between two lots of villains. But now the compass needle had swung around to point in a totally unexpected direction. The file felt hot to the touch.

"This is for SB," the first d.c. said.

That was pure routine, just as it was for Special Branch to send round for the file the moment they knew it existed. It was also pure routine for them, once they had decided the language was Czechoslovakian, to tell M15 about it, and for Five to borrow it, since they had immediate translation facilities.

◙ 11

The motel had once been yet another famous old coaching inn; perhaps all coaching inns had once been famous. This one had had two rows of stables facing each other across a coach-yard at the back; now one row had become bedrooms, the other lock-up garages. Maxim and Zuzana sat each on a bed and looked at each other.

He felt nervous. It might be his puritan streak, or the memory of Jenny or just that it was a situation forced on him rather than chosen. He had a growing feeling that Zuzana would just as happily have taken a double-bedded room.

Towards the end of his £50 he had bought a half-bottle of Scotch and Zuzana seemed willing to share it. All the expenditure—suitcases, whisky, toothbrushes, nightgown—it was going to look Highly Irregular on his Form 1711, and he hoped to hell he'd find somebody prepared to sign it.

They clinked glasses. Maxim sipped, then asked casually: "Was there any particular reason why you chose today—last night—to come over?"

"I had become disgusted with a regime which represses its own citizens but does nothing to eliminate the abuse of power among its leaders." The statement had a rehearsed ring to it, and it didn't answer Maxim's question, but Zuzana seemed to relax once she'd got it said.

"Were you going to tell us something about the bears' contact in security?"

"You are sure I will be safe?"

"If you keep telling the truth, yes. You know why they caught us back there?"

"I know, I know." She flopped back flat on the bed, spilling some of her drink, and talked at the ceiling. "I will tell you about my work. Mostly I did research and

76

keeping the files on your people. They were not so important people, but perhaps they would become important, you understand. They all had animal names: Lisák, Lasicka, Krtek, Veverka."

"A real animal farm."

She didn't get the joke. "Veverka means squirrel. But his real name was Professor John White Tyler."

"I see." Maxim made two long words of them.

She turned her head on the pillow and smiled at him mischievously. "You know him. You went to Warminster with him, but we did not find out why yet."

"I see," Maxim said again, feeling a twinge of discomfort. "And you kept the file on him?"

"Yes. I read his books, I cut all the pieces from the newspapers, I read the lectures—oh Mother, how I tried to understand about atomic wars and how they could happen in a thousand ways . . . And I knew all about the wives and the girls."

She went back to staring at the rough-plastered ceiling. The whole room was like that, not a straight line or an even surface anywhere, and all painted white that looked grey as the light died outside. Maxim guessed that she felt safer in the gloom.

"He had the first wife when he was still in your Army, after the end of the war. It went only six years, when he went back to Cambridge to work for his doctor of philosophy degree, I think it was. It is in the file. She went to work at the Pye factory while he read his books, she typed his . . . his thesis. She did everything for him."

"Did you talk to her?" It seemed very unlikely.

"No, no. For that we had this American boy, he was trying to be a journalist in London, one of our good friends in Italy was pretending to be a publisher, he asked the American to research your Tyler and two others for a book that will be published in Italy. And he was well paid, and of course, he does not read any Italian."

"Of course," Maxim agreed softly.

"The second wife, she was an American, she could have been his *daughter*." Zuzana sounded rather disgusted. Mrs Tyler Mark II—the one Brock had

77

remembered—had married him at Princeton. Tyler had originally gone over for a sabbatical year, then earned a research grant and stayed on. There he was caught up in that glorious crusade when the academics, led by Herman Kahn and the Rand Corporation, stormed the seedy bastille of nuclear war theory and transformed it into a Camelot of soaring intellectual complexity, all politicians and military men please use the back door only. Those two years changed Tyler's life, but not his habits. That marriage lasted only five years.

And all the time, during, between the after the marriages, there had been the girls. Virtually as a reflex, the STB had tossed a few of its own sisters in his path, but whether he snapped them up or not hardly mattered. You could no more blackmail Tyler for his sex life than you could next door's tomcat, because he was no more secretive about it. And as women don't usually read military studies, you couldn't even accuse him of seducing his own students, not that Cambridge would have cared anyway. Zuzana was distinctly shocked to learn that.

"So I had all that in the file. And then, then Mother Bear said to work harder on Veverka."

"When was this?" Maxim offered her the whisky but she shook her head on the pillow.

"It was last year. Before Christmas."

"Did they say why?"

She looked at him, eyes wide. Silly question: Mother Bear never says why.

"Sorry: but did you know if something had happened about Veverka?"

"He was to become chairman of the defence policy review committee."

"And you knew this when? Can you remember?"

"It was . . . about the middle of November."

That was well before any public announcement.

"And then. . .?"

"Then they said to work just on Veverka. Just him."

"You in charge and others working for you?"

She couldn't hide a quick proud smile.

"Your first real command?" Maxim asked. She didn't answer, so he rambled on, provoking her to interrupt. "I remember my first command, out in Malaysia—it was still Malaya then. Just twenty-two of them, almost half the platoon was off sick or skiving, and every one of them hadn't shaved or had got something wrong with his equipment, just to see how I'd take it. You're told to rely on your sergeant, but—"

"So I worked on Veverka. I worked and worked. I read again all the books, *The Gates of the Grave*—have you read that? I tried to find the people who were in that, if they are still alive." She suddenly sat up. "I will have a drink."

Maxim poured it. They sat facing each other, knees almost touching. "Did you ever meet Tyler himself?"

"I heard him at a lecture in London one time. But they would never let me try to meet him." She went quiet again, perhaps imagining—Maxim certainly was—the likeliest result of her meeting Tyler. A car's brakes squeaked in the stableyard, and doors slammed. They listened in secret as new arrivals clumped in next door.

Maxim whispered: "And so you worked on Veverka."

"It is funny. You say Veverka, I say Veverka, and all the time I know it is Tyler, but when I hear Tyler I think Veverka."

"Codenames actually work. Sometimes. So. . . ?"

"I tried to find the bears something, to find them *anything*." For years Moscow had just dismissed Tyler—publicly—as a normal fascist warmonger. But now they really wanted to nail a handle on him, and Zuzana did her best to find one that would fit. She tried everything, even getting long and contradictory opinions from the best Czech psychiatrists about what made the English 'Doctor X' bed as many young girls as they did themselves. It didn't help. Nothing did. The accounts grew longer but the sum at the bottom stayed a stubborn zero, while Mother Bear got more and more impatient.

"Then one of them, he sent for me and he told me, all the work I had done, I had done nothing. He said *nothing*. All that work, NOTHING!"

The noises in the next room stopped abruptly. Their

secret cocoon shattered, Maxim and Zuzana listened to others listening to what had seemed an empty room.

After a time, somebody beyond the wall moved something cautiously. Life had to go on.

"When was this?" Maxim asked softly.

"It was two days before yesterday. He said they would control the Veverka file themselves now, I would just work for them, a waitress, a messenger, *tah*."

"Did they say anything about why they could do better?"

"Oh, the bears know everything."

"Fine, but did they know anything special?"

"They said there was a letter. An old letter about Veverka, and why had I not found it."

"Have they got this letter?"

"No. But of course they will get it soon. Of course." She clearly didn't believe in the letter at all.

Maxim took her hands; she squeezed back, but maybe only instinctively. "Did they say what was in this letter?"

"It was about Veverka, something that would spoil him, just what they wanted, and why had I not found it."

Maxim was beginning to lose the thread of his interrogation; she was too close and he should let go of her hands, but . . .

"They didn't say how they knew there *was* a letter?" Had he asked that before?

"No."

"Did they say what you should do next?"

"That I should go to Ireland for them. It is more difficult for the bears to go around. To Shannon, because I work for the tourists . . . Veverka has nothing in Ireland."

What did he ask now?

The outside door in the next room slammed and footsteps faded away on the cobbles. They were alone again. What did he ask next?

He stood up without letting go of her hands, and she stood up in front of him. Her eyes caught a glint from the window, a spark in the gentle darkness around them, and he let go of her hands . . .

She was wrong. She was too short, her shoulders too wide as he pulled her against him, her breasts too big . . . She wasn't Jenny. But she was warm and welcoming after the cold lonely months . . .

Maxim lay drained and drowsy, his bones limp as skeins of wool. Behind the relief, like the big wheel at a distant fairground, turned the slow thoughts: *I have been unfaithful to Jenny . . . Jenny is dead . . . But I have been unfaithful to her . . . I told you, she is dead . . . That makes it worse . . .*

"I am hungry," Zuzana said.

He shook himself awake. *You have also been wallowing with a Czech defector,* his thoughts reminded him, much closer now. *How are you going to phrase that in your report?*

She lay mostly naked, tangled in a riot of sheets and blankets on the other bed. And she had a right to be hungry: at the pub they'd picked up only a couple of saloon bar sandwiches suffering from advanced rigor mortis. That had been enough for him, but being shot at can take people different ways.

He started dressing. "Do you want to go up to the village and see if there's a hamburger bar or something?"

"No." She moved her head a fraction on the pillow. "You will get me something. Can I have the gun?"

"Do you know how to use it?"

She took it, flicked out the magazine and pushed the safety off and on. "I know." She obviously did. Maxim wrapped the pistol in a handkerchief and pushed it under his pillow.

"Lock the door and for heaven's sake don't shoot unless somebody kicks it down." *Defector Shoots Chambermaid While Sharing Room With Major From Number 10.* Not that this motel ran to anything that could be called a 'chambermaid'.

He touched the end of her nose, and walked out.

Zuzana lay there for a few minutes. Then she got up, stretching languidly and yawning, cat-like, to lock the door. She left the lights off, fumbled for the radio, and turned it on to try and get the half-past-four news summary. She began to dress slowly.

I wonder if they will kill this sad, strong major, she thought. They may hide me, but they cannot hide Number 10.

◨ 12

The village had nothing like a hamburger bar, and the only teashop was shut. Maxim wandered around, instinctively getting the feel of the place, but also finding a non-vandalised telephone box. He wondered about ringing George, but what did he have to say? Then he came across a 'supermarket', which in this village meant a help-yourself grocer's not much bigger than the motel room, and bought a pocketful of tinned and packaged food. Then he had to buy some paper plates and plastic knives, as well.

He whispered at the bedroom door, and Zuzana put off the light to let him in. She leant against him in a quick, rather practiced gesture, and he kissed her hair. When the lights went on, he saw she was rather pale, and her hands were nervously rubbing the pleats in her skirt.

"It's all right," he said. "They can't find you here. They won't even know who to look for."

He had registered as Mr and Mrs Maxim—which was now a shade truer than it had been—because Maxim had no 'tradename', and would have to use his own credit cards, driving license and so forth. Zuzana had been professionally offended by that, but it had been the PM's decision. "We brought him in here," he had told George, "because he was Major Maxim and *not* one of the creepy-crawlies. So Major Maxim he can stay." And that was still that.

But even if he had been spotted as Maxim, the Bloc embassies hadn't got the manpower to ring every hotel in the Home Counties.

He spread out the food, expecting Zuzana to pounce. But she just began decorously spreading a little paté on a biscuit.

"Drink?" he suggested. The whisky was running low;

she'd taken a snort while he was out. She took another now.

He saw the radio and tuned it to a programme of classical music—not loud, but continuous.

"We're very happy to learn about Veverka, but is there anything you can say about the bears and our security? You do see how important that is."

She nodded with her mouth full, swallowed, took a gulp at her whisky. "It was when your minister sent home so many of the bears, do you remember? It was two years ago. The bears kept bringing in so many joes, your security could not afford to watch them all. It was, what you call it, like saturation bombing. Then for one time your minister did the right thing."

Maxim remembered: a great slaughter of the guilty when over a hundred Russian embassy and trade officials had been declared *personae non gratae*. Aeroflot had even sent a special plane to collect them. It had made headlines everywhere. Except Moscow, probably.

"So then, the bears went crazy. Suddenly they had nobody to make the drops, they thought all their sources would forget them, they would have nothing left. So they had to use us, of course. And some of the Poles and Hungarians, but . . ." the *but* and a little shrug relegated the Polish and Hungarian services to the fourth division. "Of course, they did not tell us who we were posting messages for. But it was the usual ways, the dead drops, always Moscow Centre chose them. I did not believe it before, but it is true. They could say in Moscow for me to post a message in the springs of the bed near the window of number 6 bedroom in this motel. They do not trust their own people here even to decide things like that."

Maxim had heard the same thing and hadn't really believed it, either.

"So, I tell you, it was a crazy time." They were back sitting facing each other, not touching. "We were running all over to the places Moscow said was a good drop. It was mad." And in the panic, there had been an unguarded discussion about which of two missions was more important, and Zuzana had heard enough to know she was acting as a cut-out for a source within British security itself.

"It was a moving drop, you understand. In a train, it came into Victoria just about ten o'clock each morning. I must go down to Gatwick first, then get on it there and post the message up under the towels basket in the lavatory at the back of the third first-class carriage. Then I stayed and went again just before the end to pick it up if it had not been collected, so the cleaners would not find it."

Maxim's experience was that British Rail cleaners might just be getting around to finding messages posted in the Boer War, but he smiled and nodded encouragingly.

"It was a good drop," she conceded. "It was simple, we used it often. Of course, there must have been a crash contact for the emergencies, but I would not be in that."

The radio concert ended with a burst of applause; it turned out to have been Schubert. Zuzana stood up, glanced at her watch, then prowled the room restlessly, but still with an animal grace. In an odd way, she reminded Maxim of the cat who sat on his papers.

"So I thought," she said, "why do I not find out who is this source?"

"And did you?"

Somebody next door flushed a cistern and in the silence after the music, it seemed to startle her. "I want to walk a bit. We can go down the back way."

It was quite dark by now, the sky sharp with stars. The stableyard rambled downhill into a small vegetable garden and then a field where they must once have grazed the horses. In a few seconds, Maxim's thin town shoes were soaked in freezing dew. Zuzana had on strong, well-polished ankle boots. They walked hand in hand.

Once they were clear of the buildings, she said: "It was not easy to find out, you understand. I could not wait in the corridor—those carriages were never so crowded—to go into the lavatory after each one to see if the message was gone. And the real man would have known me before I knew him. So I had to take some time. I would go in early to see if the message had gone, like that I knew he came on before East Croydon

. . ." Gradually she had eliminated the other regulars, bringing it down to one man.

And that man must be *the* man; a spymaster can use cut-outs, messengers who are no great loss when pinched, but a traitor can trust nobody. He has to collect his own post.

"Did you find out his name?" Maxim asked incautiously. But she wasn't to be hurried. They had reached the bottom of the field, where an overgrown stream glinted slow and sullen in the starlight. Zuzana shivered, folded her arms as if to cradle her breasts, and rocked gently against the quiet cold, sniffing at the sky.

"It will snow," she said suddenly. "Here you almost never have snow. It will be beautiful, like at home . . . He was I think fifty years old, or some more, about 185 centimetres in height, he is bald in the middle with grey hair . . ." the description rambled on, but it was by a trained observer and it added up to a complete man.

But what man?

"You didn't get his name?"

"Did you want me to *ask* him?"

"Once you'd spotted him, you could have followed him from Victoria, to see where he worked."

"He was in the trade. He was in both our trades, he would have noticed me. And . . . they took me off that drop. I think they had some new joes in by then, and he was too important . . ." Her voice was flat and mumbly.

Maxim said: "Have your people got a photograph of me yet?"

"Oh yes, of course."

"So you must have photos of everybody you know in British security?"

She didn't say anything.

"And you've had nearly two years to look through them, haven't you?"

"It was not easy, you must have a reason—"

"In two years you couldn't think of a reason? Who was the man you described just now?—your favourite uncle? *You never worked out which man was the contact, did you?*"

"I had to have *something!*" she shouted. "I had to bring *something* over! I had brought the Veverka file, I had it in my bag, but . . ."

Like a voice over his shoulder, Maxim could hear the Ashford instructor saying: "They all do it, they all build themselves up to make themselves more of a catch. If one says he's a KGB major, you can bet he's just a captain. If he tells you he can name six illegals, don't count on getting more than three. Just accept that you're going to be lied to, don't lose your cool, and at least you'll get all that there is to get."

I did brilliantly, Maxim thought bitterly. My first defector and the only cool thing about me is my feet.

He put his arms around her, awkwardly, since he wasn't used to her height and she was as stiff and unhelpful as a lamp-post. "I'm sorry. It's all right. You've given us quite enough to find him anyway. And the file, the baboons won't have got it. The police probably picked it up, so that's all right."

She relaxed and leant against him. "The police, of course. Yes. But what will they do to it?"

"I'll ring in and make sure we get hold of it. Come on." He put an arm round her shoulders and they started back up the field.

After a while, she said carefully: "There is something I can do for you, something else. I cannot say what, but soon."

"Fine." Maxim wasn't really listening. "Do you want to wait in the room?"

"I will wait. Can I have the gun again?"

He gave it to her along with the key, and this time waited until he heard the door lock before going up the yard.

He walked briskly out to the telephone box, since he wasn't going to trust the motel switchboard. But telephone boxes, taxies and parking spaces are never empty when you need them. He waited, almost dancing with the pain in his feet, while two girls made a long giggly call, and then another.

At last they rushed out in a flurry of long coats and laughter, not even noticing him.

Number 10 came on as a matronly voice saying:

"You should have told us where you are, Major. We've had more than one—"

"I'm not anywhere," Maxim said. "Just find me George Harbinger."

He told George about the motel, then about Zuzana's work as a cut-out and her little white lies. George took it better than he'd expected, just muttering: "Bloody woman." But he would have had far more experience of defectors' habits, if only indirectly.

Then Maxim told him about Veverka and the file. "That must have been what the wild bunch were after. There doesn't seem any reason why they should think she's even heard of the contact in security."

George grunted dubiously. "Has she said anything about why she's Seen The Light?"

"Just that she's tired of a repressive regime repressing its citizens, or something."

"Bullshit. She tried to identify that contact just so that she'd have something in the bank if she ever decided to come over. Every agent pinches some little secret, just in case. I suppose when you start in that work, you soon realise there may be only one safe place for you: the other side."

"Actually why she came," Maxim said, "is that they just took away her first command. She just grabbed the file, out of spite, and ran. Or that's my guess."

"She doesn't sound all that bright . . . What's that noise? Have you got the Brigade in there with you?"

Maxim realised he'd been stamping his almost numb feet on the floor of the box. "Sorry. She's no master-spy, but at least we know the Tyler letter's probably still around."

"I'm not at all sure I like that. We'll go into a huddle about it when you get back."

"When's that going to be?"

"Ring me in an hour or so. Oh—there's one other thing, Harry, and I don't think you should mention it to her. Wing-Commander Neale's dead. I asked the fuzz to put a guard on him but I was too late, blast it. Some of your roughnecks seem to have got in and worked on him a little. I believe it was his heart that gave out, so they probably didn't mean to kill him."

"They certainly meant to kill her."

"Yes, well . . . Keep in touch."

"Is the news about Neale on the radio?"

"I imagine so . . ."

Suddenly it wasn't just Maxim's feet that were cold. He ran all the way back to the motel, slowing down just for respectability as he entered the arch into the stableyard. The bedroom was dark, and there was no answer to his gentle knock and whisper. He tried the handle and the door opened. He knew then that she'd gone; a few seconds later, he knew the gun had gone with her.

The receptionist hadn't seen her go. "To tell the truth, I haven't seen her at all, have I? She's a foreign lady, your wife, isn't she?"

"Yes." Maxim was turning away when he realised what that meant. "She made a telephone call from the room, then?"

She could hardly deny it, but wasn't going to admit she'd tried to listen in. She must have been around fifty, with the thin bedraggled look of a bird with a broken wing. "She did make a call to London, yes."

"Just now?"

"Oh no. Nearly an hour ago, I should say."

"Can you give me the number, please?"

She was looking it up when the first shot sounded. It hardly registered on her; to Maxim it was a bomb.

Zuzana was certainly no master spy. She had rung her office as soon as the radio had told her of Neale's death: an almost purely emotional reaction, seeking revenge. But she remembered enough of her training to pretend that she had heard nothing and offered to discuss her own return to the fold *provided* nobody went near the Wing-Commander. They had promised that straight off, so she knew that when they came to meet her it would be in bad faith but perhaps without too much suspicion. But she had no time to scout the meeting-place she suggested: the porch of the church glimpsed as she and Maxim drove in. And her worst mistake was not to get there first: she had over-estimated the time they would take.

The only real error the two baboons made was not

to think that in the darkness she might have a gun in her hand.

The younger and smaller of them grabbed her from behind as she came through the lych-gate; the bigger reached for her from in front. She fired before the pistol was level, and the bullet smacked into his thigh bone. The second shot missed as the gun kicked higher, and the third went through his throat.

The other let go with one hand to reach for his own gun and she swung away, firing and missing as she turned. His shot hit her ribs with a punch that had no immediate pain, and then they were shooting into each other, barely three feet apart, until both fell down. Compared with the noise, the big baboon made almost no sound as he drowned in his own blood.

Maxim was first there, dodging from shadow to shadow across the churchyard until he could see the three bodies. He kicked the guns away; Zuzana and the younger one weren't dead, not yet.

"Did I kill them?" she muttered.

"I think so."

"I had wanted to do it . . . and be alive, but . . . *No!*" He had tried to lift her head out of the blood. But half her right eye socket was shot away. He laid her down very gently.

"They killed . . . the Wing-Commander . . ." After that she lapsed into a murmur of Czechoslovakian until she shuddered and died.

A small timid crowd had formed outside the gate. A burly man with a raincoat on over his shirt and carrying a torch, pushed through and shone it around. What had looked like black oil suddenly turned into a pond of blood.

"Great Jesus!" He swayed and put a hand on the gate for support, then turned the torch on Maxim. "I'm a policeman—"

"I'll get an ambulance," Maxim said. "You get onto Special Branch."

90

13

"At a rough guess, I would say that he broke just
about every rule in the book and quite a few that
aren't. Of course," Agnes added, "that's merely one
person's opinion."

"He had an impossible job," George said defen-
sively. "He couldn't know the girl was going to turn
into Calamity Jane."

" 'It was the girl started it'. Adam never knew what
a long-running excuse he'd thought up." They were sitting shivering in the front of George's Rover, parked
on the Horse Guards Parade behind Number 10.

"If *we'd* had her," Agnes went on, "she wouldn't
have been left alone for a second, let alone get near a
telephone or—Dear God, I still don't believe it—a
gun."

"It was all understandable the way Harry explained
it. And she wouldn't have come to your people anyway."

"She'd have done what she was told. Where else
would she go?—back to the embassy and say sorry?"

"She could have gone to Grosvenor Square. The Ivy
League can always use another defector to polish their
image with Congress."

One of the attendants, whose job was to keep the
Horse Guards exclusive, drifted up and glanced in
through the misted windows. But there was the correct
sticker on the windscreen and he wandered off down
the ranks of exceptionally clean and neatly-parked vehicles. There should be a new class in the Honours
List, George thought, with Her Majesty sticking a
parking permit on your lapel while wife and eldest
beamed tearfully in the background. It would certainly
rank above a C, but perhaps not quite a K.

"Have you any idea," Agnes persisted, "how much
work the Branch had to do to keep Mr and Mrs

Maxim's name out of it? God knows what they threatened or promised that motel. Half of Fleet Street booked in there that night. There's nowhere else to stay."

"Police get paid overtime. I do not."

"That's not what I mean. It's all being written down on tablets of stone and one day the Branch is going to need a favour from Number 10. *Then* you'll have early carol singers in Downing Street. And what was our Harold up to in that motel with Miss Kindl?"

"You write down your guess and I'll write down mine and we'll open each other's envelopes on New Year's eve. What does it matter?"

"It was in another county and besides, the wench is dead."

"When did Box 500 take up sexual prudery? Is there any news from the hospital?"

"Only that he's still critical. Fifty-fifty. It could be the uncertainty that's keeping the other side quiet."

The second baboon hadn't died, not quite, not yet. Meanwhile, stories about Gun Battle In Lonely Churchyard With Girl Defector flashed around the world, and the mystery about the two men guaranteed they would flash for days yet. The police had announced that the dead man had false German papers, but said nothing about the other. He might live to stand trial, and his papers would be evidence.

The Czech embassy had put out a statement saying just that they were sure Miss Kindl wasn't defecting, and they certainly didn't know the sort of people who carried false papers.

"Were they from sunny Russia?" George asked.

"Never in your life. The Centre wouldn't do anything so crude. That was the STB, they panicked and called in the Al Capones to try and sort out the defection before Moscow ever heard of it. Somebody really must love Professor John White Tyler—but then, I believe he loves quite a lot of people, one at a time."

George ignored that. "And have you found out who in your mob might be a traitor and comes to work on the Gatwick line every morning?"

Agnes took a couple of calming breaths. "Your dashboard clock isn't working."

"Dashboard clocks aren't supposed to work. Well?"

"George—how do you expect us to go about that?"

"Rather fast." He rubbed a clear patch on the misted windscreen. "You know—when the up-state vote comes in, we may find we're actually in the black. We did get a defector—"

"For about five minutes."

"Long enough to learn that Greyfriars has a steer on the Tyler letter, if it still exists. And a line into a bad apple in your barrel. They've also lost two trained cads—"

"Those come ten to the koruna."

"Never mind. Now everybody knows who sent them even if it can't be printed. So the STB comes out of it with a reputation not just for dirty work but incompetent dirty work. Moscow won't be minting any medals for that. And if Wing-Commander Neale gets tied in—and some bright reporter might do it—then Greyfriars have killed an MP on top of it. *They* might be ten a penny as well, but it does look bad on paper. With possibly a big show trial in six months."

"You surely don't want one?"

"Of course we don't. You never know what witnesses will say. But Greyfriars wants one even less. No, I see a distinct possibility of an increased dividend. Who do we talk to in the STB here?"

Agnes shook her head slowly. Whatever Moscow Centre and Prague were feeling, George obviously wasn't suffering, which meant that Number 10 wasn't. She'd expected a raging gloom about a scandal far worse than Jackaman having been avoided by—she believed—sheer luck.

"Josef Janza seems to be their open end right now," she said thoughtfully. "You could have met him at their National Day party. Fortyish, about five-ten, balding, very cheerful, gold teeth—"

"Yes, yes, I think I did. Right, then—" George turned suddenly brisk, snapping out orders as if he were still a Dragoons subaltern. "You meet this Janza and tell him more or less what I've said. Take a tough line. If his people even hint that anybody on our side is involved—and I mean anybody, not just Harry or Number 10—then he can start building himself an ark

93

and not to waste time waiting for the animals. Any questions?"

"Is this the Headmaster speaking?"

"No comment. None of this is avowable, of course. All your own work."

"I know." In the patch of windscreen George had wiped clear, snowflakes hardly bigger than dust swirled around as if too timid to risk a landing. Agnes shivered and reached for the door handle.

"And one other thing," George said. "See if you can chase up that STB file on Tyler. I believe your people had it to translate. It's more or less academic interest by now, but we'd like to know . . ."

"Will try. By the way, what's happened to our favourite fighting man?"

"We gave him a couple of days off to re-group."

"Ah yes. Well, at least you can't say this time that nobody's got killed."

"Not by Harry."

"And not for lack of trying. Give him time, give him time." She opened the door and skipped out. George glowered after her, then turned on the car radio. He'd wait a couple of minutes for her to get clear. Outside, the snowflakes suddenly thickened, gained confidence and started to settle.

Later that day, the second baboon suddenly died, leaving everybody else feeling much better, thank you. Now all the vote was in and could be counted. There would be no public trial with unpredictable witnesses, just a well-orchestrated inquest and—a rare treat—no relatives of the deceased around. Josef Janza quickly accepted Agnes's invitation to lunch at one of the old high-ceilinged railway hotels with wide-spaced tables. Only George, who mistrusted happy endings, seemed to have doubts.

He stayed late at Number 10, working on the draft of the PM's speech in the defence debate and worrying. Certainly the baboon had had every excuse for dying: one lung collapsed by a bullet and with pneumonia, diagnosed too late, in the other. And there was no chance that any cad or rotter could have reached his bedside, where Special Branch men and friends of

Agnes far outnumbered the doctors and nurses. But *quis custodiet ipsos custodes?* And how do you phrase such a delicate—or indelicate—question?

He was still wondering when Agnes rang to ask if the PM was home and if so, could she bring her Director-General over to see him. Urgent. George established that the PM was already on his way back from the House and told Agnes to come on round.

George shook hands with the D-G, a rather sombre, lean man in thick spectacles, and showed him straight into the Cabinet Room where the Prime Minister was waiting quite alone. Then he took Agnes next door, to the Principal Private Secretary's room, away from the young ears of the duty clerk.

She wore a sexless old sheepskin jacket and an oddly blank expression. George offered her a drink and she shook her head. "The Tyler file. I'm afraid it's gone."

"Gone? Gone where?"

"Home, I imagine." Her voice was blank, too; deliberately drained of expression. "It had been about half translated when Rex Masson—I don't know if you've met him, he's been deputy head of our vetting section the last couple of years—he asked to borrow it. He rang in later last night to say he thought he was going down with flu. Nobody got around to asking any questions until late today, then . . . he's gone, his wife's gone, the file's gone."

George walked a slow quiet circuit of the nearest desk. "Where did Masson live?"

"Just outside Reigate. He caught a Victoria train at Redhill every morning, so it sounds as if that girl was telling the truth. The Branch is pulling his house apart by now."

"This is what your D-G's telling the Headmaster?"

"Yes."

George walked another circuit. "The vetting section . . . that would be how they knew about Tyler's appointment. He would have had his vetting topped up as soon as he was chosen . . . Did this Masson of yours have anything to do with the hounding of Jackaman?"

"I don't know." She wasn't even looking at him, just staring blindly at the wall.

"Well," George said, "at least now we know. You

win one, you lose one. I can't say how the Headmaster'll take it, but I don't suppose that file would have told *us* very much. And they had to blow a prime asset to get it back. It must have been the only copy—funny, that."

"You know how they are about copying machines." Then she suddenly burst out: "What *is* it about Tyler? I know he's a great military theorist, but anybody would think he was the *Pope* . . ."

George looked mildly surprised but ignored the question. Agnes looked as if she might be going to cry; George couldn't have stood that. "It isn't your fault. These things just happen. All you can do is keep on carrying the banner with strange device through snow and ice . . . peculiarily apposite, on this evening." He had left one of the curtains open so that he could see the snowflakes spiralling down outside. It was a rare and restful sight.

"Oh *bollocks*." Agnes turned her back and blew her nose vigorously. "You just think that it's something that only happens to the Other Mob. Then when it's somebody in your own service . . . they'll be serving free champagne in Century House tonight." Agnes's view of the Intelligence Service was that the best of them were merely alcoholic transvestites. George had heard her on the subject often.

"That's out of date. *Now* have a drink."

She glanced at the tall double doors into the Cabinet Room. "All right. Make it a strong one."

George poured them both stiff whiskies. "Enough ice outside, I imagine. Confusion to the enemy." They both drank. "And what now?"

"We spend the night going through every file that Masson could have known about. And the next night . . ."

They chatted vaguely until the doors opened and the D-G came out. He looked pale: after Jackaman and now this, his job and reputation were teetering on the high wire. No, George thought, his reputation's already hit the sawdust. The job's all he's got left.

"Would you like a drink, Director-General?"

"No thank you, George. Agnes and I will be running

along. The Prime Minister said he'd call you in a few minutes."

Politely, George saw them to the front door, then went back to work on the speech. *The war in Europe ended on the river Elbe . . . Our front line is still there . . . no island has been an island since 1940 . . . Europe's defences are in Europe's hands, not in a begging bowl . . .* Apart from that last phrase, it was still crude and certainly too hawkish. But the strange device on their banner had to be Europe. Not NATO, but Europe, Europe, Europe.

Outside, the snow lay smooth and certain. London would be chaos tomorrow. And he hadn't mentioned that second baboon to Agnes. Now he never would.

14

Professor Tyler dined with the Master of his college that night. Just the two of them, alone in the big warm twinkling room, huddled at one end of the long triple-pillar table, backs to a crackling log fire. A silent maid came in and out, offering second helpings of everything, which they always refused.

"I imagine you would have to be very rich," the Master said, "to live privately in the style we decree for ourselves." Tyler made an agreeing noise, knowing that the Master had married quite enough money to live in any style he chose, private or public.

"Was it still snowing when you came in?" the Master went on. "So I suppose that tomorrow there won't be any trains or aeroplanes or buses, just because we live in a country which lies on the same line of latitude as Minsk and Hudson Bay." He gave a whimpering laugh. "But I like snow. I didn't see enough of it in London. How is London these days?"

"Cold," said Tyler. "That was nearly a week ago."

"Oh yes, your committee. When do you expect to report?—or is that Top Secret?"

Tyler smiled politely. "The final report won't be much more than a public relations exercise, Master. It's what we can persuade the joint chiefs and politicians about before then that will really matter."

The Master's bleary, baggy eyes lit up suddenly. He had decayed to a fat blotched grub of a man who moved in slow motion and occasionally missed his mouth with a forkful of food, but he remembered thirty glorious years of academic and political intrigue as one of Whitehall's top scientific advisors. A whiff of conspiracy was like cannon smoke to an old war-horse.

"But do you believe you can achieve anything significant, I mean really significant, without the *imprimatur* of our Big Brothers in Washington?"

"I think," Tyler said carefully, "that it isn't so much a question of whether we can, but that we're going to have to."

"They've come to thinking that, have they? De Gaulle really must be grinning in his grave. So you think the Americans are going to retreat from Europe?—or let their forces come down below—what do you call it?"

"The hostage level."

"Ah yes. Do you believe that?"

"Let me put it this way, Master. Ten years ago it would have been unbelievable. But the last ten years of American policy, in the White House particularly, have been unbelievable. Now nobody's sure about what can be believed any more."

After a time, the Master said vaguely: "Yes, I suppose it has come to that. But you're going to need the French, John. Of course, you get on well with them. They don't respect anybody who doesn't speak their language properly. And who isn't a bit of a gangster besides." He shook with wet, almost silent, laughter. "I suppose you'll be looking for a common nuclear targeting policy. Do you have anything to offer Paris on that?"

Tyler's smile was quick, almost defensive. How, in this great collapsing grub of a man could there still be a small bright worm of intelligence gnawing its way to the heart of every question?

He put his knife and fork down very precisely. "I think it matters less what we can offer than that we can get them to accept the principle of joint targetting. We can always change the targets later."

"Do you think they're ready for it?"

"I think they may be. They haven't had a really coherent nuclear policy since de Gaulle, and some of their *Force de Dissuasion* is getting a little tired by now—it was never very long-ranged anyway. Their Mirage IV's are all of fifteen years old, you know."

"Ummm." The Master rang a small handbell, then got up very slowly and carefully, tiptoeing along the edge of pain. "We'll have coffee by the fire, shall we? Will you take port? The Mad Doctor says I mustn't touch it any more. And a cigar?"

He gave orders over his shoulder to the expression-less maid, who collected the dishes and went out. Tyler stared after her, trying—for no good reason—to guess at her age.

"Don't seduce this one, will you, John?" the Master called from the fireplace. "It's so difficult to find a maid who's even half way competent, no matter what you pay them." He lowered himself into a stiff wing chair. "Have you met them yet?"

"No, but we're trying to arrange a little get-together. With somebody from Bonn as well."

"In the hope that they'll pay for it all."

"That's perhaps too much to hope for, Master. But West Germany has to accept that she is really a nu-clear power already, with those thousands of tactical warheads stored on her soil and sheltering behind the American atomic sword ever since NATO began."

"You aren't proposing that the Germans get their own nuclear weapons, are you?"

"No, Master. Not this year."

The Master made a long reflective humming noise. The maid came back with a coffee tray, a decanter of port and a box of Jamaican cigars. They had been Havanas when the Master still smoked. She poured coffee for them both, then the Master waved her way with a hand that went on nodding like a forgotten met-ronome.

"You'll help yourself to anything you want, John? And you know where to find the whisky." He sipped plain black coffee. "It isn't being forbidden things that's really so bothersome, it's discovering that you don't want them any more. I'm not sure what would be a vice, at my age. I suppose if I were still a believer I'd have the consolations of blasphemy . . . Are you going to propose anything specific to our Parisian target-teers?"

"I have one or two ideas that we've been discussing in committee and with the chiefs of staff. Nothing I've published, but I've been thinking along these lines for some time now . . ." Tyler selected a cigar; the end was already cut. "The problem is to find something that the Russians will believe in. I don't think they're going to believe that we can inflict damage of quantity on them. We have to find a way to inflict damage of quality."

"Ce n'est pas la quantité qui compte, mais la qualité . . . It translates well." He hummed tunelessly for a time. "But you're getting into muddy waters, John."

"We're small fish now, Master. It's the pike who likes a clear stream."

The Master said nothing more, so Tyler went and poured himself a glass of port. Before he sat down again, he lifted one of the heavy green velvet curtains at the window. The sky had cleared to a hard star-sparkled black, as clear as the desert night in the old days . . . Below, the small court was filled with rich deep snow under the blue lamplight. Just a single track of footprints went diagonally across it, and he felt a shiver of fear, but then decided it must be some young don exercising his new rights to get his feet wet across the lawn. He let the curtain fall again.

"It's going to be a cold night, Master."

"I'm sure you're right. And none of this has gone before the Cabinet, I assume?"

"I don't think targetting policy has ever been a Cabinet affair. But it's been raised at the Cabinet committee on defence, so I understand."

"Where you don't get any missionaries from Education or Social Services." He put his coffee cup down very carefully. "And you say it's fifteen years."

"What was, Master?"

"Since the French formed their first nuclear strike force."

"More than that."

"Nothing happens and yet it all goes by so quickly. When I was up as an undergraduate, in a single term you could fall in and out of love, discover a new poet and change your political views completely . . . all in eight weeks . . . John, I suppose you want me to keep this to myself?"

"We'd prefer the meeting not to be mentioned, but if we do get a targetting policy, we'll have to let it get out for it to have any deterrent effect."

"So I'm just a leaky old pump that you're priming." The great body quivered with his own joke. "Take some more coffee, John. What do they say is behind this business of that Czech girl defector?"

On the south coast, the snow lay thinner and patchier, but the wind came off the grey sea like a frozen scythe. Maxim and Chris tramped the pebble bank at the top of the beach, their feet shifting and sliding, stopping to pick up the smoothest stones and fling them into the waves. Hunger, sex and throwing stones into water were the three primitive drives that had made the human race what it is, Maxim decided.

At ten years old, Chris had grown sideways as much as upwards: he was now a miniature Welsh fly-half. Indeed, there was something of the original Celts about his long dark hair and his pale skin—but the eyes, when he turned a sudden direct stare on you, were the golden-dark of Jenny's.

And he mustn't know, Maxim thought. I must see only him in his own eyes, nobody else.

"Daddy," Chris asked, "when are you going back to London?"

"When somebody rings up. When they want me."

"Is it very secret, what you're doing?"

"Not very, no," Maxim said glibly. "I'm there to answer military questions—if I can. And all military things are at least partly secret."

"Do you see the Prime Minister all the time?"

"Not to speak to. He's around, but I usually work to one of his private secretaries, George Harbinger. I don't think you'd better mention his name around school, by the way."

"Of course I won't." Chris hunched his shoulders— in the inevitable plastic rally jacket—and trudged on, frowning over what he would say next. "Daddy—what sort of aeroplane was Mummy in when she crashed?"

"A Short Skyvan. Very square-shaped, twin engines, twin tails, high wings, fixed undercarriage . . . don't you know it?"

Chris nodded; he could identify most modern aircraft from the swamp of books and magazines in his bedroom. "I thought it was a Skyvan."

"Why did you ask, then?"

"Some of the boys at school . . . they said they

didn't believe Mummy was really dead, that she'd just gone away and left us. I thought if I could be sure what aeroplane it was, they'd believe me."

I will kill those boys, Maxim thought. One by one I will pick them up and beat their little heads to a pulp and then it won't matter *what* they believed . . .

He realised how fast he was walking, crunching ahead of Chris at a Rifle pace. He slowed. It isn't cruelty, he thought, it's just that a broken marriage is something all these kids know about, and death is something that only happens on TV. Particularly in a blown-up aeroplane. He stopped and threw three stones, trying to cut them through the crests of the breaking waves.

"I saw the aeroplane crash," he said in a flat voice.

"Yes, Daddy," Chris said. "So you're quite sure she won't come back?"

If there were hope I *would* kill them, for giving Chris such a terrible false hope.

"No," he said. "No chance. It's just you and me."

He put his arm around the boy's shoulders and they walked back through a gap in the ramshackle bathing huts onto the pebble-strewn seafront road and Maxim's car.

After a while, Chris asked: "Do you have to keep on taking exams in the Army?"

"Yes—them, or something like them."

"Ugh."

"Well, you could always become a tramp, or even go into the Air Force."

"Daddy!"

They were laughing by the time they reached Maxim's parents' house. There was a message to ring George.

15

The Massons' bungalow was a rambling affair thrown together by a speculative jerry-builder just after the First World War. It had been built for summers of tennis, cocktails and open sports cars. Under the snow, fifty years later, it looked like a group of Army huts that had melted together. Maxim drove cautiously up the thirty yards of driveway, already squashed into rutted ice by other vehicles. At the top there were four parked cars and a plain van. He just squeezed into a space beside the rickety wooden garage that was two cars long instead of wide. Odd, that.

It was also odd that there didn't seem to be a front door, just french windows that had curtains drawn across them. But a uniformed policeman hurried out of a kitchen door wanting identification. Maxim took time finding his ID card, looking around at the perfect snow on the tennis lawn, at the bulging laurels and evergreen shrubbery.

Agnes was sitting at the kitchen table, which was covered in mugs, milk bottles, cups and teapots. She still had her sheepskin jacket on, and her face looked stale. "Hello, our 'Arry. Do you want a cuppa as well?"

"If it's going," Maxim said automatically, and sat down, unbuttoning his car coat. She poured him a mug of tea. The whole room, which wasn't very big, looked slightly askew. Somebody had moved the refrigerator, the dishwasher, gas stove and a cupboard and not quite got them back in line. Deeper into the house, he could hear mutterings and tappings as the searchers moved on.

Agnes passed him a mug. "In a while they'll be testing the floorboards and stripping paper off the walls. Some of the plaster, too."

"Have they found anything?"

"Enough to be sure he was on the take from Moscow. What did George tell you?"

"Just that he was the man Zuzana Kindl was telling me about."

"Yes." Agnes gave him a brief history of Rex Masson's work at MI5. "He must have handed the file back to the bad fairies and jumped off that same night while you were explaining yourself to the Special Branch in Buckinghamshire. He'd have a crash escape all planned . . ." she shrugged inside her sheepskin jacket, which barely moved. To Maxim the house seemed quite warm, and he wondered briefly who paid for it now. And for the stripped wallpaper and plaster. Whose house *was* it, now?

He sipped the lukewarm sweet tea. "We don't know how or where?"

"The first flight he could get. Berlin or Vienna for choice, but any capital with a sizeable Russian embassy. There's no point in trying to find out. In six months time, when they've taught him to sit up and beg nicely, he'll surface in Moscow and give a press conference telling how sickened he was with the work he had to do for his fascist imperialist bosses here. And then he'll settle down in a nice little concrete flat and a small summer dacha outside Moscow—not too far outside—with a Party card so his wife can go to the head of the queues and he can buy the latest Juilliard Quartets at the foreign currency store and then just *sit* there and drink himself to death. Because that's all he's got left. All he's left himself."

She sounded very vicious.

"How old was he?" Maxim asked, then wondered why he'd said 'was' about a man who was presumably still alive.

Agnes gave him a tired smile. "Just the right generation, maybe the last of them. He was up at Oxford in the late forties, when Moscow still had some sex appeal. With the kids at the universities today, you couldn't give them Russian communism with a free pound of Mexican grass. They're into Chile or black Africa . . . I suppose even China's unfashionable now that they're playing footsie with America. More tea?"

"No thanks. What are you doing here when you're not playing mother?"

"Keeping an eye on the service's interests and telling George what's going on. I assume you'll do that now."

"I don't know. *Is* there anything going on?"

"Go and have a look. One of the coppers says he knows you."

As Maxim turned away, Agnes added: "Have you got your gun this time?"

"No. Why?"

"Oh, nothing." She grinned privately into her teacup.

Beyond the kitchen was a badly-lit corridor with doors on both sides and two men rolling up the carpet. But the mutterings seemed to come from an open door opposite. Maxim went through a dining room with heavy tables and chairs all pushed out of place, and opened a door on the far side.

It was a big low-ceilinged room, the one with the french windows at the front end, and windows on both side walls. The fourth wall was mostly a wide fireplace with a basket grate and the ashes of a log fire. It was rather cluttered, originally with knick-knacks of furniture—small tables, poufs, standing lamps along with several soft chairs, a sofa, an upright piano—but now also with five plain-clothes policemen. One of them got up from where he'd been poking the floor beside the piano and came towards Maxim grinning and holding out his hand.

"It's *Major* Maxim now, isn't it, sir? I don't suppose you remember me." There was a sly challenge in that: an Army officer is supposed to remember people. The man was very square and solid, with short fair hair, a snub nose and a slight Welsh accent.

"Ferris," Maxim said. "Sergeant Bill Ferris. You were instructing at Hereford when I started my first tour with SAS. Parachute Regiment, weren't you?"

Ferris was delighted. "I told you Mr Maxim never forgot a face, didn't I?" They shook hands. "It must be all of twelve years ago, at that."

Maxim tapped Ferris's stomach. "That's something I don't remember."

Ferris grinned again. "In Special Branch we don't do

so much doubling up and down hills as I used to." He introduced Maxim to the other policemen; most of them were sergeants, and Ferris the only inspector. They shook hands politely, then faded back to their work, one of them taking Ferris's place down by the piano. They were pulling at the floorboards, probing the walls with large needles, carefully dismantling the standard lamps.

"Take your pick, sir," Ferris waved his hand at a collection of objects on a small table. There was a torch battery, a talcum powder tin, a large table lighter, silver cigarette box and a few others.

Maxim hesitated. "If I choose right, do I get my hand blown off?"

"This isn't Aden, sir. Nor Londonderry. Just pick one."

Maxim chose the talcum tin. Ferris unscrewed the cap, sprinkled a little powder to prove it worked, then screwed the cap back on and gave it an extra twist and push. The tin slid apart, a tin within a tin. The powder was held in a narrow central compartment, with empty hiding places on either side.

"Beautiful work," Ferris purred. "Beautiful. Moscow Centre does a lovely job. But of course—" he went on showing the secret compartments in the torch battery, the table lighter and all the others; "—they've always had a tradition of craftsmanship. I don't say Russians make good artists, mind. But they're craftsmen. I read the other day about a Russian who carves little temples and things out of bits of ivory that you can only see under a really powerful glass. He makes a cut in between his heartbeats, the article said, to keep his hand steady. They give his work to visiting VIP's and people."

As a policeman, Ferris had flowered surprisingly. Maxim remembered him as a very plodding instructor in communications. And that reminded him. "Have you found any radio gear?"

Ferris looked up, shocked. "Oh no, sir. Moscow Centre wouldn't use radio these days. Not in this country, anyway."

Maxim felt he'd made an indecent suggestion by

mistake. "Sorry. But then how did he get in touch with his friends in Kensington Palace Gardens?"

"I thought you knew something about that already, sir." Ferris looked sly again. "The dead letter box on the train, wasn't it?"

"That was only a one-way street. He wasn't sending anything."

"Then any other way. There could be a thousand. He could think of a few for himself, I expect, him being so much in the business already." Maxim realised that Special Branch wasn't totally dismayed at MI5 being caught in the wrong bed. "Of course, most of what he'd be passing on would be film, undeveloped 110-size film cassettes. You see?" He held up the talcum tin again. "Just the right size, made for it. He'd photograph some documents in his office, then leave this at some drop. It isn't suspicious to own one of those pockets cameras, now everybody's got them. But he couldn't exactly take it down to the corner shop to be developed, now could he, sir?"

"Hardly."

"The trouble we take to make it easy for other people's spies," Ferris sighed. "We invent these cameras and button-sized microphones and put copying machines in every office . . . Did you know that in Russia every typewriter has to be registered with the police and they take a sample page from it, in case you start spreading those *samizdats?*"

"Really?" Maxim knew that already.

"It is a fact. And——" Then one of the policemen called him over. Ferris said: "Excuse me," and went back to the suspect floorboard beside the piano.

Maxim watched for a while, then got bored. The operation had the leisurely thoroughness of an old lady doing embroidery; a proper house search like this could easily last a week. He drifted back through the dining room to the corridor, where the other two policemen had finished rolling up the carpet. They looked at him, but said nothing.

If the Massons had had children, they didn't live at home any more. There were four possible bedrooms, one of which had been turned into a study and another which had no clothes or character and was obviously a spare room. Then husband and wife had each had a room, with a linking door. He was fumbling among the clothes in Rex Masson's built-in cupboard when Agnes came quietly up behind him.

"How are you doing, Sherlock?"

"You know my methods—and they don't seem to do any good. I can tell he went in a hurry. I wouldn't walk out on a wardrobe like this." The clothes were all good quality, most of them tailored, and the shoes expensive.

"If you're moonlighting for Moscow you can afford to be a snappy dresser. I doubt he'd risk even coming home. Just ring her and tell her to meet him. He can't have known how much time he had. She left behind a lot of good stuff, too."

"Was she in it with him?" Maxim went on rummaging.

"You can't tell. All that gimmickry—the talcum tin and the cigarette lighter and so on—that came from his room or the study. Philby's wife didn't know. But you get some husband-and-wife teams as well."

Masson obviously had the habit of putting tickets—theatre, car-park, cinema—into his outside breast pocket. Half the jackets in the closet had some. And once, in his first Latin lesson, the young Harry Maxim had noticed that the objectives had the same endings as the nouns to which they applied. Perhaps he, he alone, had spotted this and for him Latin was going to be easy! Perhaps putting ticket stubs in your breast pocket was a sure sign of treachery. Life should be that simple.

"D'you notice anything about the house?" Agnes asked. "Taking everything together?"

Maxim stopped and looked around and tried to remember. Overall, the house was rather dark and worn; the furniture wasn't expensive, the central heating radiators were the heavy old-fashioned kind you found in barracks and schools—big enough to sit on (it was supposed to give you piles or chilblains, he couldn't remember which). But the clothes . . .

"He spent his money on things he could take with him," he decided. "Not on the house. What car did he have?"

"A five-year-old Renault 12. She had an eight-year-old Mini. That's right: he was always going home to Moscow in the end."

"I suppose they always have to."

"Sometimes faster than they expect," Agnes said grimly. "Those bastards are not going to like the Moscow clothing shops."

In fact, the house did have a front door, but as it was set at ninety degrees to the sensible, it was invisible from the drive. And since the uniformed policeman wasn't guarding the house in any serious sense, Mrs Barbara Masson walked up to the door and let herself in on her key before anybody had seen her.

She stood in a tiny hallway, lined with coats, between the two big rooms and asked loudly: "And just who on *earth* are all of you?"

Agnes came quickly across the dining-room. "Hello, Barbara. We're us. Plus Special Branch, of course."

"I do hope, Agnes Algar, that at least you've got a search warrant."

"Oh yes, we're all being very legal. We even brought our own tea and sugar and milk. That's standard procedure on occasions like this."

Mrs Masson put down the suitcase she had in one hand and the airline bag she had in the other and slowly knelt down between them and began to cry and cry and cry.

◉ 16

"He said we were going on just a short trip to Vienna and the service had said I could go. I've been on these things before. It's something about a couple looking less suspicious than a single person. That's right, isn't it, Agnes?"

"That's right." Agnes spoke very gently.

"He said he wouldn't have time to get home, it had all been arranged at the last minute and that I should pack for both of us. He told me some special things he wanted." She was lying flat on her bed, staring at the ceiling. The room was darkening as evening crept in, but nobody moved to turn on a light. Maxim had found her a drink and Agnes had rummaged out a packet of tranquilisers from the bottom of her vast handbag, and Inspector Ferris had been chased back to his mouseholing. Now they just listened.

Barbara Masson had a very English elegance and the face you see in society magazines: lean, high cheekbones, a slightly large mouth and very good teeth. That sort ages well, and the silver in her long fair hair suited her. She could have worn pearls to hose out the pig-sty and not look overdressed.

"What special things?" Agnes prompted.

"Oh, two of his newest suits and his favourite ties—quite a lot of them, I thought, and his new shoes and to be sure to bring his best cuff-links. And he wanted the two little cameras. It all sounded rather *grand* for a two-day jaunt, but I didn't suspect *anything*." Her voice was a Knightsbridge flute that frequently hit a word *fortissimo*.

"Two cameras?" Agnes asked. But of course Masson would need two, no professional dared trust only one. And he had certainly been a professional photographer.

"Yes, one of them was mine, he gave me it. But I

111

never really *liked* it. It was too small and fiddly. He borrowed it sometimes."

"So you took both."

"That's right. Well, when I got to Heathrow, he gave me a new passport. It had my picture in it, I don't know where he got *that*, and it said I was Margaret Franklin. I'd never seen it before, of course, but it had quite a lot of stamps and visas in it as if I'd got to all these places." She lifted her head to stare at Agnes. "I thought it was the service who'd done it, but it must have really been *them*?"

"They're good at their job."

"Yes." It was a sigh. Mrs Masson let her head fall back. "Actually, I was quite excited, being somebody else, somebody unreal. A bit like taking over from Sarah Bernhardt and making an absolute wow of it." She giggled and waved an arm in a gesture slightly unstrung by vermouth and tranquilisers and probably lack of sleep. An empty glass thumped onto the carpet but didn't break. Nobody moved.

"We put up at a hotel down in the old city, but it was a modern hotel. We didn't get there until after dinner but it didn't really matter because we'd had one of those ucky airline meals. You *have* to eat them because there's nothing else to *do* on an aeroplane except get sloshed. Rex said he had to go out just to make a contact. He was gone, oh, about three-quarters of an hour. When he came back he said he'd arranged a chaffeur-driven car for us to go sight-seeing the next morning. I *thought* that was a bit odd because Vienna was full of snow so heaven *knows* what it would be like outside. But at least we wouldn't be doing the driving and the service was paying, so . . . In the morning he told me."

"Before you got in the car?"

"This was before the car even came. He told me to pack, and then he said we weren't going back to Britain, not ever again. We were going to Moscow instead. I just didn't *believe* him, I thought he was making some terrible joke. Then I realized we were only *about* thirty miles from Moscow—if you see what I mean."

Agnes nodded. "The Czech frontier at Bratislava.

That's probably where you'd have gone over. Did he say . . . why you were going?"

"He talked about half-baked *socialism* mixed with half-baked *capitalism* and governments that didn't dare take any decisions so that Britain was run by the civil service and the unions. I must say it's funny he was blaming the *unions* and here we were on our way to Moscow." Her voice was suddenly strained and bitter.

Agnes said softly: "They don't have strikes in Moscow, Barbara."

"I suppose not . . . But I wasn't really listening. It was all as if he'd said he'd been sleeping with somebody else for years . . . No, I *really* think it was worse. If he'd been sleeping around there would have been just *part* of him I hadn't understood. But this was *all* of him."

Treachery, Maxim thought, is a balloon. It has to be complete or it's nothing.

"And what did you do?" Agnes asked.

"It's quite terrible how you fall back on clichés. I just said: 'I'm leaving you, Rex. Good-bye.' And I picked up my bags and I walked out."

"He didn't try to stop you?"

"No. Nobody did. But why do you think he didn't wait until we were actually *in* the car before he told me where we were going?"

"Maybe," Maxim said, "that after all the years when you didn't have a choice, he owed you one at the end."

Mrs Masson lifted herself on one elbow and peered through the gloom at him. "Yes. Yes, I *suppose* you could be right. He wasn't an *unkind* man."

Agnes said: "Also you couldn't have been dragged unwillingly through the Austrian frontier post. And so you flew back home?"

"It wasn't that easy," Mrs Masson said reproachfully. "This is *yesterday* I'm talking about." She had done a slow frightening journey quite alone—more alone than she'd ever been before—and now, perhaps, she wanted to blunt the memory by doing it again in company.

When she reached the airport, she realised she hadn't

even any Austrian money for the taxi and had to over-
pay heavily in sterling. And then there wasn't a flight
to Britain for another three hours. She began to worry.

Rex might have let her go, but that didn't mean his
new masters concurred. And there she'd be, sitting in
the most obvious place, for three hours . . .

She pulled herself together, changed the rest of her
pounds into schillings and took a taxi back to the city,
to the railway station. Which station? She hadn't realised there were two. Then where did she want to go?
She didn't know that, either, but then remembered that
Germany was to the west, away from the Iron Curtain.
Then she must go to the Westbahnhof.

"How were you going to manage for tickets and a
passport?" Agnes asked.

"Oh, I had my Diner's Club card, thank heavens. I'd
only taken it out two years ago. And I actually had my
real passport. You see, Rex hadn't told me *not* to bring
it when he rang, I suppose that would have sounded
odd, so I just naturally *did*. But he'd taken back the
Margaret Franklin one."

There was a stopping train to Munich, and as she
watched the white countryside rumble by, the terrors
began again. For over twenty years of marriage she
had been aware of the KGB as a giant enemy, but a
distant, misty one. Now the giant was aware of her,
knew she was scuttling around somewhere on the floor
of Europe, would be leaning down to look closer . . .
At every stop, anybody getting on could be an agent,
and most of them looked like it. She reached Munich
almost in hysterics.

She staved them off until Munich airport—and by
then the snow had hit London, catching Heathrow with
its boots off, as usual. Flights to London were backing
up all over Europe, nobody knew when . . . at that,
she hauled her case into the lavatory and sat down and
burst into tears. Her whole life had fallen in on her,
and she was still trapped in the rubble.

At least German lavatories are clean enough for a
good long cry. And after that, she remembered the
duty-free bottle of Scotch in her airline bag, a rare and
expensive brand that Rex had insisted on—and she
now knew why. She didn't much like Scotch, especially

neat, but a few cautious gulps made the giant seem smaller, and shorter-sighted. She took a taxi back to the station and bought a ticket to Frankfurt, remembering vaguely that the airport there had more flights than anywhere in Germany, and anyway, she wanted to keep moving.

"You could have gone to the British consul," Agnes pointed out.

"You mean just walk in and tell some little *trade* official that my husband's defected to Russia and I think the KGB's after me? Oh no *thank* you, Agnes. He'd've thought I was *mad*."

"You could have rung us. You know the number."

There was a tense silence. Maxim got up, switched on a lamp with an old parchment shade, then fumbled the curtains shut. The room took on a warm, firelight glow.

"Perhaps," he said, "you didn't want to risk being the first to break the news."

"I *think* perhaps that was it," Mrs Masson said gratefully. She swung her feet onto the floor and sat up, flexing her shoulders. "I suppose he *might* have changed his mind and come back. And anyway, would you have believed me, Agnes?"

"It's our job to believe things like this," Agnes said tonelessly, watching Maxim.

"And *there*," Mrs Masson said, "they *did* catch me."

Probably they'd spotted her at the airport but not risked making a pass then. Now they found her alone in a corner of the concourse, searching for change in her handbag. One snatched the bag, the other stepped in to block her from view, and she thought he had a gun in his hand. Then before she had time to decide whether to scream or not, the bag had been thrown back at her and they were gone, hurrying but not running, and lost in a crowd that looked quickly at her and quickly away, uninvolved.

She was shaking so badly that she could hardly stand as she reached down for the bag to see what they had left her. And the answer was everything—except her little camera.

"Was there a film in it?" Agnes asked.

"Well there *was*, yes, I'd just put it in. I'd noticed there were only two shots left in it, so I used them taking a picture of the house—I don't suppose they'll come out, in that light—and bought a new film at Victoria."

"What did you do with the old one?" Agnes asked, her voice very controlled.

"It's somewhere in my airline bag. I was going to get it developed."

"We'll do that for you."

There was a distant thump as the police moved some heavy furniture. Mrs Masson shuddered. "It's like having the *burglars* in, grubbing through your clothes . . . Oh, Agnes, just tell me *who* I married."

Agnes had come down by train and Maxim offered to drop her at Redhill station. His own drive back to London was going to be murder in that weather, and she had the film to develop. Ferris watched, shivering, as he backed a cautious three-point turn among the parked police cars and vanished as they started down the rutted ice of the drive.

"What happens now?" Maxim asked. "I mean to her. What does she live on?"

"Tricky question. I suppose we might get his pension paid to her—somehow. We can do things with money that would have you jailed in more respectable departments. So she could be lucky that far."

As they turned onto the wooded suburban road, the car slid broadside across the camber until it hit the piled snow on the verge. Maxim eased it out with very delicate use of the clutch. "D'you know what she told me, while you were getting your coat? That he made love to her, that last night in Vienna. It seems they hardly ever slept together any more. She thought it might be a sort of fresh start."

"The bastard," Agnes said unemotionally.

"So probably he guessed she wouldn't go with him."

"Always leave them laughing."

◙ 17

It was past nine o'clock when he parked in the bright, wide empty stretch of Whitehall. The journey had been a crawling chaos, even though he was running against the commuter tide, but central London was spookily quiet in the snow. It could have been three in the morning.

For once there were no tourists, just the policeman stamping his feet and punching his gloved hands together outside Number 10, Maxim went through to George's room, but there was only the duty clerk there.

"They're in the Cabinet Room, Major. Would you go straight in?"

Back down the corridor to the corner, where visitors to the Cabinet Room passed through the haughty marble gaze of Wellington—whom the French politely believed was Julius Caesar—and tapped on the door. George shouted: "Come!"

He and Agnes were alone in the tall room, seated together at the near end of a vast boat-shaped table, with red-leather-padded dining chairs all around it. There was a scatter of glossy black-and-white prints on the brown baize tabletop.

"D'you want a drink? I should think you must." George waved at a trolley of bottles and glasses by the fireplace. There wasn't any beer, so Maxim mixed himself a long whisky and water.

"That's the film, is it?"

"See what you make of that." George shoved a photograph into his hand.

It was a negative print, white lettering on black. It seemed to be a straightforward typed document, with unfamiliar numbers and letters as references, then a heading:

Maxim sat down and began to read. The print was almost life size and only slightly blurred by the grain.

When he'd finished he said: "We knew just about all this already. You could have worked this up from the files."

"It gets better later," Agnes said. She seemed surprisingly cheerful.

George pawed among the prints and thrust another one at Maxim. "Try that for size." Agnes's cheerfulness certainly wasn't infectious.

This page began: *Joint account in the names of Gerald and Mary Jackaman at Compte Nationale d'Escompte, Boulevard Heurteloup, Tours.* The rest was a mixture of figures—mostly francs and dates—which Maxim might have been able to analyse if he had the time. But he felt he had to say something.

"There's no classification," he said, inspired.

"The Other Mob," Agnes said, "don't classify their documents. They regard every piece of paper they handle as above and beyond NATO Cosmic. I believe they file used loo paper under—"

"Shut *up*," George said.

"This was put together by MI6, then?"

"In *direct* contradiction to a hands-off order distributed by the Headmaster. Then, in a rare fit of brotherly love, they showed it to Box 500—"

"Masson probably asked for it," Agnes said.

"With what excuse?"

She shrugged. "Nobody believes excuses in our trade so you don't usually give them."

"What a beautiful world."

"If you want to send a gunboat instead, go right ahead and send a gunboat."

Hoping he was peace-making, Maxim asked: "Has the Prime Minister seen this?"

George glowered. "He's still at the House. There's the Defence debate on, remember?"

"Yes. Sorry." Maxim realised that George, as the PM's defence adviser, would far rather have been down there playing nanny. "I'm not used to the idea that debates really happen except in the newspapers, and that people have to be there to make them happen."

"You share that simple failing with most of the Honourable Members of Parliament. At one time, there were only seventeen, *seventeen* of them in the Chamber while the Defence Secretary was speaking. And this is about war and peace, the lot, everything."

"Perhaps," Agnes said, "they've just come to realise that it's the civil service and the trade unions who run the country."

"What?"

"Just a quote from our latest traitor."

George stared at her, then got heavily to his feet. "I need a drink."

Agnes caught Maxim's eye and smiled gently. "We're waiting for a gentleman from Six to come round and explain his service's little antics. Don't stay if you can't stand the sight of blood."

Maxim smiled back, sipped his drink and looked around. The room seemed cold, or perhaps it was just that it was so empty. He had been in here only once before, being 'shown around' by George. It was longer than the Private Secretaries' room next door, but built in exactly the same style except for two incongruous pairs of pillars holding up the ceiling at one end where a wall had been knocked down to add an extra few feet. The walls were painted oyster white and had only one picture, a portrait of Sir Robert Walpole, over the fireplace. The writhing brass chandeliers had been put in by Sir Anthony Eden, he remembered George saying. He wondered if the cleaners had got around to thanking him yet.

The man from the Intelligence Service said his name was Guy Husband, so perhaps it was. He was about forty, gangling and donnish, wearing an expensive tweed sportscoat that was rumpled and smeared with pipe ash. He had a high forehead, a breaking wave of wiry brown hair and a long nose. His teeth were rather yellow, and he tapped them constantly with his pen.

"In fact," he said, "this shouldn't really have been circulated at all, even on a limited basis. One might say that it wasn't really developed."

"That's what one might say, might *one?*" George asked coldly.

"I only meant that our researches are far from complete. I think it was a mistake to pass it on to our sister service—" he smiled at Agnes; "—and indeed, we now know it was a mistake, bearing in mind the loyalties of the man on whose desk it landed." He smiled again.

"Oh quite," George agreed. "The Headmaster will be, *one* might say, interested to know that the only way he can find out what his Intelligence Service is up to is by routing through the house of a traitor."

"Well, I don't really think—"

"*Particularly* when it turns out that they're working on an operation that he has specifically forbidden."

Husband smiled and gave a coquettish wriggle of you-and-I-know-what-prime-ministers-will-be-old-boy. "I do understand that it was Box 500 that was told to cease and desist."

"It was distributed!" George snapped. He took a deep breath. "All right. This material—" he slapped a hand on the glossy prints; "—hasn't got a summary. Give me one."

"I did say it was undeveloped."

"When the Prime Minister gets back here I would like to have something to say to him other than suggest he gets your Director-General around to tell him personally. Just give me everything you've got, developed, undeveloped or still stuck in the mangle."

"We-ell," Husband took a folded paper from an inside pocket. "What it boils down to is that Jackaman had a perfectly legal bank account in France. They owned a holiday cottage in the valley of Loire, and Exchange Control allows one to have funds over there to pay the plumber and window-cleaner and so on. . . . A very nice part of the world."

"I know the Loire valley. Get on with it."

"Ah . . . then they sold the cottage a couple of years ago, and brought the money back into this country. Unless they were buying something else there, that's legally what they had to do. But the account was allowed to stay open: there would be lingering debts, legal fees and so on. Quite normal. But then the account started building up again. Now, I'm sure you appreciate that France isn't Switzerland—"

"Dear God," George breathed; "although I was not born with football studs growing out of my feet like most people who read Geography, I *do* know the difference between France and Switzerland. Get *on*."

Untroubled, Husband continued. "France has nothing like Switzerland's ideas of banking secrecy, nothing like even our own, which really aren't very impressive. They seem to be most amenable. As I say, in the last eighteen months the account has grown, not regularly, but fairly steadily, until it now stands at something a little over fifteen thousand pounds—at the current rate of exchange."

"This would be a non-resident account?" Maxim asked. "Usually only fed with money from abroad?"

"That's quite right. You would need French exchange control permission to put in francs."

"But the account itself can be in francs? Safe from any devaluation of sterling?"

"Oh yes."

"How the hell do you know this, Harry?" George demanded.

"I've spent more of my life abroad than you have, I expect."

There was a short silence. Husband watched Maxim covertly, intrigued to find him in on a meeting at this level. Over at Six, they still weren't sure what to make of the Downing Street soldier.

"And this was all clearly illegal?" George asked.

"In British law, yes."

Agnes said: "Clumsy, too."

"I agree there are more subtle ways of secreting money abroad, but it probably wouldn't have come to light unless we—I'm sorry, I mean first your service—had started looking."

"When was the last payment made?" George asked.

"Last year, shortly before Jackaman died."

"Is there any suggestion," Maxim asked, "that Jackaman was taking Moscow gold?"

Husband and Agnes looked quickly at each other, then shook their heads. This at least was one thing they agreed on. She said: "No. The Centre would never let one of their people do anything so risky."

"So the money now belongs to Mrs Jackaman?"

"A nice point," Husband smiled. "As a true patriot, one really ought to tell the Inland Revenue that Jackaman's estate is some fifteen thousand pounds larger than they first thought. However, perhaps one doesn't want to drag the Jackaman name any further in the dust."

"One doesn't," George said. "Not unless one wants one's Director-General around here on his hands and knees pleading for a job scrubbing out the loos."

Husband's boyish smile became a little strained.

Agnes asked: "Has probate been granted?"

"Yes. He left quite a small estate, but very tidy. Most of the money was tied up in the English house. It's for sale now."

"Where's Mrs Jackaman?" Maxim asked.

Husband now had no smile at all, and his voice was petulant. "You see, that was one of the reasons why we regarded this material as being undeveloped. Her pension is paid into the local bank, but she hasn't drawn any of it out, yet. Their only child lives in America now, and—"

"You mean," Agnes said sweetly, "that you have no bloody idea at all."

18

"And *that*," Agnes said after Husband had gone, "is all that stands between us and the Red Peril."

"There's me and my pistol as well," Maxim volunteered.

George said: "He obviously isn't a field man."

"He isn't even a field mouse."

"They've got some good men over there. I tell you, you're just being old-fashioned." George poured them all another round of drinks and looked impatiently at his watch. "Why the *hell* don't they broadcast debates? At least they could do it on a land-line to here and the Cabinet Office and the Departments. All right, where are we now?"

Maxim had been picking through the photographs—which Husband had made a feeble attempt to take with him, since they were his service's documents—and found that they spent half a page on Mrs Jackaman's background. Until then he'd known nothing about her except that Who's Who gave her family name as Brennan. He read it carefully.

"We assume," Agnes said, "that Greyfriars' interest in Jackaman is because of their interest in Tyler. And that centres on the famous Tyler letter."

"If it still exists," George said quickly.

Maxim lifted his head. "It sounded from what Zuzana Kindl said that the KGB had only just heard about it. And they weren't working directly on Tyler at that time. So they either tripped over it or somebody . . ." he let the idea hang in the air like an unmentionable smell.

"Could it have been your little chum Charles Farthing?" George asked hopefully.

"No. He's a bit of a nutter, but a patriotic nutter. He didn't think Tyler was pure enough in heart for us."

"You don't think Greyfriars actually have this letter?"

Agnes said: "I doubt they'd be going through all this hoop-de-ha if they had it already." She looked at Maxim, who shrugged and went back to the blurred typescript in the photograph.

"It all comes back to Mrs Jackaman," Agnes said remorselessly. "If anybody's got that letter, it's most likely her."

"Why did Jackaman commit suicide in the first place?" Maxim asked.

"Or, of course," Agnes added, "the last place."

"Because," George began with the reined-in patience of a kindergarten teacher, "Box 500 confronted him with rumours of his illegal French bank account."

Maxim shook his head slowly. "I don't follow that. Most suicides are despair, hopelessness, things are only going to get worse . . . I'm assuming Jackaman wasn't a complete moron, so he must have known that account could wreck his whole career. So—did he simply say to himself, Okay, if I'm found out, I'll shoot myself? And if he hadn't decided that, why did he do it? I just can't get hold of it."

George started a slow circuit of the Cabinet table. Since it seated about thirty, that took time. He stopped at the far end and called back: "You aren't, God help us all, trying to turn this into a country house murder mystery?"

"I'm just asking."

"And," Agnes persisted, "why wasn't there a suicide note?"

"Oh blast it, there aren't any *rules* for committing suicide."

"Yes there are. Look at Japan. And Jackaman was a senior civil servant; paperwork was his daily bread. Minutes, memos, reports, letters, just let me have a draft paper about that, will you, old boy?"

Maxim said: "Perhaps it wasn't anything to do with the bank account, but he just despaired of paperwork."

"Or perhaps," George snapped, "he had a horrible prevision of his life being batted around by you two clowns." He cruised slowly back down the fireplace side of the table, past the PM's chair.

Maxim asked calmly: "Who found his body?"

George stopped and looked at him suspiciously. "His wife. There were only the two of them in the house and it was fairly isolated. She heard a shot but thought it was him having a crack at a pigeon or something, then after a time she went to see and . . . I read her statement."

"I don't call that very sensitive of him," Agnes said. "He can't have expected to look very palatable."

"He wasn't a very sensitive man, not in an imaginative way. He just had a strong sense of honour and duty."

"Except where money was concerned," Maxim suggested.

George slumped into a chair, took a thin cigar from a case in his top waistcoat pocket and stared moodily at it. He sighed, clipped the end, and lit it with a plain match. He looked defeated.

"He left a note," Agnes said quietly, "and he left the Tyler letter. She suppressed both. I don't know why. Then she let the KGB know that she had it. Again, I don't know why. And we don't know where she is to ask her."

"I rather think," Maxim said, "that I do. But if I do, then so does Greyfriars."

It was past midnight. Whitehall was still brightly lit, still empty. The ministerial palaces on either side wore, for once, a stark blue-rinsed beauty, with fringes of snow on their cornices where they reached up almost out of the light.

"Sometimes this town remembers its past," Agnes said, huddling in her sheepskin and breathing like a dragon. She began to quote:

"Ne'er saw I, never felt, a calm so deep!
The river glideth at his own sweet will:
Dear God! the very houses seem asleep;
And all that mighty heart is lying still!"

"When I first joined the Army," Maxim said, "most suicides happened in the lavatories. I suppose it was

125

the only place the poor kids could get any real privacy."

She stopped dead and stared at him. "Bloody flaming hell's fire. Did you hear one word of what I said?"

"It's Wordsworth, isn't it? The one about Westminster Bridge."

They walked for a while in silence, then Maxim asked: "D'you want a lift anywhere?"

"No thanks. I'll drop in at one of our offices around the corner. I want to know if they've turned up anything more."

But she wasn't in any hurry, and it was a rare privilege to have the centre of London to yourself. They drifted past Maxim's car and instinctively headed for Westminster Bridge.

"Where do you get a handle like Maxim?" Agnes asked. "Are you descended from the restaurant or the machine-gun?"

"Neither, I'm afraid. But it's supposed to be a French Huguenot name, so perhaps we're all umpteenth cousins."

"I should try and inherit the restaurant; the patents on the gun must have run out years ago. You don't come of an Army family?"

"I'm the first, as far as I know. My father tried to join up in '39, but he was a skilled tool-maker by then, a reserved occupation . . . I think he's always felt bad about not having Done His Bit. His father had been in the Navy in the First War. No—" he shook his head as she was about to ask something. "He didn't push me into it. He doesn't have a very high opinion of Army officers in peace-time. He'd rather I was doing something useful for exports."

Agnes gave a sympathetic grunt.

They came out of Bridge Street below Big Ben into the blast of Siberian air funnelled up the Thames, and scurried across the road to the bridge.

"And how did a nice girl—and all that?" Maxim asked.

She thought about it. "I don't know if I was pushed or just fell. I was reading Modern Languages at Oxford and I hadn't got much idea of what I wanted to do afterwards, and one of the dons suggested I might pop down to London and have lunch with an old friend of hers . . . so you do that, and gradually you begin to realise what they're talking about. It sounded more interesting than translating French comic books for a publisher, so . . ."

"Why you?"

"My father was a civil servant all his life, mostly at Agriculture or the Home Office. The head-hunters at universities look for sons and daughters of people like him—my sister was at Defence until she married, and my young brother's in the Treasury. We're supposed to have a bred-in sense of duty and patriotism. I suppose we do—for a time."

Maxim scooped crusted snow off the bridge parapet, waited until his bare hands had melted it into a ball, then threw it into the swirling water below. There was no 'glideth' about the Thames tonight.

"What happens after that?" he asked, shoving his hands deep into his coat pockets.

"What happened to you?"

"I asked first."

"So you did." She folded her arms on the parapet and stared down river, against the wind. "I suppose it was because I'd taken the Queen's shilling. And she always seems to want thirteen pence in change. Maybe I should have held out for fourteen pence, like our dearly beloved Rex Masson."

Maxim didn't say anything to that, so she asked: "And what about you, now?"

"I don't know . . ."

"That's a good start."

He grinned and made a useless attempt to stop his hair blowing in all directions. At least in uniform you wore a hat . . . "I just wonder now if anybody joins the Army they thought they were joining. A few generals and sergeant-majors, probably, and the odd one like David Stirling or Popski and Tyler. For the rest of us . . . there's always enough small issues to keep you busy. Maybe it's only when you get to Whitehall that you begin to wonder about the big picture—even about whether there *is* a big picture. Perhaps I let Je—, my wife, do too much of the thinking for me."

"I heard about her." Agnes didn't say any more.

"You weren't married?"

"No." She paused. "I'm not in a nine-to-five job. The big picture is that there's a war on. Or at least you have to believe there is." She swung around and pecked him on the cheek. "G'night, ahr 'Arry."

He watched her walk briskly back across the bridge, then followed more slowly.

19

From the air, Ireland was an opaque stained-glass window of delicate greens and browns, the hedges and walls making strong lines of shadow in the low afternoon sun. Then a glance of the soft feminine shapes of the western mountains, with only a dusting of snow on their northern slopes, and the Boeing 737 slammed down on Shannon's wet runway.

"Are you commercial?" the girl at the hotel desk asked. Maxim just stared, wondering what the answer should be, before asking what she meant.

"Well, we find . . ." she was suddenly rather embarrassed, ". . . that the commercial gentlemen don't usually want a bath. A *bathroom*, by that I mean. We don't have any rooms left with *bathrooms*."

"Let's say I'm commercial."

Maxim grinned to himself as he unpacked, then deliberately went and wallowed—free—in a deep tub in the communal bathroom down the corridor. The flight had been two hours late since Heathrow still hadn't got itself defrosted properly, and his job in Ireland could only be done in working hours. It had also been a cold fifteen miles from Shannon to Limerick, the only car left for hire at the airport being an Escort with a busted heater.

He had booked nothing in advance, getting the air ticket at the last moment. The name Maxim hadn't gone ahead of him—they hoped.

"Once you're on that plane, you're out of the United Kingdom," George warned him, quite unnecessarily.

"Most of the serious soldiering I've done has been outside the UK."

"If you do any serious soldiering in the Irish Republic, you needn't bother coming home again. You haven't got that pistol with you, I hope and trust but don't really believe?"

"No." All he had was a totally illegal flick-knife in among his shaving gear. He wasn't sure how illegal it was in Ireland, but assumed it must be.

He walked the damp drabness of O'Connell street until he found a telephone box, and rang a London number Agnes had given him. All he said was: "H at hotel number one."

A man's voice said: "Right," and rang off. George would be told that he'd got in at the first hotel on their list.

Then he rang a number up in the Silvermine Mountains, twenty miles north, and made an appointment for nine-thirty the next morning. The man at the other end was very willing but played his part like the first read-through at a church hall dramatic society. Maxim hurried back through the drizzle grinning wryly to himself. The poor put-upon bastard. Being an old chum of George's and owning a retreat in the right part of Ireland could suddenly become a nervous hazard, particularly since they couldn't tell him what it was all about.

Maxim had vaguely expected a run-down castle. What he got was a run-down cottage. It sat in a field ringed with walls that were just lines of dark stone piled together, and at some time it must have burned down. But long ago, because now the remaining roof timbers were almost smothered by some climbing evergreen, making a green thatch above the empty window-frames. In good weather it would be the perfect meeting-place for lovers from a bad historical novel. Now it seemed like a mistake in map-reading.

But there was a nearly new silver-grey BMW saloon parked in the yard behind, and an unseen wing of the cottage had been restored, slate roof, double glazed windows and all. Jonathan St. John Rafford hurried out and snatched open the door of the Escort.

"My God, isn't the weather awful? Get yourself inside." He scampered away again. Maxim picked up his briefcase and followed. The restored rooms were warm, bright, cosy, with books jammed into every space.

Rafford was pouring coffee. "Black? Do you take sugar?" He was a few years older than Maxim but still trying to be twenty-six. He wore very tight faded jeans with his tummy bulging over them, and a rough-knit fisherman's sweater. His face was slightly puffy, with a sharp aristocratic nose and long dark hair that he had to keep sweeping out of his eyes with an elaborate gesture.

He wrote, so George had said, very sensitive biographies of minor but well-born European politicians.

"Aren't you having any?" Maxim asked. There was only one cup poured.

"No, no, I'll be away. There's the phone, and I've put out the directory. You did want the Yellow Pages as well?"

"Thank you. If you ever have to explain why I was here, and we don't think you will, it was to look over this property in case you'd let George and me buy into it, as a shared holiday home."

"Actually," Rafford said thoughtfully, "that might not be a bad idea."

"Oh Lord."

"I'm terribly sorry." He really looked it. "No, what I meant was: I spurn your offer, after due consideration, as being far below the market value. Is that better?"

"Much."

Rafford picked up a worn duffle coat, turned to the door, then turned back. "This is absolutely nothing to do with North and South, is it?"

"It's nothing to do with Ireland at all," Maxim said firmly.

"Oh, that's fine. Help yourself to anything you can find in the kitchen or the drinks and . . ." he smiled boyishly; ". . . just look the property over."

Maxim sipped coffee until the BMW had growled away, then sat down at a telephone which wasn't in a call box and didn't go through a hotel switchboard, and started on the first of a long list of numbers.

He began with what were, or might be, Mrs Jackaman's relatives; Brennans were very thick on the ground in southwestern Ireland. Maxim was a London estate agent who only wanted to know who was handling the sale of the English house because he might have a client; did they know where he could contact

Mrs Jackaman, née Mary Brennan? No fish bit on that one, though once he thought he sensed a nibble. He underlined the name.

Then he became a furrier and tried the bigger shops of Limerick, Ennis, Nenagh and Killaloe: did Mrs Jackaman have an account with them?—she'd left Britain after ordering this fur jacket and said she'd send her Irish address when she had one, but . . . Nothing.

After nearly two hours, he got up and walked around the room, shaking the creases out of himself and rubbing his dialling hand. For the first time in his life he felt some sympathy for journalists who must spend whole days doing this sort of thing, carefully sifting through pan after pan of gold to discover one speck of dirt.

He made another pot of coffee and sat down to try the long shots. They'd wondered about the doctors and lawyers, but decided not—not yet, anyway. Those would be professionally secretive and suspicious; you weren't speaking to some dumb blonde in Accounts.

"You're a Citroën agent, I think?"

"We are that. Can I help you?"

"I hope so. I was talking to a Mrs Mary Jackaman some time ago and she asked me to get her a couple of fog-lamps for her Citroën GS when I was next over in France, so I did that——"

"Why should she ask that? I could have got them for her meself, easy."

"No idea. But she does come to your garage?"

"We've had her car in here, sure."

Crunch. The fish had bitten. Now slowly, Harry, *slowly*.

"Oh good. I just don't know how to get them to her. She hadn't got a proper address there when I last saw her. Should I drop them off on you? I'll be down that way early next week."

"Surely you can." Maxim held his breath. "She's living in a houseboat on the Lough, up beyond Ballina. But you leave them with me any time, we're a deal easier to find. Did I have your name?"

"John Rhodes, from Bristol. Thanks for your trouble. I'll be seeing you."

Maxim put the phone down very carefully and un-clenched his hand from around it. The fingers were white. Funny: he'd never have gripped a weapon that fiercely.

◩ 20

On the way, he stopped at a tiny village grocer's and bought himself a rough picnic: cheese triangles, potted meat, biscuits and a couple of tins of beer. He didn't want to show his face in any restaurant or bar around there. Then, once he had passed Ballina, he worked carefully up the east side of the Lough, snooping down every side road or track that could possibly lead to a boat. It took time and the drizzle turned to rain. He wished he'd thought of going up the far side of the Lough, where the road ran right along the shore, and using his field glasses. There couldn't be many houseboats around at this time of the year.

Then he saw the Citroën, parked beside a gate in a field that stretched down to the water.

It might have been converted from one of the vast range of small landing craft sold off after the war. There had been dozens of different types, but all of them looking like half-sunken shoeboxes, and a lot had ended up as houseboats or small ferries. This one had a tall, split-level cabin built atop it, with wide windows and their inevitable net curtains, and even a window-box under each one. It was old and needed painting, but it still had a certain spartan strength. High as the cabin was, the wind might blow it over but wouldn't blow it to pieces.

He walked over a creaking gangplank that was as good a warning as any barking dog, and stepped down into a tiny cockpit. There was a small steering-wheel on the cabin wall and a slot for an outboard motor at the back. Or did you say 'stern' for houseboats?

After a moment, he tapped lightly on the cabin door, where the varnish was peeling off in long thin scabs. Nothing happened for a minute, then there was a scuffle and a clang, and more silence.

134

Then a woman asked: "Who is it, then?"

Maxim took the chance. "I'm Major Harry Maxim, British Army, and I work in Number 10 Downing Street."

A pause. "Why don't you bugger off back there, then?"

"We traced you, Mrs Jackaman, because a Czech defector told me where to look. They won't be long, if they aren't here already."

"Just suppose I went down and told the boys in the bar that the British Army's invading Lough Derg?"

"I don't know, Mrs Jackaman. I don't know what'll happen when the other side gets here, either."

Another pause. "I might be more interested in seeing them than you buggers." Her voice, if not her language, was very pure and precise, as if she'd once taken elocution lessons.

"Then why are you hiding out here?"

"Bugger off."

"I'll be in my car in the lane."

He walked back across the gangplank, feeling her stare piercing his back, and up the soaking field to the lane. In the car, he turned on his pocket radio, and started to eat the cheese and potted meat. At some time, the Escort's steering-wheel had been taken off and put back ninety degrees wrong, so that the plaque in the centre read

FORD

He daren't tell George that; he'd say it was Very Irish, when it wasn't, it was Very Garage. He cut and spread the food with the illegal flick-knife, then wiped it carefully clean and put it back into his trouser pocket.

After twenty minutes she trudged up the field. He got out politely and waited.

She was smaller and dumpier than he'd expected—though he wasn't sure what he *had* expected—in a green tweed skirt, a short black leather coat cut like a double-breasted mac, and a headscarf knotted at the back of her neck.

"What if I asked you to drive me into town to see the Gardai?"

"I'd say it wasn't a bad idea."

"Let's see your ID, Major Whosit." She'd been a Ministry of Defence wife for a dozen years. Maxim took out his card; she studied it, grunted, then slumped into the passenger seat. He walked round and got in the other side.

"Do you want to go anywhere?"

"Just drive around. I get cooped up in there."

Maxim backed fast up the narrow lane. "Would you like some rather nasty processed cheese?"

"Sure." She fumbled the box, spilled the cheeses, rescued one from between the seats and started picking it open. She was lightly and inoffensively drunk, and Maxim wondered how much of that had happened after he knocked on the door. A round, plump and rather flushed face, a piggy nose and at least a double chin. Put kindly, she was a bit short on royal blood. Perhaps the elocution lessons had been a touching attempt to become a proper Diplomatic Wife.

"What's an infantry Major doing at Number Ten?"

"I hope I'm the first to find out. I was attached there after your husband died. The Prime Minister was rather annoyed with the security service."

"Oh, *that's* nice. Our masters are good at being right—after the event. Very well, Major, what's all this about?"

"Why is the KGB looking for you?"

"I put in a question and all I get back is a question. You're like one of those fruit-machines in pubs where all you get is tokens, never real money. And you said it was the Czechs, not the Russians."

"They usually use the Czechs or Poles for their leg-work outside London. Their own people can't go more than thirty miles without giving notice and saying where and when—it's retaliation for the rules they slap on us in Moscow. The same thing works for Dublin. I thought you'd have known that."

"I expect Jerry told me at some time. You can't remember everything."

"And did you approach them, first?"

"Who told you that?"

"I did say there'd been a defector."

She was quiet for a while. The rain kept coming down, and the tracks feeding into the road from the Arra Mountains on their right spread fans of mud and twigs across it.

"This is a bloody cold car," she said at last.

"The heater's on the blink."

She gave a cackle of laughter. "More cuts in defence spending?" The elocution hadn't reached as far as her laugh; it was plain raw meat.

"How did you get in touch with them? I wouldn't know where to start."

She looked at him sideways. "Really? You should read more spy thrillers. What you do is, you write them a letter—on MoD paper so they'll take some notice of it—and then you don't post it or deliver it yourself. You drop it in at the Aeroflot office in Piccadilly and hope they'll have the sense to see it gets to the right people."

"And they did."

"If they hadn't, I'd have tried some other way. I wasn't going to risk another little visit from bloody Security."

He glanced at her; her mouth was clenched shut and her eyes fixed.

"And then?"

"Then . . . then they put a message in the *Telegraph*, a meaningless one I'd given them, to show they'd got my letter. So I sent them another."

"Did you say who you were?"

"Of course I did, man. I had to or they wouldn't have believed a thing."

Maxim had a weird disembodied feeling, like going under an anaesthetic. At Ashford they'd told him about traitors who *had* to confess, but this was ridiculous.

She had cheered up. "So then I told them they had to give me a telephone number which I could ring, and they did. They put it in the *Telegraph* in code: you added one to the first number, subtracted one from the second, that sort of thing, I'd told them how to do it, but I'm sure they'd be used to it anyway."

"I'm sure," Maxim murmured.

137

"So they never got to know where I was."

Abruptly, the high wooded banks on either side of the road ended and they came out onto an open headland overlooking the Lough. On a whim, Maxim swung off onto the turf and parked facing the water that rippled like stretched grey silk in the wind.

"Would you like a can of beer?"

"Surely."

He found the two cans on the back seat. She snapped hers open, took a quick drink, then started running the broken-off can ring up and down her finger until it just squeezed over the knuckle to touch the wide wedding band. She didn't know she was doing it.

"Could you tell me why you began all this?" He wasn't at all sure it was the right question.

She looked up, sharp and sly, and reached into her handbag. "I'm not breaking any law, Major, not a single bloody one. Because do you know what is the best book I've ever read in my life? It is this book, Major Harry of the British Army."

She waggled an Irish passport in his face.

"When I married I got dual nationality, but Ireland won't let you have but one passport so of course I had to have a British one. But now, now I'm back home again. And I'm not breaking one single Irish law, Mister Major Harry." She took a triumphant swig of beer.

"That doesn't tell me why you approached them."

"I don't have to tell you any reason at all."

"No."

She stared ahead through the windscreen at the misty hills on the far side of the Lough. "It is a gentle land. And now at last it is making some money. Have you been here long enough to see that?"

Maxim nodded. Every little house he had passed seemed freshly painted and the cars on the road were new and shiny and plenty of them. It had impressed him.

"He promised that when he retired," she went on, "we should buy a place here, in the old country. He had been very careful about his life insurance. But do you know what happens to life insurance when you are driven to suicide, Major Harry?"

It was as simple as that. Agnes's Mob had robbed

her of a husband *and* a second home and real security. Of course she hated them, and this was a beautiful two-pronged revenge because it could turn into money as well.

"I'm sorry about that," he said lamely. "I hadn't thought . . ."

"They could do it to you, too."

"Not quite . . ." Maxim squeezed the steering-wheel very tight for a moment. "And . . . have they made you an offer yet? We know they want that letter badly."

"What letter?"

"The letter about Professor Tyler. If we aren't talking about that, then I'm sorry to have troubled you."

He watched her as she carefully and rather drunkenly tried to work out whether it was in her interest to lie to him.

"The funny thing," he went on, "is that Tyler says the thing must be a fake. He never even knew that chap in Canada, whats-his-name . . ."

"Etheridge," she said automatically.

"That's him." Maxim tried to keep his voice calm. "Tyler says publish and be damned. Anybody who does will just make fools of themselves."

"You're a bloody liar," she growled.

"I'm not," Maxim lied. "But Tyler could be, I suppose."

"Somebody bloody is," she said, suddenly happy. "Or why would he be wanting to buy it off me as well?"

Oh God, why hadn't he thought of that, of her offering it to Tyler as well? If she was trying to turn the letter into money then an auction was so *obvious* . . .

"You're into a rather high-stakes game, Mrs Jackaman," he said thoughtfully, "trying to play off Professor Tyler against the KGB. *They* won't mind a bit of argy-bargy about money—they're quite used to that—and they don't have cash-flow problems. But had you thought how they'd feel if they believed they were going to lose, not going to get the letter? They've already been looking for you, ever since you contacted them."

She glanced at him suspiciously.

"Oh yes. All the letters and classified ads and telephone calls aren't what they really want: they want to meet you. And a lonely houseboat is just where they'd choose. We knew you were in the Shannon area because the defector told us. After that, it took me just two and a half hours of phoning around until I found out just where—"

"Who told you?"

"It wasn't their fault; they didn't know you wanted it kept a secret. The point is that if I can do it, anybody can."

She brooded on that for a moment. "I'm getting cold. Can we go back?"

"Of course." The car skidded across the greasy grass as he turned around onto the road.

He walked her to the gangplank and as she unlocked the door she said: "You'd better come in and get warm, Major."

They went through a small cabin that was just for summertime, with big windows and wicker furniture that had once been gilded. Then down past a tiny kitchen—or galley?—into the main cabin. It was stuffed with furniture and as precisely tidied as a Victorian parlour. Everything that could be centred—the fruit bowl on the table—was centred, everything that could be polished was polished, and the books and magazines in the shelves stood rigid as Guardsmen at a Trooping.

From the corner, she said: "I'm having a small Jameson—will you join me?"

"Yes, please." He moved carefully through the cabin and sat on an utterly un-seagoing chair at the table. None of the furniture was particularly good, or even matching, but it was clean. Probably she had nothing else to do, except drink. A warm paraffin smell crept up on him; she had turned up an unseen heater.

"Well, Major Harry," she put a heavy glass down before him, on a small embroidered mat to save the table surface. "Well, and what do you really want me to do?"

"Tell me what's happened to the letter."

"Ah, now that *would* be telling." She smiled coyly.

"Will you sell it to us? You know there are secret funds for this sort of thing."

"Perhaps I've sold it already. I might have sold it to Professor Tyler, mightn't I?" She took a big sip of neat whisky. "Shall I tell you something about Professor Tyler, Major Harry? He gets people killed."

"I don't think he had anything to do with your husband's death."

"He put the Security people onto him."

"I doubt he did, Mrs Jackaman. Your husband was making his objections to Tyler in the Whitehall circuit. Not in Tyler's world."

"It's the same thing." She got up to refill her glass. He waited until she came back.

"Has that letter really gone to the Russians?"

"You're thinking like an Englishman, Major Harry."

"If they ever come across the Elbe, Mrs Jackaman, do you think they're going to stop at Holyhead?"

She sloshed the whisky around in her glass, looking moodily down at it. "Do you know what Gerald wrote before he died? Do you know that? No, of course you don't. You never saw it and nobody else did either. Except me. Now you're going to ask me why I didn't show it to the police. A bloody silly question, Major Harry Whatsit. Bloody silly." Quietly, she had gone over the top into real drunkenness. Maxim sat still and folded his hands around his glass.

"I can translate it for you, Major Harry. I can remember it. He said that the Security Service had been planting money in our French account just to discredit him. He'd found they'd been doing that. Now what do you think of that, Major Harry?"

Maxim took his time answering.

"But it wasn't, Mrs Jackaman. It was you, putting in money without him knowing."

She stared at him with watery red, deep-sunk eyes. "I should have had to get to the bank statements from the *Compte Nationale* before he did."

"I think you did. You must have handled that side of the marriage anyway, or you wouldn't have risked it."

"And where do you think I got that much money?"

"Nobody said anything about how much money."

141

There was a long silence while she frowned and tried to remember, then took a mouthful of whisky and shrugged. Maxim went on: "It was probably an inheritance or selling property in your own family, over here. It might be easier to move money out of Ireland to France. I don't think it's any more legal."

Outside, the afternoon was beginning to darken, and a new wind made the water slap irregularly but monotonously against the metal hull. She eased out from the crowded table and went to the corner cupboard, then came back without having refilled her glass.

"All right," she said wearily. "What do you want me to do?" She took a small orange from the bowl and began tearing the skin off; the sudden sharp smell cut through that of paraffin.

Maxim was suddenly tired of the whole Tyler letter business, of Mrs Jackaman and her whisky breath. Next time. But he had to make sure there would be a next time.

"The first thing," he said firmly, "is to get away from here. Forget the car, the boat, everything. Don't worry about the cost. I've said that others could find you just as easily as I did. You do see that?"

She moved her head, half nod, half shake.

"Is there anybody you can stay with?" Maxim asked. "A friend, not a relative, somewhere it would be difficult to trace you?"

"I can think of one or two. If you haven't found a few friends by my age . . ."

"I'll drive you wherever you want. An airport or main-line station. A hotel."

"It's like that, is it?"

"This is the first division, Mrs Jackaman. With the Cup Final coming up. Three people have been killed about that letter already."

He'd over-done it. Her face was tight and suspicious. "Really? I'll pack my case."

She went through into a cabin in the bows that must be a bedroom. Maxim tore a small orange apart for himself, dunking the segments in his whisky and chewing them angrily. The oblong aluminium-framed windows were misting over, but he could still see the gentle green lines of the far shore. *How can anybody*

142

live in Ireland and not believe that people get killed for politics?

She came back with her black coat on, carrying a heavy suitcase of battered fawn leather, held together with plenty of straps. Maxim took it. She turned off the hidden stove, gave one look around, then led the way out.

He had stowed the case in the back of the Escort when she joined him, rattling the houseboat keys.

"I'll take the car into Nenagh and leave it at the garage there. It's quite all right, Major." She had seen the look on his face. "I was sick when you weren't looking. I'm never sick when anybody is looking. I learnt that much from the Diplomatic. I can drive." She opened the Citroën. "You go ahead."

He was parked about twenty yards in front. He had backed away perhaps another twenty when her car exploded.

There was no sharp noise like a normal explosive. Just a heavy *thud* and flames surging out of every window as if there had never been any glass in them at all. Then it was a shapeless blistering bonfire, rolling black smoke into the air and reminding Maxim of something . . . He began running towards it, but mostly so that he could later say to himself that he'd done so.

There was nothing he could do, not even get within ten feet of the furious blaze. Perhaps if she'd rolled out in the first two seconds, and without taking a breath . . . but she hadn't.

He remembered now. A Land-Rover loaded with petrol cans that some idiot had managed to drive over a land-mine in the Yemen . . . He also remembered what had been left when the fire died out. It wasn't enough even to be horrible. He got into the Escort and drove away from the smoke signal.

The letter wasn't in the suitcase, not even in the lining, though he hadn't really expected it to be anywhere. Perhaps somebody in London would complain about lost evidence; if so, he could tell them precisely where he dumped the case, weighed down with rocks, into the Lough.

After that, he drove on up to Nenagh and turned

back southwest on the main road to Limerick, bypassing Ballina and the Lough-side road. There probably wouldn't be any Gardai checkpoints set up yet, but it would be silly to get involved at all. An innocent man can be convicted, but not a man they don't even know exists, have never met.

How had he got to thinking like that? He'd joined up to be a simple soldier, hadn't he? The rain blattered down again, and he grinned sourly. That should wash out his tyre-marks in the lane, and the lane's mud from his tyres. How *had* he got to thinking like that?

▣ 21

In Limerick he found a telephone and rang the number
that was probably some MI5 office or safe house. A
man's voice, perhaps a different one, said: "Yes?"

"H here. I'm afraid the project's been terminated.
There was some prejudice, extreme prejudice."

There was a silence at the other end. 'Terminate
with extreme prejudice' was CIA-ese for 'bump-off', or
so Maxim had heard; he hoped the man had heard
that, too.

The line crackled. "I see. Yes?"

"I don't think they'll even bother to send us a letter
about it." He was proud of that sentence, though God
alone knew how he'd explain it if anybody was listening in.

"Right," the man said. "I'll ring the Automobile Association for you, as well." The phone clicked.

Maxim stared blankly at it. The AA? What had *they*
. . . Then he realised that they were Agnes Algar's initials, as well. So that was her office name, or one of
them.

He hurried back through the rain to the hotel and
sank himself in another hot bath. For a commerical
traveller, he was being remarkably clean. Then he listened to the six-thirty radio news, but there was no
mention of the fire.

The beef at dinner was over-cooked.

The ten o'clock news had two sentences about a body
in a burnt-out car near Ballina, County Tipperary, but
nothing about what the Gardai thought of it. Maxim
lay on his bed and tried to watch them work—assuming they went about it much the same was as in
Belfast after a car bomb.

First, put the fire out, if somebody else or the rain
hadn't done it already. After one look inside, there

then wouldn't be any hurry. Block off the road with plastic cones, seal off the area with white tapes tied from hedge to hedge, and maybe poke around a bit. In Belfast there wouldn't be any doubt about what had happened. Down in County Tipperary they would have less experience in jumping to the right conclusion.

So they'd wait for the experts to arrive and the wreck to cool, which could be a fair old time after such a fire. Meanwhile, the job was identification. The car's number plates might still be readable, and they'd know it was a Citroën GS, so all they'd have to do was call at the nearest farmhouse door. You might stay secret in the middle of a city, where nobody wants to know, but never in the countryside. He'd proved that by finding her so quickly. Come to think of it, so had somebody else.

Now they knew she lived on the houseboat. Knock on that door, and get no answer. Would they then kick it down? Why should they? If it was an accident, then there was no point, and if it was murder then they might be lousing up the evidence.

They wouldn't be looking for an important letter.

The Lough ran north and south at that point, so he came from the south, against the damp chill wind and the noises drifting down on it. He had spent half an hour waiting in the parked car for his eyes to adjust, and there were glimpses of a quarter moon above the restless clouds, so he could move accurately. Even then, after two minutes creeping through the reeds and nettles at the water's edge he was soaked through, particularly his feet, in bedroom slippers. But he also had somebody else's raincoat, pinched from the hotel coatroom. He felt worst about that than concealing evidence of a murder or being about to effect a burglarious entry, but his own coat had to look fresh and clean tomorrow.

Up beyond the field there was a faint glow among the trees where the Gardai were still working on the burned car. Ahead, the houseboat was just a dark shape on slightly less dark water. He lay and listened carefully, feeling cold but confident. Nobody out there in the night belonged as much as he did. It might be their country, but darkness and stealth were his trade.

There was no-one on or in the houseboat, no lights, no sounds. And why should anyone be there? What was there to guard? He crawled the last twenty yards because he would be outlined against the Lough, and crawled the creaking gangplank, too.

He worked his way all around the boat, trying the windows and a hatch on the foredeck, but they were all shut tight. It had to be the cabin door. Like most boat doors, that slid rather than swung on hinges. He took a small metal beer-can opener, rather out-dated since cans had grown pull-rings but still hardly a suspicious possession, and started levering at the top glide track. It came loose gradually, except for one sudden jerk and a *crack* that sounded nuclear, but probably wouldn't carry twenty yards against the wind. Then the door sagged loose, hingeing on its lock, and he slipped inside.

Now I really am on my own, he thought. No story in the world, up to and including the truth, can help now.

He pulled the curtains—they were reasonably light-proof—across the shore-side windows, and started working under brief flashes from a pinhole torch. This was no police search, slow and meticulous, but a whirlwind burglary. He emptied every drawer onto the floor, then threw it onto the bed or sofa. Every piece of paper that could be the letter went straight into a shopping bag, the rest scattered anywhere. Clothes, books, food, cushions, bedclothes, piled up on the floor. But this time, nobody was going to come home and weep with shock at the desecration.

The gangplank creaked.

Maxim stopped feeling bad about the stolen rain-coat. He put the shopping bag down in a safe corner, the torch in his pocket and took out the flick-knife. The houseboat tilted as weight came aboard, and there was a slight sound from the cockpit, but only very slight.

One person, just one, but one who knew how to move as quietly as possible. Not a policeman. A police-man wouldn't bother to move quietly unless he had

147

suspicions, and if he had them he'd have a lot of friends as well.

A brilliant light beam stabbed across the cabin, flicked one side and the other and hit Maxim in the eyes. The light went out and the man behind it was charging for him.

Dazzled, Maxim stepped to his left to give his knife hand more room and snicked the blade open. He trod on a cushion and skidded off balance just as the man tripped on something else and crashed into his legs. Then they were flailing wildly around the wreckage of the raped cabin. This was no policeman and no simple burglar either, but a trained fighting man who acted and reacted like a crazed cobra. Every move was supposed to be deadly, and everything became a weapon. A foot stabbed past Maxim's left ear, then an empty drawer smashed against the table leg above him. He got his left hand on a piece of clothing and rammed the knife blade into it.

The man let go a snarling gasp, and jerked away.

Maxim flicked on his pinhole torch. Sitting in the carnage but six feet away—a surprising distance—was a square-shaped man with a square face blinking in the feeble light. He was holding a hand to the outside of his left thigh, where the knife had gone in.

"Stay just where you are," Maxim said. And he stayed where he was himself, playing the thin beam over the man. He was probably a few years younger than Maxim, with a rather blobby nose, wide mouth and coarse grainy skin, a face that made you think the sculptor had meant to spend another day on it. He was wearing a dark muddy anorak, with the zip now torn loose.

"The police are up on the road," the man said. He had a very slight accent.

"I know. Any good reason why I shouldn't scream for them?"

"I perhaps could think of one or two. And so could you."

Maxim let the torch beam droop, but he wasn't going to get any closer. If they tangled again, one of them was going to get killed and he wasn't too confident about which one.

"If you can walk away from this," he said, "you can walk away."

The man considered it. When the Gardai came down the field, there would be a lot of explaining to do, and a lot of time in which to do it. Neither of them wanted that.

"Okay." He levered himself to his feet. By now the wound must be stiffening the leg, something else that Maxim had been counting on. The gangplank creaked again, the boat swayed and steadied, and Maxim lifted the curtain of one window to watch the figure hobble quickly away.

Now he was really hurrying. Allowing himself little squirts of light from the torch, he kicked the papers and clothing into a heap, added some of the lighter furniture and soaked it all with paraffin from the stove and a two-gallon can he found in a cupboard in the bows. Then he cut three two-foot lengths from a handful of thick white string and left them to soak in the paraffin.

On deck, he undid the anchor and the stern line, and loosened the one at the bows. Then down into the rancid fumes of the cabin, where he laid the three fuses on a dry patch of floor and lit them. They began to burn steadily, like wicks, creeping towards the heap. At least one should stay alight, giving him, he reckoned, a two-minute start. He ran up into the fresh cold night air, threw off the bow rope and pushed the houseboat out with the gangplank. It moved very slowly and ponderously, but it moved, the bows swinging as the rain-fed current in the Lough caught hold. Already it was too far out for anybody to reach. He started running.

He passed one wall and nobody had shouted, then another. There was no sound, but a ripple of light on the water made him stop and look back. The houseboat was about fifteen yards out, still swinging downstream, the curtained windows glowing. Then one of the curtains vanished in a flare of pink-white light and the window cracked like a shot.

Watching fires, especially those you've started yourself, is as basic a human instinct as throwing stones at

149

water. He forced himself to run on. Up at the lane, somebody called out and a car engine started.

An hour later, after the hotel had locked up for the night, Maxim climbed off the furnace room roof and into his bedroom window, jammed slightly open by a wedge of folded paper.

At Shannon airport they had set up a trestle table even before the check-in desks so that they could search all your luggage. And it was nothing to do with terrorism or hijacking: the searchers even looked at the soles of Maxim's shoes. But the slippers were in the Lough, along with the stolen raincoat and the flick-knife. He would miss that.

Standing beside the table there were two professionally hard-eyed men, and a third who was elderly and had a plump ugly face and a sad expression. One of the plain-clothes men stepped forward. "Excuse me, but would you mind showing me some identification? It's just security."

Don't be too co-operative. Maxim frowned, looked puzzled, and said: "Yes. All right." He gave them his driving license.

"Would you have anything else?"

"Why?"

"Just security." He was thin, with a long sour face.

Maxim shrugged. "Here, take the bloody lot." There was nothing in his wallet to let him down: no ID card or calling cards or MoD pass. He could even have brought his passport, since like most officers he had put his occupation as 'Government official', but the pattern of visas in it would be a giveaway to anybody who knew those places where the sun still hadn't set on the British Army.

The older man was staring at him with a sorrowful anger.

"You'll have been staying here how long, sorr?" the second detective asked in a soft apologetic voice. He was larger, a comfortable man in a short tweed coat.

"Just a couple of nights."

"Was it a business trip, sorr?"

"Not really. I was looking at a property a friend and

I were thinking of buying into. Up in the Silvermine Mountains. What's this about?"

"Did you ever hear of the name Jackaman?" the first one asked.

"I don't think so." *You bloody fool: if they ask what you do, you'll have to say you work in Whitehall. Of course you know the name Jackaman.* "Yes. There was a civil servant. He committed suicide. Is that the one?"

"Sort of. You didn't know Mrs Jackaman?"

"Didn't know either of them."

"So it's just a coincidence, you being here?" They were playing it sweet and sour; the first one asking the tough tactless questions, the second being gentle and sympathetic. Damn the flight for being so empty that they had time for that charade. Maxim would have liked a queue of impatient passengers behind him. He'd even have bought them their tickets.

"What the *hell* do you mean by coincidence?"

The old man burst out: "My sister was burnt to death last night!"

That was where he'd seen the fat piggy face before.

"I'm very sorry. But . . . do you mean she was murdered?"

"There are some unexplained aspects, as you might say, sorr," the second policeman said quickly.

"Well, I'm sorry. But I don't go around burning people."

Only houseboats.

He was wearing his 'civil servant' blue suit, striped shirt and a tie that would have looked dull on an undertaker. Of course, if that was the way arsonists and murderers were dressing this season . . . Then, thank God, there were a couple of more roughly dressed characters getting their luggage searched behind him.

The first detective gave an impatient snort. "Can I have the address of the house you were looking at?" He played his part well, unless he was just anti-English anyway.

Maxim gave them Rafford's address and phone number. They already had his own address, from the driving license.

"Will you be buying it?"

"It needs more work than we'd realised. We'll see."

"Thank you for your help, sorr."

Maxim said to the old man: "I hope they . . ." The old man ignored him, and Maxim walked past.

Jonathan St. John Rafford would be climbing the wall if they mentioned boobytrapped cars and burned-out houseboats. Maxim decided to ring him, but not hastily. The police wouldn't have time to check for a while.

The flight was delayed. He drank a cup of coffee, then walked around the windowless, timeless hangar of a departure lounge that was far too big for the number of passengers at that time of year. The duty-free display was a supermarket in itself, and he was startled by the prices until he realised they were in dollars. Then he was only half startled. But he ought to get something for Chris and his parents . . . why did you feel compelled to buy something in an airport? Pilots obviously didn't.

"Did you hear about the terrible fire?" a slightly accented voice said.

Maxim turned slowly. "What fire?"

"Two of them, in fact." On the far side of a rack of candles shaped like Guinness bottles and flowers and apples, there was a square coarse-grained face with rather unfinished features.

The face smiled. "There was a fire in a car and then there was a fire in a boat. You should have heard it on the radio."

"Did anybody get hurt?"

"In the car, somebody was killed."

"Did anybody get hurt?" Maxim repeated.

The face smiled again. The hair above it was dark and neat, brushed straight back from a high forehead with a slight widow's peak. There were heavy bags under the dark eyes, permanent ones, not just from a late night.

"Nobody got hurt very badly," the face said.

"I'm glad to hear that."

"So you had no trouble with the search? There was no mud on your shoes, and no smell of paraffin on your clothes? And your coat is so very clean. You are

153

very careful. I think . . . I think you are Major Maxim of Downing Street."

"I didn't catch your name."

"Suppose I told the searchers who you are."

"Then I would tell them to look at your left leg."

The loudspeaker announced a flight to Paris, and the face turned away, still smiling, and saying: "Perhaps we'll meet again . . ."

Now Maxim could see the square body, wearing a dark brown suit that was well cut but not by anybody in Britain. The walk was absolutely upright, with no hint of a limp. If he was working alone, he must have bandaged the leg himself: nobody would dare take such an obvious stab wound to a doctor. He might be full of pain-killers, of course, or well trained to pain. Or most likely, both.

Maxim picked up a candle moulded as a pineapple. He was rather afraid his mother would like that. But first he had to ring Rafford.

◉ 23

The room was neon lit and deliberately featureless, without any decoration or pictures to remind you of anything. Just the shelves of big leather-bound albums and an oak lectern like the ones where you spread out a newspaper in the public library.

Maxim sat on a hard chair and turned the album's pages quickly. Each right-hand one had a dozen or so photographs, about the size of a patience card, slotted into it. He wouldn't easily have believed there were that many ugly people in the world.

He went right through the book, then turned back to a page in the middle. "That's him, if anybody is."

It wasn't a normal mug shot, not the usual full-face of a convicted man, but a snatched picture that the victim wasn't supposed to know about. Maxim wondered if this one really hadn't known.

The Branch man leaned over his shoulder and lifted the photograph out to see what was written on the back. Without a word, he handed it to Agnes.

"I admire your taste," she said. "He goes around as Lajos Komocsin, Hungarian businessman. He must be at least part Hungarian or he wouldn't get away with it, but the current theory is that he's a Major Azarov from the KGB. Not known to be assigned anywhere."

"Whoever he is, he's a professional. As well trained as I am, and younger."

"But just as modest with it, I've no doubt." She passed the photograph back to the Branch inspector. "And now he's got a distinguishing scar on the outside front of his left thigh, is that right?"

"Around there."

"So if he ever comes at us with his trousers down, we can shoot without asking questions."

"Yes, Miss." The inspector made a note and went on looking at Maxim with a wary smile.

155

"It wasn't on your patch," Agnes reassured him. "Not even in this country. Come on, Harry, the pumpkin may be back from the ball."

The ball was really, in George's phrase, a 'Common Market rave-up'. To celebrate the end of a conference on energy conservation, the two big drawing rooms on the first floor were flooded with light and heat and jammed with guests in evening dress. Maxim and Agnes sneaked up the staircase feeling like very poor relatives.

The butler recognised Maxim, looked apprehensively at his suit, and asked: "Should I announce you, sir?"

"No thanks. But could you get word to Mr Harbinger that I'm in my room?"

"Very good, Major." He sounded relieved. Beyond him, Maxim glimpsed the Prime Minister, weaving politely through the roar of cocktail chatter, stalked a few feet behind by a tall hawk-faced woman who ran the Press Office but was now busy brushing aside anybody she thought wasn't worth the PM's time. Most of the world fell into that category. Maxim wasn't even in the world.

The working parts of the house were discreetly closed off with elegant ropes attached to little wooden pillars. A uniformed messenger lifted aside the rope to the next staircase, winked, and said: "Nice to see somebody's minding the shop, sir."

In his cubbyhole, Maxim turned on the light and drew the curtains. Agnes looked around.

"Gawd, how you ruling classes do live. Swung any good cats recently?"

Maxim had forgotten she'd never been there before. "I can do you tea or instant soup. Nothing stronger."

"Never mind, I'll wait." He didn't realise just what she'd meant until George came in a few minutes later, wearing a very old-fashioned dinner jacket and carrying a nearly full bottle of champagne. He flopped in the desk chair, leaving Maxim leaning against the desk itself.

"Oh God, but good causes do make bad parties. Have you got any glasses?" He pulled open his collar and unwound his tie, then poured champagne into

Maxim's collection of tea/soup mugs. "So—how far have we got?"

"We've established that the Other Side was represented there," Agnes said. "Harry's identified one."

"How did they find her?"

Maxim shook his head slowly. "A dozen ways. She'd read a couple of thrillers and thought she knew it all, then hid out a few miles from where she was born. She'd left a track like a tank going through a wheatfield."

George grunted.

"Probably a Major Azarov," Agnes said. "We had him down as just a support agent, but Harry says he's a trained tearaway as well. Luckily we had our trusty flick-knife with us . . ."

"A flick-knife?" George said heavily. He was slightly drunk, but knew it. "A flick-knife. You didn't tell me you were taking one."

"You didn't ask."

"I didn't ask if you were taking one of the new FH-70 howitzers, either, but next time I'll have a complete list. And you really burned down that houseboat?"

"The letter might have been on board; it wasn't in the papers I'd pinched. I was just trying to stop as many rabbit-holes as I could."

"If she was going off with you," Agnes said, "it was most likely in her handbag."

"If she read thrillers," George said, "she probably left it in a sealed envelope with her solicitors and orders to send it to number 2 Dzerzhinsky Street in the event of her untimely demise. Do we know who her solicitors are?"

"I can find out tomorrow," Agnes said. "And then . . ." she delicately took a book of matches from her handbag and laid it on the desk beside Maxim.

"Thank you," he said politely. "But I prefer my own."

"Dear Heaven, are you two *trying* to give me a stroke?" George asked. From the floor below, there came a gentle rumble of applause; somebody had just finished a speech. "And now where are we?"

"If Professor Tyler was bidding for it, we know the

letter's real," Maxim said. "At best it could have been burned. At worst we know who wrote it."

"Who?"

"Robert Reginald Etheridge." Maxim took a notebook from his pocket. "Born 1923 in a place called Bishop Wilton near York. He was a farm boy brought up on tractors. He enlisted in 1940 and the Yorkshire Dragoons took him as a driver . . ."

"Whatever happened to them?" George asked instinctively, pouring more champagne all round. The room was small enough that nobody had to get up, just reach.

"The Yorkshire Dragoons were amalgamated with two other regiments to form the Queen's Own Yorkshire Yeomanry in 1956. Since then, they've been reduced to just a squadron in the Queen's Own Yeomanry."

After a while, George asked: "Did you just happen to know that?"

"I never look these things up just because you might ask."

Agnes swallowed a chuckle and choked on it.

"Go on," George said stiffly.

"He was in Egypt with their motor battalion and volunteered for the Long Range Desert Group in 1942. They accepted him with a drop from corporal to private, and the only mention of him in *The Gates of the Grave* is on the last patrol Tyler led in the LRDG. Etheridge was one of the three survivors. After that he was shipped home and never went abroad again. He finished the war as a sergeant driving instructor, demobbed late '45. No claim for any disability pension."

"Why d'you say that?" Agnes pounced.

"There seems to be a doubt about his mental stability. Just a hint in his records."

"Doubt?" George said. "I should have thought it was a crystal certainty. The man went to Canada voluntarily, didn't he?—and then changed his name to Bruckshaw and drank himself to death. Guilty on all three charges."

Maxim smiled politely and sipped the lukewarm

champagne. He didn't much like champagne, even cold.

"You say three men survived," Agnes said. "Etheridge, Tyler himself, and . . .?"

"A French lieutenant, Henri de Carette. We don't have his records, of course, but it's in the book. He was a career officer, commissioned just before the war and retired as a full colonel something over ten years ago. He's still alive."

"*That* can't be in Tyler's book," George said suspiciously.

"I rang our military attaché's office in Paris. They're going to find his address."

"God, I hope they go carefully. The French get paranoid at any hint of us playing the Great Game on their pitch. No, they'll know what they're doing . . . So now where does that leave us?"

Maxim shrugged.

"There's one other person who knows what's in that letter," Agnes said.

"I know that," George said. "But we can't exactly walk up to him and say, 'Excuse me Professor but what horrible thing did you get up to in the desert in early '43 that could be the subject of a letter from the late Sergeant Etheridge?' We *need* that man."

"What for?"

George held up the champagne bottle, stared moodily at how little was left, and poured it out. "The state provideth and the state drinketh, blessed be the name of the state. The taxpayer can always eat cake." The bottle clanged into the wastebucket. "You two can keep shut up; you wouldn't be in your jobs if you couldn't . . . In a couple of weeks Tyler goes to Luxembourg to talk to the French and West Germans about nuclear targetting policy. All this is rather behind the Americans' backs.

"He's the only person we've got whom the French will listen to on defence, particularly nuclear. He speaks the language well, he doesn't trust Washington, and he really seems to believe in a third world war. What more can they ask?"

"I believe in a third world war," Agnes said. "It's the fourth one I've me doubts about. But thank you for telling us this, since Greyfrairs must have known long ago, the way they've stepped up their campaign on Tyler."

"They knew he was going to head the review committee; we don't know if they know about Luxembourg."

"If Bonn's involved, then they know." There had just been a new eruption of security scandals in West Germany, with lonely secretaries to important officials getting seduced by trained gigolos from East Germany. It was an old story, but to Box 500 it didn't get any better in the constant retelling.

"Maybe, maybe." There was another rumble of laughter and applause from the drawing rooms. "At least I'm missing the speechifying . . . So it seems as if we'd better talk to this de Carette, once we know where he lives. I'm not farming it out to Six; Harry, can you do it, the soldier to soldier approach?"

"I can try."

"Also try not to take a flick-knife this time."

Back down in the Private Secretaries' room, George checked through the tray of paperwork that had arrived in the last two hours. Agnes sat on the edge of his desk, listening to the guests clumping down the stairs outside in seven languages.

"Would you have thought of simply burning that houseboat?" George asked.

She considered. "I hope so."

"You *hope* so?"

"He *might* have destroyed the letter, and I assume that's what we want. Especially now we know whatever it says is true."

"Ye-es." George made it a long, unleavened word.

"And if he hadn't had that flick-knife, he could be dead, the way he told it. I assume that's something we *don't* want; British Army officer attached to Number 10 found dead on Irish houseboat of woman murdered in—"

"Yes, yes, *yes*." George glared at a paper in his hand. "Why don't they write to the AUC? The Headmaster isn't responsible for the ice at Heathrow . . .

You don't think Harry blew that bloody woman up himself, as well?"

"Why should he? And the funny thing is . . . I think he'd have told us if he had."

George let the letter drift back into the tray but went on staring at it, unseeing. Then he said quietly: "I hope you won't tell Harry, but I advised the Headmaster to pick somebody else. I think he chose Harry not because he's going somewhere in the Army, since he's quite likely not, but because he doesn't care where he's going any more. I still don't know if we did the right thing, but yes, I think he'd have told us. So who did it?"

"There was a certain Major Azarov also in the cast."

"If he lit the fuse, wouldn't that suggest that Muscovy already has the letter? They wouldn't want to kill her *before* they got it." George shivered. "But if they'd got the letter, what was Azarov doing on the houseboat?"

"Setting up our Major Maxim for a nice Anglo-Irish scandal? He could have tailed Harry from Limerick. He's a good soldier, but . . ."

"Yes . . . Will you go with him to France, once we've located this de Carette?"

"I'd love to watch him in action." Agnes grinned mischievously. "Perhaps we'll get ourselves into another war with France and see Britain restored to her former glory."

"Agnes, do not *say* these things."

Opening the door to his flat, Maxim knew immediately there was something wrong. A smell? A draught? The way the lock had turned? He stayed very still and carefully took the revolver from his briefcase. For once he had it when he might need it.

But he didn't. There was nobody there—not any longer. They seemed to have taken nothing and done nothing like vandalise the place. There were just tiny things like a few books upside down in the bookshelf, the tea and sugar jars switched around in the kitchen cupboard, his usual chair moved out of line with the

TV set. Little things that said: we could have done big things, and next time . . .

He threw out the tea and sugar, just in case, and took a can of beer from the fridge—left with its door slightly open. It had all been nicely done, because the local police would give you one of those ay-ay-he's-one-of-those looks if you complained that someone had broken in just to change your tea and sugar jars around, then relocked the door on the way out.

Nicely done, perhaps too nicely. It was frightening how easily they had got in, but no more than frightening. Maxim couldn't share Barbara Masson's feeling of being despoiled by strangers picking over her property, because he had no property to be picked over. The flat was just the ninth—or was it tenth—place he had rented since his marriage.

Both the gas fire and the record player seemed to be working. He put on the first side of Ralph Kirkpatrick playing 'The Welltempered Clavier'—Jenny had given him the album, to show there was more to the keyboard than Ellington and Basie—and sat down yet again with *The Gates of the Grave*. The twenty-year-old paperback was coming unbound in lumps, but he knew which lump he wanted.

The patrol started from Zella oasis, the new head-quarters of LRDG, about 200 miles south of the coast road . . .

◙ 24

Nice airport was swarming with would-be skiers off some cancelled or diverted flight. The floors were piled with tartan-coloured luggage and skis in long red plastic cases, the desks surrounded by suntanned men in short fur jackets of the sort women wore to the 1953 Coronation.

Maxim and Agnes hired a Citroën Deux-Cheveaux and, after a few mistakes, untangled themselves from the complex of fast new coast roads and began weaving up into the hills behind the city. For the first twenty miles the land was all used up, busy and untidy with olive groves on every slope, red-tiled villas, garages, souvenir shops and pylons. But after that it thinned out, and the rock bones of the hillsides showed through.

"The French," Agnes said, as they passed a very old farmhouse, "let their buildings flourish but keep the trees very much pruned and in their place. In Britain it's the other way round: it's an offence to enlarge your house or cut down your trees. What a basis for *entente*."

Maxim smiled and went on winding the bouncy little can of a car around the sharpening bends. Above, the sky was a hard cold blue, and against it they could suddenly see the place they had come to visit. And, miles before they got there, it could see them.

The Chateau de Carette had always been small, by castle standards. Now it was just the tall square keep, a shaft of grainy honey-coloured stone rising firmly out of a rabble of extra buildings and wings that had been built on down the years. There was almost no sign of the curtain wall and its gatehouse that had originally defined the boundaries, but Maxim could see just where it must have led around the subtle curves and

163

advantages of the hilltop. A soldier's eye is the same, whether he's positioning a laser target designator or a frightened peasant with a crossbow.

The rough driveway—the French don't take gravel seriously—led around to a small door set in one corner of a newish wing. A worn Citroën Safari was parked untidily by the edge of a bank of rough grass that slid down towards the valley. Maxim put the Deux-Cheveaux in beside it.

"He's watching us," Agnes said suddenly.

"Yes."

"Do you feel it, too?"

"Not particularly. But he would be; it's what the place was built for." The keep reared above them, its narrow top windows still holding an all-round view: down the valley, up the valley, across the hills to either side.

The arched door, criss-crossed with ironwork, opened just before they knocked on it. A dour old man-servant poked his head out and grunted at them.

"Nous sommes M'mselle Algar et Major de Chasseurs Maxim," Maxim said in a very flat accent. He had already learnt that Agnes spoke the language almost perfectly, but she was letting him lead.

"Vous avez des cartes de visite, M'sieur, M'mselle?" The old boy had wet blue eyes and the look of a Dracula with indigestion.

Solemnly, they both handed him calling-cards. What on earth does Agnes put on hers? Maxim wondered. They were led down a stone corridor into a wide reception room, and motioned to stay there.

The interior of the keep had been torn out, or possibly fallen down, and rebuilt recently in a more-or-less medieval style. But real money has been spent: you don't pick up floor beams over twenty feet long just by strolling around Cannes market. The furniture was thick, dark, square, and the walls partly rough-plastered, partly raw stone that felt slightly warm to the touch, the way southern stone does even in winter.

Agnes was humming: "Robin Hood, Robin Hood, *riding* through the glen . . ."

The servant came back and led them upstairs, breathing in dry gasps like the swish-swish of a stiff broom. At each floor, the glimpses of decor got more and more personal: thick rugs in front of fireplaces that were obviously used, the sparkle of silver and glassware.

The last flight was a steep stone newel curling up a small turret at one corner. The old man stayed at the bottom, wheezing loudly.

At first sight, Colonel de Carette was both dapper and plump. He was shortish and Maxim knew he was just about sixty. The face was round but not fat, with a sharp nose and very expressive thick eyebrows. He had a neat little moustache, still a lot of silvery-black hair and he could never be anything but French, or think of trying to be.

"*M'mselle Algar.*" He brushed her hand with his lips. "*Enchanté.* And Major Maxim." They shook hands. "Will you take a glass of wine? It is from the region only, so you will not expect too much . . ." The bottle was waiting, misted with cold, on a silver tray. He poured three glasses.

"May I ask you not to smoke? The doctors . . ." he waved a hand. "And I believe the weather in England hasn't been too good? We even had a few flakes around the hills here. But I think perhaps we *see* more snow than most of England." Beyond the tall windows on the east wall they could see a grey corner of the Mediterranean and then the jagged white peaks lifting out of a hazy horizon. The Ligurian Appenines, far across the Italian frontier.

The room was the whole top floor, with windows on all sides and a fireplace with a small wood fire burning in between the two on the west wall. It was low-ceilinged, for its size, and obviously de Carette's private hideout. There was no mock-medievalism about the furniture and panelling, just comfort and a respectable untidiness: piles of books and papers but no dirty glasses or full ashtrays. On a big table at the north end, dozens—maybe hundreds—of model soldiers were laid out in the formal patterns of an eighteenth-century battle.

Maxim glanced at Agnes and wondered if she was thinking what he was: we're privileged to be met in this room instead of downstairs. That means he's going to talk to us. It doesn't mean he's going to tell us the truth.

De Carette chattered on, pointing at views through the window, picking up little silver and china ornaments and showing them to Agnes. His English was very fluent, contrasting with his French habit of cocking his head, bird-like, at a fresh angle for every new phrase.

When they had finished the first glass, he poured refills and then they all sat down. Now it begins, Maxim thought. De Carette had dressed the part carefully, in a dark green velvet smoking jacket over narrow check trousers, a precisely folded silk kerchief at his throat.

"And what, if it is not a secret, is a major of the light infantry—I believe you said you were a *chasseur?* You know of course that I was once of the *Chasseurs d'Afrique?*—what is he doing in Number 10 Downing Street?"

"What's any major doing without a command?"

"Yes . . . it can be an . . . an *uncertain* rank."

"It can last a long time."

"But for you, obviously it will not." It was politely put. He didn't ask Agnes what she did, so he probably knew. There would be well-placed friends in London.

"And now, what may I do for you?"

They had talked over this moment and hadn't managed to think of any better tactic than honesty, though Agnes had certainly tried.

Maxim began his party recitation. "A couple of years ago, a man called Bob Etheridge died in Montreal. When he knew he was dying, he wrote a letter to a man in our Ministry of Defence, Gerald Jackaman." But de Carette gave no flicker of recognition. He smiled and nodded. "Jackaman committed suicide last November. His widow took the letter and—we now know—offered to sell it to the Russians. Whether or not they have it, we have no idea. Somebody killed her. We do know the letter says something about Professor John White Tyler. We hoped you might be able to tell us what could be in it."

"Ah yes. John is somebody quite important, now."

Agnes said: "He's coming up to some delicate negotiations on European defence, soon. Of course, we'd rather you didn't spread that around."

De Carette smiled again, accepting that she had passed a little of the responsibility onto him. "Yes . . . John would be good for that work . . . But why do you ask me?"

"You, Tyler and Etheridge were the only survivors of that last Long Range Desert Group patrol," Maxim said. "It's the only thing that connects you. He doesn't mention either of you in his book again."

"You might always ask John himself."

"We may have to," Agnes said. "But that won't stop the Other Side, if they haven't got the letter, coming and asking you. They can read books, too."

De Carette's eyebrows leapt into a sardonic slant. "Are you trying to frighten me, Miss Algar?"

"Am I succeeding?"

But he just sipped his wine and cocked his head back at Maxim. "This letter seems . . . like the jewel one takes from the idol and then, whoever owns it, he must die. What did poor Etheridge die from?"

"Drink."

De Carette slanted his eyebrows again and began a cold chuckle. Abruptly it became a retching cough. He stiffened and went very pale, Maxim and Agnes leaning forward but unsure how they could help. Then de Carette lifted his hand feebly and waved them back. For a long time he sat very upright in his seat, seeming to hold his chest together with his hands.

At last he took out a folded handkerchief and wiped his lips, ignoring the sparkle of sweat on his deep forehead. After a sip of wine, he said carefully: "I am very sorry, but it is all right now. But tell me . . . what is John Tyler dying from?"

Maxim blinked at him, puzzled. Agnes shrugged and muttered: *"Le baisage."*

"John? That is strange . . . in the desert, he was like a monk."

"In the desert, did you have any choice?"

"A . . . small amount. And certainly a choice of conversation."

Maxim asked: "And what are you dying of, sir?"

De Carette seemed to ignore him. He got up slowly

and walked around the room, weaving carefully between the furniture until he reached the south wall. That was the only one with window seats built into it. He stared down into the valley.

"I saw you coming. I have watched for a long time because I knew that one day somebody would come. And I thought they might be too late. The doctors told me I have *la tuberculose*. You see, they cannot call it cancer of the lung because the government owns the monopoly of tobacco and so we do not have cancer of the lung in France. It is probably forbidden by some law of some thirteenth of July . . ." He lifted his hands in a weary gesture, and turned back from the window.

"So you are right, Major. And . . . I also thought to write a letter. But I could not decide where to send it. My wife is dead, my sons . . . I am not sure they would understand. Perhaps you will, Major." He came back and sat down. "Some more wine . . ."

Maxim got up quickly and poured it; that just about killed the bottle, and de Carette took a small telephone from beside the fire and gave orders.

"The family de Carette has always been of the Army. Some to the Navy, but most to Saint-Cyr. You can see . . ." The panelled walls were lined with austerely framed photographs of groups of officers, some sitting in rigidly posed rows, some grinning across the crumpled mudguard of a Sherman tank. Many were far too old to be of this de Carette, but his career was all there: the stiff-necked graduate of Saint-Cyr, the sous-lieutenant among black troops in Africa, sharing a jeep with Leclerc, being decorated by de Gaulle, in Hanoi with de Lattre de Tassigny . . .

But not in the desert with John White Tyler.

An old lady came into the room carrying a new tray of glasses and a bottle, the cork already drawn. De Carette thanked her brusquely.

"And so . . . when I had my commission, I was humiliated to be posted to Africa. We all knew, we young officers, that a war must come in Europe—was that hope, perhaps?—but nothing could come to Fort Archimbault or de Possel. But a soldier who argues with orders is arguing with his luck, perhaps his life. We listened on the radio as France died, day by day, and we cursed God. Yet the officers who stayed there were defeated or dismissed. And the few—there were some—who tried to maintain the Army of the Armistice at Vichy, to keep something sacred from the politicians and Germans, something they could one day build on again (perhaps I understand those men better, now), after the war they were assumed to be collaborators and anybody who had been in Africa was a hero."

He smiled at Agnes. *"Enfin,* I became a hero."

But not quickly. He was among the first to come north and join up with 8th Army in the desert, but his knowledge of English doomed him to a series of liaison jobs with the Staff. He saw little action except in Cairo bedrooms—"They were all spies, those girls, but they learned nothing from me, not in any way, alas. I was very young . . ." Then it was 1942, Alamein, and what really did seem like the last push westwards. He was to go forward to Benghazi, and on by single-engined Waco down to join the Long Range Desert Group, who needed a French officer. His contact would be Captain John White Tyler.

"But, of course, you know all this from John's book."

"We'd like to hear your version, sir," Maxim said.

De Carette took a mouthful of wine and cocked his head as if he were tasting it for the first time. "It is bizarre. What I most remember is how we all smoked cigarettes, all the time, whenever anything happened or did not happen . . . I smoked far more cigarettes than I fired bullets . . ."

◉ 25

The patrol started from Zella oasis, the new headquarters of LRDG, about two hundred miles south of the coast road where the armies fought and where—thank God—the insects stayed. They kept just over the horizon from the next oasis at Hon, where the Italians were supposed still to have a thousand soldiers in residence, and near the end of the first day came out onto the flat gravel of the Hamada el Homra, the Red Desert.

It was a small group, just ten men spread among two jeeps and two much-converted thirty-hundredweight Chevrolet trucks. They were looking for a unit, or advance guard or patrol—call it what you like because it could be pure rumour—of French colonial troops coming up from somewhere in West Africa.

From the beginning of the war there had been over 120,000 French soldiers in Africa—regular, colonial, native and Foreign Legion—vaguely loyal to Vichy but mostly just counting their fingers. A few, Leclerc and de Carette himself among them, had come up to join 8th Army long before. Now, after the Allies had landed in Morocco and Algeria and the Germans had torn down and thrown away the Vichy government like old Christmas decorations, there was a rush from the other French garrisons to get back into the war.

They appeared almost anywhere. They raided and even captured Italian outposts, they ambushed convoys and sometimes each other—but the one thing they never did was tell anybody else what they were doing.

"If a French officer came to me," a choleric colonel in Benghazi had said, "and told me where he'd been, what he'd done, and where he was going next, I'd have him shot as a German spy. He'd be no bloody Frenchie!"

De Carette had begun to wind himself up into a cold

fury, but then remembered that he was very young and junior, and that this colonel was his door into the romantic behind-the-lines warfare of LRDG, so shouldn't be slammed carelessly. And anyway, he knew there was enough truth in the comment to agree politely. Very coldly, but politely.

That was their only task: to find the rumoured French unit. Contact with the enemy was to be avoided. On the other hand, it was a big desert and the enemy might not know contact with him was to be avoided, so they carried the more-or-less standard armament of twin Vickers K guns fired from the right-hand seat of the jeeps, with a single Lewis and a belt-fed Vickers machine-gun in the Chevs. They also had rifles, pistols, Tommy-guns, grenades, land-mines, 808-type plastic explosive and a few incendiary candles. Just standard equipment.

The patrol seemed to be one big family, perhaps more than a family, since the ones who didn't fit had been thrown out. They came from any unit in the desert and wore any bits of uniform they happened to have—most of it all at once, in the January chill, topped off with a greatcoat or goatskin jacket. Nobody wore the flowing *keffiyah* head-dress any more: it looked splendidly romantic, but it also caught in the steering-wheel or the chattering bolt-knob of a machine-gun. A knitted woolly 'comforter' didn't.

Nobody seemed to use ranks or even real names. Tyler was 'Skipper' and only de Carette was 'sir'—the newcomer, the outsider. He wasn't sure he really wanted to be part of the family, but he did want to be asked.

"They were very fair," de Carette recalled. "They saw I could drive perhaps better than any of them, so they let me have one of the jeeps. John drove the other. You are too young, both of you, to remember, but before the war most French and English soldiers could not drive at all. Except a few who had been drivers of trucks for a job, and the boys of parents with some money. My family had some money, and I had driven a car in Africa since I was big enough to see over the steering-wheel. I expect it was illegal even then, but . . ."

An hour before sunset they stopped for the night. Just stopped, because on the flat plain there was nowhere to hide. The Signals sergeant from the wireless Chev erected his flimsy aerial and started tapping out a position report. Others unloaded just as much as they needed for the night and no more, because they might need a fast getaway. They serviced the vehicles, cleaned the guns and everybody filled his waterbottle. Nobody went anywhere without a full waterbottle.

They had done 150 miles, not bad considering the basalt rocks above Hon and it being a first day when newly-stowed stores could shake loose and even fall off. But Captain Tyler was strict about things like that, preaching gently that a tin of meat and veg wasn't important in itself, only when you couldn't find it. At twenty-seven he was older than any of them except the Signals sergeant.

One of them cooked a stew of tinned M and V over the traditional 8th Army stove: one of the old flimsy petrol tins bodged with holes and half-filled with petrol-soaked sand. It burned surprisingly tamely for a surprising time. The tea came thick and horribly sweet, made with condensed milk. De Carette made no comment.

At the moment of sunset itself, the Red Desert suddenly lived up to its name. The rusty plain turned to blood in the horizontal light, then richened through all the scarlets and purples of raw meat as shadows stretched out from inch-high pebbles. Only the colours moved; everything else was quite still. Everybody stopped and watched; none of them had been this far west before. They lit cigarettes and the smoke drifted almost straight upwards. Then the colours faded and darkened to colourlessness, and the patrol gave appreciative grunts and went back to their jobs.

"Always something new," Tyler said, his long face becoming an opera devil in the red light. *"Ex Africa semper aliquid novi.* We may impress ourselves with what we're up to, but I doubt we'd impress old Pliny. Although it was some Greek who said it first . . ."

He rambled on in his slow, serious voice, and de

Carette flattered himself that Tyler might be glad to have a companion to whom he could quote Latin. Yet the scholar and soldier seemed to blend without a seam showing, and Tyler wasn't condescending when he argued with Corporal Bede about the unnecessary complication of the Tommy-gun. Was this some Anglo-Saxon duplicity?

But he was right about the desert: always something new. To some it was a mysterious woman, to others an old bitch who never knew her own mind. Neither pretended to know the 'desert'. It would change subtly, from gravel to tiny stones to bigger ones and then sharp rocks that carved at your tyres until your arms were limp with winding the steering-wheel and your speed had dropped at least ten mph (or ten mih— miles in the hour—as the Army put it, just to remind you this wasn't a Saturday afternoon picnic). And then the lady might throw a real change of mood at you, like a crumbled escarpment that fell away a full three hundred feet that you wouldn't have chanced even in one of the new Sherman tanks.

Or perhaps a miniature mountain range, jagged as broken glass, poking out of the plain like the backbone of some vast dinosaur. All quite unexpected, of course.

The desert was a very *old* lady. And there were almost no maps of her face.

Tyle poured everybody a mug of rum, lime-juice powder and water, then one by one they wrapped themselves in sleeping bags under tarpaulins stretched from the vehicles like tent-halves. The night turned viciously cold under a sky crowded with stars that shone, not twinkled, in the diamond-clear air. They were all young, fit and well rested, so nobody felt very tired yet. There wasn't much talking, but matches flared and cigarettes glowed until well after midnight.

Around noon on the third day they slid down the western escarpment off the Hamada and, according to dead reckoning navigation, crossed into Tunisia.

Unexpectedly—as you'd expect—the desert changed to short, sandy-grey hummocks wearing toupees of crackly brush that broke off and jammed in the track rods and exhausts. It had a depressing and unnatural nastiness, like the man-made deserts of rubbish and broken cars beside the railway yards outside big cities. It slowed them anyway, but they also went more cautiously.

That night they leaguered three-quarters of a mile before a track that wasn't properly a road but had been in use long before most other roads in the world. From the Mediterranean in the north it reached down some 1800 rambling miles through the real Sahara to Tamanrasset and finally Kano in Nigeria, and camel trains had been plodding it since Hannibal's day.

If the French had got this far, they had almost certainly used this track. But so would any Afrika Korps unit which had picked up the same rumour. They put a watcher at the trackside while the rest of them went on with the evening chores.

About half an hour before sunset, two aeroplanes flew northwards on the far side of the track. Through glasses, Tyler identified them as Stukas. They were flying suspiciously low and slow, although the nearest landing-ground was at least seventy miles away. De Carette felt a ripple of unease run through the patrol, and when the aircraft noise had faded, several of them quietly went around checking the camouflage nets and bushes piled on the vehicles.

"We shan't see them again today," Tyler said. "They don't have the night-flying lights and whatnot on the landing-grounds here. It's probably safer lighting a fire at night than by day. There must be dozens of Arab fires up and down the track." He gave a little chuckle, but went on frowning at the humps that were the Chevs. "Oh well . . . if you knows of a better 'ole, go to it."

Then he had to explain the old First War cartoon of the soldiers in a shell-hole to de Carette.

They kept watch on the track, in relays, until midnight. De Carette felt left out at not having been chosen, but the last watcher let him know why. It was a corporal called Bede, rather quiet and serious.

"Only a few camels," he reported. "But when it was clear I went down and took a shufti and there's been a lot of wheeled stuff recently. No tanks or half-tracks, just wheels. Some Opels and Kübels and some I don't know, Skip. I tried drawing a couple of them." He shone his torch on the signals pad and held it out—but to de Carette, not Tyler.

"I tell you," de Carette smiled, "I thought it was fantastic, quite absurd. How could I recognise the patterns of some old French tyres? I could not even tell you the patterns of my own cars or the jeep I had just been driving. But then I saw: all of them would know just that. Like their own signatures. I was ashamed and angry, but now I know they were telling me something. I might tell them about Africa, but they could tell me—the only professional soldier—about war. John knew it, of course."

He chuckled at the memory, coughed carefully, and said: "He asked Bede if he could tell which way they had been going, these tracks. But he could not. So John sent him back with his torch, a long useless walk, to have a look. It was his sort of discipline."

◙ 26

They renewed the watch again from before dawn. At half past nine, Tyler went off to take a stint himself. Without him, de Carette felt even less a part of the family, and suddenly very frightened. Here they were, behind enemy lines (insofar as that part of the desert had 'lines' at all) but they weren't dashing about, blazing away with machine-guns and watching fuel dumps go up in fountains of flame. They were crawling under the camouflage nets to tinker with the engines and guns, brewing up tea, smoking, re-reading tattered old letters from home, snoozing . . . it was all so *normal* that it made the war seem very much more total than just the bombing of children and old women.

One of the Chev drivers, a lance-corporal known as Griff, came over with a blackened tea-can. "Cuppa *shay*, sir?" He was a handsome boy from somewhere in London, his hair ink black except for the dust, and the lower half of his face looking as if he'd washed in ash. By now they all had four-day beards, ranging from the True Explorer to the Sadly Adolescent. Nobody shaved in LRDG; it was a waste of water but more than that a waste of *hot* water, which took fuel and time. What they heated, they drank as *shay*, though no Arab would accept Griff's brew as real tea.

"Thank you very much." De Carette offered him a cigarette.

"Ta, sir." Griff squatted down and puffed. "Is it true what they say about the Arabs around here, sir? I mean them not being like the Sennoos?"

"I am afraid that it is. Here, I think it would be a bad mistake to trust them."

"Yer." Griff frowned as he thought out the implications of this. In Libya, the Senussi were the LRDG's best allies against Italian overlords who shut them in concentration camps and, occasionally, took their

176

chiefs up in an aeroplane and pushed them out without benefit of a parachute. But in Tunisia the French were the hated overlords, and de Carette had spent too long as a child in North Africa to have any illusions about it. Vichy had gained some popularity with its anti-semitic laws, but most popular of all—according to Intelligence—were the newly arrived German troops with their rigid good manners and open-handed payments for food and services rendered.

If 'liberation' meant a return to tight-wad French rule, most Tunisian Arabs wanted nothing to do with it.

"Yer," Griff decided. "Could make it tricky, that, sir. Mind, the Skipper speaks Arabic, did you know that?"

"He speaks it better than I myself do, and I was born in Algeria. He also speaks better French than I speak English."

"Yer." Griff nodded, satisfied. "He's dead clever, the Skipper. Wonder what he'll do, after the war? I s'pose he'll go to Oxford or Cambridge and be a professor. I can't see him wanting to be a bleedin' general."

It was a simple assumption, but Griff didn't live to see it come true. Ten minutes later, the aircraft found them.

The first was a lone CR 42, an old biplane fighter and just about the last of its type that the Italians dared fly over Africa. It droned along, weaving lazily, parallel to the track. The pilot was obviously searching the ground but whether he was looking for anything in particular . . . In any case, all they could do was lie still in the best cover they could find. Even if the vehicles hadn't been immobilised by camouflage, they couldn't have dodged among those hummocks.

The pilot could have seen something as small and chancy as the glint of a well-scrubbed cooking-tin; more likely it was the sheer bulk of the Chevs. They stood at least five feet high when loaded and even parked between the hummocks couldn't be made to look like small bushes. But whatever he saw, the moment was quite clear. The fighter stiffened out of its curving flight, then its engine howled as it climbed flamboyantly against the sun.

The patrol swore vividly and scuttled around, re-arranging themselves to meet the line of attack. They rammed magazines into the Tommy-guns and cocked them—and so did de Carette, although he hadn't much faith in pistol-calibre bullets bringing down an aeroplane. But there was no time to tear off the camouflage nets and get at the machine-guns on the vehicles, even if anybody had felt suicidal enough to try.

Fired simultaneously, four heavy machine-guns make a single stretched-out explosion: *brrrrrap*. The recoil checked the aeroplane for a moment in a sprinkle of falling brass cartridge cases, and dust erupted all around the wireless Chev. The Tommy-guns burped back. De Carette knelt up, the gun stabbing against his shoulder like a pneumatic drill.

The biplane climbed away, followed by the thin rattle of a single Lewis gun.

It was sheer chance that Bede had been working on the other Chev at the time. And it was probably his strict but unimaginative sense of what was right and proper that made him knock aside the bits of bush over the Lewis gun and pull down the netting until the barrel poked through. He might have run away from a Messerschmitt, which was a proper modern aeroplane, but not from some tatty old biplane.

"Get out of there, you stupid bugger!" Griff screamed, and rushed across to the Chev. De Carette saw him ranting at the shadow of Bede inside the netting, but then the biplane turned in again, wings wriggling as it straightened its aim. He heard the first few shots from the Lewis before it was blotted out. *Brrrrrrap.*

The Chev vanished in a blast of dust, and in the middle of it there was flame. Griff staggered out of the smoke, either wounded or dazed. De Carette got up—so did half a dozen others—but they were slapped down as the whole thing blew. Petrol, mines, grenades, maybe even the plastic explosive, all at once. Blazing fuel cans arced into the bushes on every side and started new fires, and when the first eruption died down, the Chev was a tangle of junk, burning steadily and pouring black smoke into the air. Somebody ran across to Griff, took one look and ran back. There was no sign of Bede at all.

The biplane climbed away rather slower than before, and went into a wide, wary turn. So perhaps Bede, or even one of the Tommy-guns, had got lucky after all. Or maybe it was just out of ammunition, because after one circle it flew away to the north.

"Get all the camouflage off," de Carette ordered. "Get everything ready to move." They hardly needed telling. The CR 42 knew it had left an unfinished job, and the smoke was rolling two hundred feet into the air before it thinned out. An aeroplane could probably see that from forty miles away. Ammunition began to cook off in the fire, spitting in all directions.

They were ready to move in under five minutes. The wireless Chev had several holes through its wooden bodywork, and there was a strong smell of petrol from a punctured can, but worst of all was a patch of damp on the ground between the front wheels.

"The bugger got her in the waterworks," the driver said. He crawled under and started feeling up around the radiator. "Shit."

"How far can you go?" de Carette asked.

"Dunno, sir . . . could be a mile or two . . ."

"Put in some water now, quickly." They moved like a circus acrobatic team. One yanked open the bonnet, another tossed down the can of water, the driver had the radiator cap off, a fourth started pouring. The bonnet clanged shut again.

"Go," de Carette said. "Spread out, go for the track. The Skipper will be coming back, one of us will see him." He slipped easily into command now there were decisions to be made. He must remember that he, unlike them, was a properly trained professional soldier. It was pure chance that they knew more about war than he did.

They picked up Tyler and his co-watcher after only a few minutes, staggering breathlessly back through the hummocks towards the smoke. De Carette gave him a quick report, and Tyler dropped panting into the gunner's seat of his jeep.

"Onto the track, then we'll head south." They

charged off again. The first thing was to put distance between themselves and that black signpost in the sky.

They had to stop once, to put another can of water into the Chev; they didn't like using it up that way, but they had plenty for the moment . . . And in any case, de Carette knew the mission was dead. The loss of a truck and two men wasn't itself so bad: any military unit has to be able to take casualties without falling apart, and the lost supplies and fuel would have been used up by the dead men and wrecked truck anyway. But a single bullet through the wireless Chev's radiator was far worse. If they had to abandon that truck and fit eight men into two jeeps already jammed with gear, they'd have to dump not only the Chev's supplies but some from the jeeps as well.

It seemed very bourgeois thinking, and de Carette reminded himself of his mother in her high-necked black bombazine, old before her time because her chosen age was old, ticking off on her fingers the tiny triumphs of a morning's shopping in Cannes market.

But he hadn't starved at home and he didn't want to starve in the desert. No, the mission was dead. Tyler would know that.

They reached the track and turned south, away—they hoped—from trouble. For about ten miles they ran at speeds of thirty and forty mph, until the Chev's driver waved them down. The radiator was steaming like a kettle.

"Another ten seconds and she'd seize solid, Skipper."

Tyler looked carefully around. There was a narrow strip of the bushy hummocks on the west side of the track before the real sand began. "Get off the road and dig her in."

They all bumped cautiously into a dead-end wadi, ran for a hundred and fifty yards, then stuck. Everybody except the gunners leapt out and started smothering the truck in netting and bushes. The gunners watched and automatically lit cigarettes. None of the vehicles had windscreens, so it was near impossible to smoke on the move.

Tyler scribbled a quick message on a signals pad and showed it to de Carette. It gave their position, then: *No clue French. Lost two men and one Chev air attack. Other Chev probably immobile. Task unlikely completion. Details follow. Tyler.*

De Carette nodded. "Does one need more detail?"

Tyler made a grunting chuckling noise and gave the signal to the Sergeant. "Encipher that and get it off as soon as you can, never mind about proper call times. We'll be back by dark."

One of the gunners called: "Planes, Skipper! Up North." He used a deliberately husky voice, as if aeroplanes five miles away might overhear, but de Carette now knew how he felt.

"Start up!" Tyler shouted. They drove out of the wadi and on southwards at a sober speed to keep down the dust.

"They're comin' this way, sir." his gunner said. They called him Yorkie, a solid squat boy from a Yeomanry regiment.

"What are they?"

"Stukas I reckon. Bugger 'em. There in't no hurry, sir."

De Carette had instinctively accelerated, but speed was no use against an aeroplane until it was actually attacking you.

"They 'ave us." Yorkie said. De Carette let the jeep coast, looking back over his shoulder. The two crank-winged Junkers 87's were following straight down the line of the track and as he watched, their engines began to strain, reaching for more height. He drove on slowly, glancing upwards. The first Stuka nosed carefully over, with the precision of a marksman bringing a target rifle into his shoulder. Yorkie muttered filthy words. The Stuka dived almost vertically but not very fast, a crippled black shape against the pale sky.

"This in't our 'un," Yorkie said. "We'll get 'is mate." He swung up the K guns and fingered the triggers. "Could you keep 'er still a moment, sir?"

De Carette turned the jeep sideways and stopped. The Stuka was already right overhead, going for Tyler's jeep, a quarter of a mile down the track. Yorkie started firing as the Stuka let go two small bombs and began a sharp pull-out.

Tyler's jeep swerved wildly away off the track and

two yellow-black spouts of smoke jumped up behind him. The jeep seemed unharmed. So did the Stuka.

"'Ere comes our 'un," Yorkie said, and went on swearing calmly as he changed the pans on the K guns. But he wouldn't be able to elevate them enough to shoot at a dive-bomber coming from right above.

"It seems so," de Carette said, surprised at how cool he sounded. He was terrified. He had been in a few night-time air raids in Egypt, and under artillery fire three times. But those had been impersonal, random affairs. Now a man in an aeroplane had chosen to kill him. There had been a choice and that man had decided to kill him, de Carette, rather than somebody else. It was unbelievable. As it toppled into the dive, the second Stuka looked like a gun barrel with wings.

He hauled the jeep around and accelerated furiously north, back up the track and into the diving aeroplane, hoping to force it to steepen its dive even further. But he was going too fast to look up.

"Bombs away!" Yorkie called. De Carette wrenched the wheel, almost overturned the jeep, and crashed into the cover of two bushy dunes. An explosion and a blast of hot air slapped him in the back. He froze, trying to decide if he were hurt, and there came another, longer explosion.

"You bastard! You bugger!" Yorkie screamed in delight. "That's t'first time tha's done that trick, you fucker!"

Shakily, de Carette looked around. A quarter of a mile south, there was a long smear of rich flame and smoke rising beside the track. The Stuka hadn't quite managed its pull-out. He had never felt so happy that somebody had died.

De Carette backed nervously out of the dunes. They lit cigarettes and watched the first Stuka circling. After five minutes it flew away and they drove down to find Tyler. He was cannily hiding his jeep in the drifting smoke downwind of the burning wreckage.

"Are both of you all right?" he asked. "And the jeep? Good show. Well—" nodding at the fire: "— that's one on the profits side."

Tyler's gunner was a Birmingham boy with a bush of fair hair and a skin that turned red rather than tanned in the sun and wind. He was called Gunner, a nickname that had baffled de Carette until he realised it wasn't because he fired the machine-guns—which they all might do—but because he came from the Royal Artillery. Now he and Yorkie were wrangling like puppies because Gunner was quite sure (so he said) that it was his shooting and not a pilot's mistake that had crashed the Stuka.

"Do we go back now?" de Carette asked.

Tyler frowned at the sky, then the track north. "I don't like leaving them, but . . . that Stuka probably radioed our position. We'd do best to keep on south. It might draw attention away from the Chev. Hell's teeth, come back *here*, you moron!" Gunner had gone searching in the wreckage for a souvenir. He scampered back with a battered inspection plate that had sprung loose.

"Did you know they was Eyeties, Skip, them Stukas? They had the three what's-its on the tail. The markings. I didn't know the Eyeties had Stukas."

"Well, I did," Tyler said. "If you join Uncle Adolf's club, you get a badge and free Stukas. Italy, Hungary, Rumania, all of them . . ." But he still made a note of it for his report.

This, de Carette thought, is a man who takes war seriously. He may be leading small patrols across the desert, but he knows somebody who knows what aircraft Hitler is giving his Balkan friends, and he remembers.

For an hour, they hurried away from this new sky-marker, stopping just now and then to look at rubbish beside the track. They found cigarette packets, mostly Italian, broken wine bottles and a few German food tins that could be months old and still unrusted in that climate. But nothing French.

Finally they stopped for a brew-up and a very late lunch of biscuits and cheese, pickles and tinned fruit. To his own surprise, de Carette found he was getting a taste for the spicy English pickled onion.

As the excitement of action wore off, the mood turned gloomy as they remembered Bede and Griff.

"He was all right, was our Griff," Gunner recalled.

"You always got a laugh out of 'im. And Jamie, he was all right, too."

"Aye," Yorkie said in a kind of sigh. "He were all right. Bit serious, mind, but there's worse things to be. And I liked that Griff."

"Right then," Tyler said firmly. "It cost them two men in that Stuka. But you won't shoot any more down with the guns all fouled. Let's get on with it."

They cleaned the guns, refilled the magazines and drove on south, a last stretch of the hand to reach a probably mythical ally. They were just about to turn back when Tyler's jeep suddenly stopped and he raised his arm. De Carette braked and waited, well back. Tyler jumped out, carrying a Tommy-gun, and ran into the dunes east of the track. Everybody lit cigarettes.

After about five minutes, Tyler re-appeared and waved them up. Leading onto the track was a wide, shallow wadi, its sandy floor plaited with tyre tracks. And a twinkling scatter of cartridge cases. Yorkie got down and picked one up, sniffing at it. "Aye, it's German, and recent. 20-mil. Likely they've had a scout car down 'ere."

"They did," Tyler said quietly. He nodded up the wadi. "Go and take a look," he told de Carette. "Stay on the side; the track just might be mined."

Two hundred yards later, the wadi opened up into a perfect flat camp-site—except that it was far too close to the track. That was one mistake this French unit wouldn't make again. The burned-out hulks of the three civilian trucks seemed somehow far more miserable than the two military ones. North Africa was covered with wrecked army trucks, and also with little humps in the sand like those along the windward side of the dunes, each marked by a small board chopped off one of the truck bodies.

There were sixteen graves, the names laboriously scratched into the wood with indelible pencil. A lieutenant, two sergeants, a corporal, the rest privates. All French names presumably none of them native troops. Why hadn't they given them the dignity of upended rifles jammed into the sand as markers? Because they were in Arab territory. A rifle was hard currency here.

Even the smallest battle is horribly untidy. The ground was littered with bits of clothing, cooking tins, tools, patches of dried blood, more cartridge cases and a sprinkling of black and grey ash from the dead fires. All the wreckage was quite cold, even where it had burned hot enough to melt the metal. More than a day ago. Two?

"Vous étes Anglais, n'est-ce-pas?"

De Carette whipped around, jabbing the safety on the Tommy-gun as it came up level. A man was standing in a small gap between the dunes, ragged and dirty, with a bloody bandage around his left calf and propping himself on a crutch that was a charred plank. As his heart slowed down again, de Carette saw that under the tiredness and the thin beard the man was younger than himself. And the baggy trousers and flared jacket were certainly French.

He lowered the gun a fraction. *"Je suis Lieutenant de Carette, Chasseurs d'Afrique."*

The man grinned and sagged with relief, then tried to pull himself to attention. He croaked: *"Soldat de la premiere classe Gaston Lecat, mon Lieutenant."*

De Carette washed and re-bandaged the wound while Yorkie brewed hot water and Gunner kept watch. Tyler asked the questions, in his careful but fluént French, and de Carette was a little miffed that he seemed to know more about the French army in Africa than he did himself.

Yes, they had come up out of French West Africa once the old Vichy Colonel had managed to go down with malaria and the young Major decided it was time they got into the real war. They might have been searching for somebody called General Leclerc—was there such a man? No, they didn't have a wireless transmitter with them. It was back at the fort, too big to put in a truck. There had been about forty of them, he thought, and they'd been on the road for eight, or was it ten?, days. They hadn't seen anybody except a few Arab camel drivers, who told them there weren't any Germans down here . . .

Tyler and de Carette swapped sour looks.

And, of course, the Italians. The Italians who had

come up the same track behind them, the day of the attack. They'd pulled off into the dunes for lunch and left a guard hidden down by the road, and he saw this convoy of Italian motor-cars go past. Five of them and one truck. The Italians in the cars seemed to be officers and two women. Yes, the Major had thought that was odd, too. So he'd taken Sergeant Foulque and probably it was four men and one of the Chatellerault machine-guns and gone off in two cars to follow.

And the rest of them had waited—and that night there was the attack. A blast of fire and grenades sweeping the camp, quickly followed by the pumping twenty-millimetres of scout cars charging up the wadi. He himself had never even found his rifle in the darkness, he'd just run until a bullet knocked him spinning down the dune and he hadn't seen anybody since then. He'd crawled away into the night and watched the glow of the burning trucks and heard at dawn the noise of digging, and then the Germans had driven away. He had waited all day, then all night, for the Major, but . . .

And, just like that, Lecat fell asleep, with a half-full mug of tea and rum in one hand and a burning cigarette in the other. Tyler carefully took the cigarette and ground it into the sand. "He's lucky to be able to do that, not to get hysterical or weepy when it's all over."

"You think it is all over?" De Carette gestured around.

"For him it is. He's found a new commander, the kitten has a new mother and doesn't have to do his own worrying any more. Most soldiers are like that, thank God."

De Carette looked down at the relaxed, very young face behind the wispy blonde beard. "He is only a lance-corporal, one stripe above nothing . . . So they did come this way. And they got caught. We have made our mission." He may have sounded bitter, hating to see French soldiers come off second best. But three years or more raising and lowering a flag over a Sahara fort was no training to meet the Afrika Korps.

"And what about the Major?" Tyler asked.

"He was caught as well." Now he was sure he sounded bitter.

"He must have gone up the track before we reached it; he left about forty-eight hours ago. And what do you think about the Italians, *Henry?*"

"I don't understand it, *Jean.*" It was a tiny joke, switching nationalities on each other's names. Tyler was trying to cheer him up. "From Ghadames?" That was the walled village—a town by desert standards—down on the edge of the Sahara, a hundred miles south. A strong Italian garrison, when last heard of. The French must have bypassed it without explaining to Lecat.

"Just officers and women in cars," Tyler brooded, "and one truck, probably with their baggage."

"*Jésus.* Can they really be leaving their own men?" Italian garrison units had no great reputation for gallantry, but *this* . . .

"It looks very much like it. Ghadames could be wide open—if we can get a message through. *Sonnez le boute-selle.*"

They went north, Lecat jammed crossways among the supplies in the back of de Carette's jeep. The sun dwindled on their left, so that would be where any wise enemy would set an ambush, but they saw nobody. Perhaps the action over the last two days had persuaded even the camel drivers that their own journeys weren't immediately necessary.

They passed the strewn wreckage of the Stuka, still smouldering in places, and reached the area of the wireless truck just before sunset. Surprised, de Carette saw Tyler drive steadily past the wadi and round a bend in the track that put it out of sight. There he stopped and de Carette pulled up beside him.

Tyler looked grim. "There should have been a guard on that wadi. The boys know a jeep when they hear one. Come on." He and Gunner took Tommy-guns and moved off into the hummocks. De Carette got out to sit at the guns of Tyler's jeep, just in case. By the time he'd slid into place, he found he had a lit cigarette in his hand.

Gunner came back about twenty minutes later, trailing his Tommy-gun by the sling in a hunched, disconsolate plod.

"They've gone. Just gone, Chev and all. The Jerries got 'em. They left a Volkswagen that got stuck, like." He started rummaging in the back of the jeep, and came up with one of the British four-gallon petrol tins. "Skipper wants a couple of gallons and some high-tension lead and a spark-plug."

"What for?" de Carette asked.

Gunner looked at him gloomily. "You could take 'em to him, sir, if you wanted."

"I will."

Gunner poured off half the petrol into the jeep's tank, and de Carette took the can back over the hummocks. Where the Chev had been there was a scatter of camouflage nets, torn bush, empty tins, cartridge cases—all the usual rubbish of an action. Fifty yards back down the wadi, Tyler was waiting by a Volkswagen that was jammed to its hub caps in soft sand. All its doors were open and there was a mess of blood on the driver's seat, but no holes in the bodywork. Somebody in the Chev had got off a burst that had hit the driver in the head or chest and the little car had run wild into the very obvious patch of sand.

"Why did they not pull it out?" de Carette asked. Given a heavier vehicle and a tow-rope—which was as vital in the desert as water—it was a simple job, even if it took a little time.

"I imagine they had one or two men wounded, bleeding badly, and I hope some of our boys to guard as well. They'd be in a hurry. But I wouldn't be surprised if they came back for it." Tyler lifted the engine cover at the back; it was the open military version of the Volkswagen, technically a Kübelwagen.

"It may be booby-trapped," de Carette said.

"It isn't, but it's going to be. I'd rather do it with a mine or some 808, but that was all in the Chevs. So now we have to improvise."

He undid the lead from the furthest in of the two right-hand cylinders, a difficult one to get at, or even see properly. He connected part of the extra length of wire to the lead and pushed it through a hole he had already bodged in the fire wall that separated the engine from the back seat. Under the seat, there was a small stowage compartment for the battery, the jack and some tools.

Tyler punched a hole through the thin cap of the petrol can and threaded both pieces of wire through it, then attached them to the spark plug: one lead to the normal terminal, the other wrapped around the screw thread. The far end of that wire went to the negative terminal on the battery. Then he placed the petrol tin very carefully, screwed the cap gently on, and put the seat in place above it. Back at the engine, he arranged the plug lead so that, unless you looked very closely, it still seemed to go to the cylinder.

Military drivers are taught to check their vehicles much more regularly and closely than most civilian drivers ever do. But de Carette could see what would happen if they came to rescue this one. They'd be in a rush. One could be arranging the tow-rope, another might lift the cover just for a glance in case somebody had wrecked the engine overnight. He might not even bother to do that. But almost certainly one of them would try the starter, to see if the battery had gone flat. And that new plug would flash in the vapour coming off two gallons of petrol that nobody knew was down there under the back seat.

They started back to the jeeps in the reddening light.

"I never thought I'd feel glad we still had one of those damned tins," Tyler commented. The 'damned tins' were Cairo's idea of petrol cans: flimsy things that leaked if you even looked at them nastily. Mostly the LRDG used the far tougher German version, whose nickname was already becoming a generic for an efficient liquids container: the Jerry-can. But you couldn't punch holes in those.

They drove a few miles north and just before sunset turned off the track, well off, to make supper.

It was a gloomy meal. For once even Tyler seemed too drained to do more than insist that they light a fire and get hot food. They ate in silence, except for de Carette trying to reassure Lecat, whose morale was slumping as his saviours slid into their own melancholia. Luckily, he was too tired to stay awake longer than it took him to eat.

Tyler sat wrapped in a great-coat and brooded over a map-board by torchlight, a mug of rum-and-lime in his hand.

"How did they get t'Chev going?" Yorkie muttered. "Her looked bad to me."

Gunner stared at him in the last flickers of the sand-and-petrol stove. "What d'you think our boys was doing all afternoon while we was getting our balls bombed off? It coulda been just the hose. I could fit a new one meself in half an hour."

"It looked like t'radiator to me. They would've filled it with porridge, most like."

"Best thing to do with porridge, that."

"There's nowt wrong with porridge."

"Bloody Scotties."

"Tha knows bloody well where Yorkshire is . . ." They mumbled on, huddled against the side of a jeep and swapping cigarettes automatically.

De Carette sat down beside Tyler. "That Boche commander must not be a fool, John."

"No . . . he's handled his side of things pretty well. Where d'you think he's based?"

"The village?" It was the only possible answer. About forty miles north the map marked a small village with a water hole, just off the track and on the edge of the Grand Erg Oriental, the real sand sea that stretched west and south into the Sahara itself, impassable even to a jeep. If the Germans weren't in the village, there was no logical place for them to be.

"Yes . . . they've probably got a dozen French prisoners and our boys, they'd need somewhere to lock them up."

"John," de Carette said suspiciously, "you do not want to go into that village . . ."

"I'd like to rescue our people, but if we can just reach the wireless Chev we could get a message through. It'll save us three days drive back to Zella—even if the Stukas don't get us."

This man *does* take war seriously, de Carette thought. He is proposing to invade a village, almost certainly a walled one, which must hold at least one armoured car and a platoon of infantry—if it held anything they wanted to find.

But then his vision of the war expanded and he saw over half a million men tangled in battle along the North African coastline. All Captain Tyler had left to lose was two jeeps and five lives. It was sheer bad luck that one life was called Henri de Carette.

They moved out at ten o'clock, with a sliver of moon due to rise around four in the morning. For them, it was probably safest to drive in the dark with headlights blazing confidently, and if anybody recognised them as jeeps that needn't mean anything. The Afrika Korps used as many jeeps as it could capture, just as the 8th Army used Volkswagens, Opel trucks, Steyrs and all the rest.

About midnight, they reached the turn-off for the village and stopped short to examine the wheel-marks by torchlight.

"There's been a scout car in and out here," Gunner reported. "But we knew that anyhow. And the Chev for a cert. And some lorry, and a Volkswagen. But we knew that, too."

Tyler stared up the little track. There was a distinct horizon where the stars ended, but you might not see a moving man at more than fifty yards. They daren't trust the map to tell them how far the village was, so two of them walked well ahead of the now lightless jeeps and their noise.

It was nearly two miles before an unnatural square shape hardened against the sky. They parked the jeeps off the track and Tyler, de Carette and Gunner went forward to reconnoitre.

The village had a wall, all right, squeezing it tight so that the outside houses and wall became part of each other. Feathery date palms stuck up among the buildings, giving the whole ramshackle place the look of a big flat flower bowl. The wall had no value against attack: it could be climbed in seconds. But here the usual enemy was the sand, ebbing and flowing with the winds and able to swamp an open village in a few days. There were occasional drifts piled as if they were trying to lift like a wave and break over the top of the wall, but none had made it yet. The only other way in was a single gateway blocked with two heavy but rickety wooden doors. Wood had to last a long time in the desert.

And it could have been an abandoned cemetery for all the sound and light coming out of it.

They crept around it at a distance where they hoped they wouldn't be seen—unless somebody had night glasses—and then made one cautious foray up to look at the wall itself. The Romans might have begun it, the Foreign Legion would certainly have done some of the patching, and two millenia of villagers the rest.

They were fingering the flaky mud covering and crumbling stonework when the first motor started.

Instinctively they crouched, Tommy-guns raised, but common sense said that if you've spotted an intruder the first thing you do isn't to start a motor vehicle. Tyler waved them outwards and they scuttled away into the night. Behind them, another engine coughed and then a third.

"The first was a truck," Tyler decided. "The second was different, maybe the scout car. Would you agree?" he added politely.

"John, it is whatever you say."

"They're not just running up their engines. They're coming out."

But it was a couple of minutes after they reached a place to watch the gateway before there was a flash of headlights inside and the gates were dragged slowly open.

Three vehicles drove out. A squat four-wheeled scout car, then unmistakably, the Chev, and finally a four-wheel truck.

"Blast, blast, blast," Tyler muttered.

"Will your Yorkie start shooting?" de Carette asked nervously.

"No," Tyler said firmly, like an order aimed a mile down the track. "Not if he wants to stay in LRDG."

In that clear night there was no afterglow from the headlights; one moment they were lighting the dunes with their rocking beams, then they were out of sight completely, leaving just the engine noise. They listened for well after that too had faded before starting to walk back, gloomily.

"That wasn't a fighting patrol," Tyler said. "They might be evacuating completely, or they could be just taking prisoners and wounded up to Mareth or somewhere, and be coming back in daylight. We can't get the Chev's wireless now."

"If there's one in the village, Skipper," Gunner said, "we could go and sort of liberate it, like."

"Could you make a German wireless work?" de Carette asked. He saw only the heads turn in the darkness, but knew he was getting an incredulous stare, and mumbled an apology. If you were prepared to drive across unmapped deserts for a thousand miles, you'd better believe you can make *anything* work.

"Let's go and sort t'buggers out—if they're there," Yorkie said.

Tyler waited a moment for de Carette to cast his vote, then said quietly: "Right. We'll do it in two stages . . ."

▣ 27

Tyler and de Carette climbed the crumbling wall very carefully, but still scabs of dried mud flaked off under their boots and flopped into the sand. They rolled carefully over the top and dropped a few feet into a tiny orange grove, itself held in by a two-foot wall. Even in the January night, the trees had a faint fragrance.

A narrow alleyway led down between the houses towards what must be a central piazza with the water hold that had first made the village possible. The buildings on either side were jammed together, their flat roofs blending to form a second upstairs village that was private to the wives, leaving the streets strictly for men and a few servant girls.

De Carette had been in villages like this before the war, but had felt hardly any more welcome. There would be plenty of rifles around that didn't belong to the Afrika Korps.

Starlight throws no shadows, just blurring patches of dark and not so dark. They paused in the mouth of the alley, where it met a sandy lane perhaps the width of a truck, leading uphill to the right towards the gateway. Tyler moved in a careful crouch across to a clump of stubby palms on the far side, and when nothing reacted to that, started moving down towards the piazza, de Carette paralleling him beside the near wall.

He had been flattered at first that Tyler had picked him, then depressed when he realised that, *au contraire*, Tyler had picked Yorkie and Gunner as the ones he trusted to handle the jeeps. Now he just felt frightened. But at least he might get his first chance to kill somebody. Yesterday's Stuka had made the war a very personal thing, and he didn't want to die that sort of virgin.

Then they were at the piazza and fading back into dark doorways to survey it.

It would have been about thirty yards square if anything in that village had been square, with a dim glitter of water in a walled pond off to one side among the date palms. Alleys made doorways of darkness at the corners, and opposite, past the palms, were the arches of camel stables and . . .

. . . and the faint hard outline of another Volkswagen. De Carette's heart seemed to give a gulp. A parked vehicle meant a guard: in a place like this the villagers would loot the gold from your teeth while you slept.

For a full five minutes they watched, but nothing moved or made any sound. Then Tyler eased slowly back up the lane and de Carette followed. They went about fifty yards and met under another palm.

"The guard must be in the stables," Tyler whispered.

"They are probably all in the stables. To be anywhere else they would have to put people out of their houses, and I think it is not German policy to cause such trouble here."

"Yes . . . I hadn't thought of that. Thank you, Henri." De Carette felt a glow of satisfaction.

"And another at the gate," Tyler went on. He looked at his watch. "Twelve minutes. Let's get up there."

They slunk quietly up the winding lane, until the gap of stars ahead showed they were in sight of the gateway. It was too risky to go any further. They slid into doorways and waited. Above, a sprinkle of real light, by starlight standards, had fallen on the highest roofs and palms. The moon was up. De Carette found suddenly that he was staring across the lane at a battered old enamel Singer Sewing Machine advertisement. He almost laughed aloud, but remembered that this was one machine that needed no power and usually no repair. The sewing machine and the rifle. The front line of civilisation.

Then he heard the growl of the jeep.

A figure that was just a moving shadow broke the line of the gateway, peering out at the sound. On the left. How would he be armed? A light machine-gun would be the obvious weapon, but that should have two men . . .

Somebody shouted from the piazza and the gate guard called back, then the night shattered as the K guns fired, throwing a burst of little tracer darts through the topmost palm fronds and spattering against the buildings.

Two men ran up from the piazza, clumping and panting. They carried rifles, but missed seeing Tyler and de Carette because they just weren't looking. They joined the guard at the gates, trying to drag them shut.

Tyler slipped out of his doorway and catfooted up the lane. De Carette followed. This was better than they'd expected: three men at the gate instead of one or two. At twenty yards range, Tyler stopped and lifted his gun to his shoulder. De Carette did the same, in the slow motion of utter certainty.

He aimed low at the figure hauling on the right-hand gate and squeezed the trigger, letting the gun track upwards with the recoil. The man collapsed like a burst balloon, and de Carette felt a surge of relief that was almost a sexual climax. He could do it, he had done it, and if he died now, the score was at least level.

He stepped back against the wall to reach into his haversack for another magazine, thumb the old one out, let it drop, push the new one into place. They ran forward.

One of the men on the left of the gate was still moving. Tyler fired two shots into him. De Carette took his own victim by the feet and dragged him clear of the gateway, which was still open wide enough to take a jeep.

He would like to have known the man's name.

The jeep charged past on the moonlit plain, and Tyler flashed his torch at it. It swung in and ran up to them.

Lecat was sitting up in the back of it, holding a rifle.

"Why the hell did you bring him?" Tyler asked Gunner, who was driving, with Yorkie at the guns.

"You try making him stay behind, Skip. He's like a fuckin' dog."

"I *explained* to him," de Carette began.

"Never mind," Tyler said. "We've knocked off three and there might be only one left. Follow us."

"I *did* explain to him, John," de Carette muttered, as they moved out ahead.

"I heard you. I forgot what I had said yesterday: he has found a new mother. He isn't going to be alone again."

They went about twenty yards ahead of the blacked-out jeep that purred gently on the downhill slope. There might be no more than one man down there. The Volkswagen only held four; it was smaller than a jeep. But that, de Carette thought uneasily, meant that it could hardly carry any supplies as well. That didn't sound like the desert.

He thumbed the safety catch on the Tommy-gun for the thousandth time, which was silly because none of them ever put it on when carrying the gun. It was too stiff and awkward, and the trigger pull was heavy enough for safety anyway . . .

A second engine roared, dropped to a rumble, then in a blaze of headlights the cubist shape of a scout car came up the slope from its hiding place in the piazza stables.

De Carette darted forward into the mouth of an alley, then lifted the gun.

"Grenades!" Tyler roared.

Of course. He reached into his haversack. Pull out the pin, glance around the corner, toss it down the lane as the lever whanged away.

The grenades went off almost simultaneously, the blast bouncing off the close walls and hitting de Carette like a slap on the ears. A cloud of dust erupted in the narrow lane, but through it he saw the flare of the scout car's twenty-millimetre. The K guns hammered back, and screaming nails of light bounced every way off the scout car, jamming the narrow lane with noise, flashes, dust and madness.

The undamaged scout car ground past the alley, the jeep's engine revved furiously, and the two vehicles charged into each other head-on with a noise like a gigantic gong. Or maybe he was only remembering it that way, because it signalled the end of all the other noises.

In the silence, Tyler ran forward and dropped a grenade into the open turret of the scout car. Somebody in there screamed and heaved into view, then the grenade went off beneath him with a hollow bang, and he collapsed out of the turret and slid down into the lane. He didn't need shooting.

Neither did Gunner. At the last instant, the last shot from the scout car had exploded in his chest. He was a shrunken, shortened object wrapped around the steering-wheel by the impact, and de Carette was glad that the starlight made him colourless.

The jeep wasn't going to move again, its bonnet steaming and crumpled.

"Right," Tyler said. "Yorkie and Lecat get the stuff unloaded. Henri, down to the stables with me."

There might have been a clever back way to the piazza, down through the alleyways, but they hadn't time to find it. War is not having time to be clever, being forced to meet things head on. As Gunner had.

The Volkswagen was still in place, and nothing moved. Tyler ran around the left-hand side, between the palms and the pond, and fired a short burst against the stable wall, just to provoke a reaction. Nothing reacted. And there was no radio in the stables.

"Damn," Tyler said. "All for not much. I'd rather have Gunner than . . . Damn."

"Listen," de Carette said, and Tyler became very still. At first there was just a whimpering sound from one of the windows around the piazza, the first reminder that this was a living village, and certainly no longer a sleeping one. But the villagers were letting the Europeans settle their quarrels by themselves. At the end of it, there would always be some loot.

Then Tyler heard the distant sound of motors.

Yorkie came staggering into the piazza, supporting Lecat with one hand and dragging a load of haversacks, water-bottles and gear with the other.

"They're coming back, Skipper. I could see t'lights."

"How many?"

"There's two of 'em."

One vehicle they might ambush, but two . . . particularly if it was a truck of infantry.

"Over the wall." Tyler decided. "And no shooting. You know the way, Henri."

As de Carette helped Lecat back towards the alley, Tyler opened the engine of the Volks and yanked out the whole handful of high-tension leads, then threw them in the pond. When he joined them at the wall itself, he was carrying a heavy Jerry-can marked with a white cross, the sign for drinking water.

They lowered Lecat over the wall and dropped down beside him. The vehicle lights were just coming out of the track onto the flat plain around the village. A scout car and a truck, which stopped well before the gate, obviously suspicious.

Yorkie simply lifted Lecat onto his back and started running. De Carette and Tyler snatched up all the rest and followed. They dodged behind the village and into the soft dunes. There they collapsed, panting.

After a few minutes there was a burst of firing, somebody shooting at a villager or just a ghost. Some shouting, then silence.

"Nobody's going to come looking for us in the dark," Tyler said. "Back around to the other jeep."

They had less than two hours to dawn and took most of it in helping Lecat through the tangle of hummocks and dunes. They had to bring him to the jeep, not vice versa; it was parked at what they believed was just out of hearing of the village—a long way on a desert night—they daren't bring it closer.

It was also parked rather carelessly, close to the track, because they had assumed they'd be back to it well before dawn. They were almost there when they heard it drive away.

For a moment, de Carette feared Tyler was thinking of a second attack on the village. But then they staggered back into the dunes, away from where the jeep had been parked because that would be the first place the Germans would come looking in daylight.

The day began with a pale light, like the first jet of a gas burner flaring across the stars. Streamers of red appeared overhead and then the bloodshot sun itself, bringing light but no warmth. They felt safe to light cigarettes and Tyler poured out one cup of water for each, in turn. They only had one cup with them.

"We're going to have to do some walking," he said.

"To Zella?" That must be 600 miles, more than the depth of France from the Channel to the Riviera.

"No. We'll head north."

"John, in the north is *Rommel*."

"We won't go that far. If we can get around west of the salt marsh, to Nefta, we'll find something. There was a rumour 1st Army had got as far as Tozeur, so they could be further by now. That's only about a hundred and twenty miles."

Instinctively, de Carette's mind began breaking the distance down into day's marches: rations, water, bivouac times . . . and it was all meaningless.

"John—we have *soldat de la première classe* Lecat with us."

"Ask him if he'd rather surrender. It has to come from you."

De Carette turned reluctantly to the young soldier, very young indeed behind the patchy beard and pain-weary eyes. He already knew what the answer would be.

They began to walk. They walked very slowly, if possible along the troughs between the crescent dunes, which lay in roughly north-south lines and curved like arches laid flat on the landscape. Sometimes they had to climb over a dune, where it was soft, deep and slippery, like wading through flour. The slightest breath of wind skimmed the sand off the crest of the dunes and drifted it into their eyes. Only Yorkie and Lecat had sand-goggles, but they were passed round in rotation.

Lecat always needed one man to help him along, since he'd abandoned the plank crutch when they first rescued him. Who needed a crutch to ride in the back of a jeep? One man carried most of the haversacks, a Tommy-gun and the water Jerry-can, which made him awkwardly lopsided like a heavy suitcase does. The third was resting from a bout with Lecat and just carried a gun, a haversack of grenades and a few odds and ends. After two days they simply threw away the Tommy-guns, which weighed around twelve pounds, and the grenades which were a pound and a half each, leaving themselves with just two pistols. It was ridiculous to pretend they might be a fighting force any longer.

Without Lecat, they could have marched over twenty miles a day. With him, they were managing five, at best seven. And just being forced to move so slowly was more tiring than a natural pace.

It was Yorkie who mentioned it first. "If t'Frenchie had been captured, Skip, ah reckon he'd be in t'ospital by now, being fixed up fine. You do 'ear that Jerry runs good 'ospitals."

"He is a Frenchman," de Carette said coldly.

"He's one of us," Tyler said, and that finished it. But Lecat wasn't really one of them. Armies are made up of tiny groups—platoons, patrols, squadrons, troops—with the fierce loyalty of shared experience and danger. Even to de Carette, Lecat was still outside the LRDG family.

They walked mostly by night and lay up by day. It was nothing to do with being seen: out in the sand, neither friend nor enemy would find them because nobody bothered to look. They were in a place that was impassable to vehicles, and in the desert war such a place was a nowhere. But the nights were too cold for sleeping without the greatcoats and tents they had lost with the jeeps, and the days often too hot to move far without sweating and getting thirsty. They usually found a bush and lay down in its thin shade, staying still even when they weren't sleeping, because movement wasted energy . . .

On the fifth night, they found the German airman. From his badges Tyler identified him as a pilot Oberfeldwebel; he must have parachuted or crash-landed somewhere in the Grand Erg, and then started walking with just his water bottle and maybe a few bars of chocolate. How long he'd been there, they couldn't even guess. Drifting sand had half buried him, but in that dry air there was no corruption. The face had mummified into something three thousand years old, rigid dry skin stretched back from the teeth. The teeth were clenched onto the stem of a dead bush.

They trudged on silently through the dunes that had an unearthly silvery beauty under the waxing moon. The landscape was so simple, so infinite, and there was no sound except the hiss of sand in the wind. They could be on another planet, where all that was asked of you was that you walk slowly through a silent black-and-silver loveliness for ever.

The sun spoiled it, coming up quickly and complicating their life with colour and heat and changes of wind, so that they had to hunt for a scrap of shade and dole out the small ration of water that was still cold after the night. The days were annoying, restless, unnecessary.

They were wearing out. They were dying.

"If one of us went ahead, Skip," Yorkie said, "like he could tell them where to find us. I mean the rest of us. I'd have to be one of those who stayed, I know. But . . ."

"You don't know," Tyler said wearily. "It's at least forty miles before we get out of this sand and go west for Nefta. That would be another four or five days supposing 1st Army's got that far. But even then they couldn't send a vehicle down here to pick you up. In any case, we're in enemy territory, give or take."

That day they hadn't found a bush, and were crouching in the lee of a crescent dune, carefully lighting one cigarette from another, and smoking them in rotation. Absurdly, they had fewer matches left than cigarettes.

"We walked into this," de Carette said, "so we must walk out of it."

"Lecat didn't walk out of it," Maxim said, after de Carette had been silent for half a minute. "Professor Tyler says in his book that his leg went bad and he died of that."

De Carette sipped his wine and, blinking as if he had just woken up, gazed around the cool-warm room that was not hot or cold, and at the bright sky and the snow peaks outside.

"It was not his wound, not that. He was a pleasant boy, from l'Auvergne—so naturally they had sent him to Africa. Naturally." De Carette chuckled to himself, without humour. "That is the way of the Army. John and I talked to him, we learned about his widowed mother, his older sister who might become a *religieuse*,

the work on the farm that he had been taken from . . .
he talked enough. He was not dying from that leg. We
shot him."

Maxim nodded and waited.

"We needed the water, and the time. After that, we
could walk thirty kilometres a day. It took us only a
few days more to Nefta."

"And Yorkie's real name was Etheridge?"

"Yes, but I did not know until after. So always I
think of him just as Yorkie."

"Did you ever meet Gerald Jackaman?" Agnes
asked.

"The young man from Algiers? He was visiting the
Americans at Tebessa, and he came down to debrief
us, when we contacted 1st Army."

"Who actually shot Lecat?" Maxim asked.

"Who would have done it if you had been in command, Major?"

For a long time, as they wound down the hillside road,
Agnes said nothing. Then: "So that's why Etheridge
wrote to Jackaman. He was the first one they'd told
lies to. I wonder if he'd suspected something all these
years since."

"He seems to have accepted Etheridge's letter without asking any questions."

"Yes . . . So, they shot somebody on their own side,
a poor wounded French boy. It haunts them all their
lives, and one of them even changes his name, emi-
grates and dies of drink. I don't know . . . I wouldn't
have thought that by the fourth year of the war soldiers would be that sensitive." She sounded disap-
pointed. "Do you believe him?"

"As far as he went."

"How much further was there?"

"They didn't just shoot him. They ate him."

◨ 28

"Are you quite sure?" George asked.

"It has to be. You have to forget all the Beau Geste stuff about water being the only thing that matters in the desert. Those three went for well over a week, mostly through soft sand, and that's like snow. It isn't much warmer, either, in January: the temperature can go below freezing. If you're moving in that sort of cold, you're really burning fuel. I'm not saying they'd have died of starvation; they'd have died of thirst because they were too starved to do anything but sit down and drink up their water."

George put his cup and saucer down with a clang and stared around the room, looking for comfort. There was little to find. He had moved into the family set of rooms in Albany when he got the Downing Street posting and it became impossible to commute from Hertfordshire. Annette had done what she could to brighten the tall gloomy rooms with fresh paint and new lampshades, but she daren't change the furniture any more than George's mother or grandmother had dared. Coming in off the chilly stone staircase, Maxim and Agnes had walked through a time gate, back seventy-five years to the days when the Empire was built of solid dark mahogany and pictures of dead animals.

"You are absolutely certain they couldn't have taken enough food?" Sir Anthony Sladen asked. They were seated around one end of a vast dining table, George and Sladen on opposite sides, Maxim and Agnes at the top, in the witness box.

Maxim shook his head. "There were three men marching for something like eleven days and a fourth who lasted five or six—de Carette wasn't precise about the dates. But that's nearly forty days' rations. George—you've been in the Army. You know what a day's rations looks like, what it weighs."

"It's a long time since my Army days."

"It's a long time," Agnes said, "since you helped Annette carry in the groceries from the car."

George scowled at her. Sladen gave a cool smirk.

"They must have grabbed up some food from the last jeep," Maxim said, "but nothing like enough."

"Oh Lord." George shook the heavy silver teapot and got a sludgy sound. "Does anybody want any more tea?"

Nobody did.

"Tell me, Major," Sladen leant his forearms precisely on the table; "why nobody, in all these years, has spotted what must be something of a, ah, *discrepancy* in Tyler's own book?"

"He's vaguer about the time factor than de Carette. He makes the whole march through the sand a poetic affair, trudging on under the moon, days and nights blending into one—"

"The St.-Exupéry touch. I'm sorry."

"He even hints they may have got to Nefta a few days early and rested before contacting 1st Army. The shorter he can make the march, the smaller the food problem. But the big worry that he writes about is whether he'd get a court of inquiry; he'd lost all his vehicles and weapons and nine British soldiers, never mind one Frenchman."

"It could have been a real worry," George reflected. "A court of inquiry wouldn't settle for the poetic approach."

"What actually happened to this town—Ghadames, was it?" Sladen asked. "I'm sure you know, Major."

"A Free French unit under Colonel Delange came up from the south-east and took it at the end of the month. I don't think there was any shooting; the officers really had deserted."

"Thank you." Sladen and George looked at each other across the table. The afternoon dimmed in the Ropewalk outside, as quietly as in a country churchyard. It was a jolt to remember that the Piccadilly traffic was only a hundred yards away.

"So we have one desert town liberated," George said ruminatively. "At least two German vehicles destroyed, plus one Stuka, half a dozen or more soldiers dead—all for the cost of one patrol. About the same as a heavy bomber getting shot down. Not too bad an exchange, for those days. But also one French soldier, cannabilised. And a third of a century later, in comes the bill for *that*."

Sladen nodded in sombre agreement.

"Thank you, Harry," George said, but his voice was still heavy. "You've done just what you were appointed for: saved us a nasty scandal. I'll have to advise the Headmaster to drop Tyler."

"I wouldn't have thought he can do that off his own bat," Sladen said quickly. "But I'll be recommending the same thing to the committee."

Maxim stared from one to the other, disbelieving. "But all this happened around the time I was *born*."

"It doesn't matter if it happened as part of the banquet before Waterloo."

"But if you really want an agreement with the French, and Tyler's the only one who can get it . . ."

"Major," Sladen said, "if there is even a hint that our chief negotiator had, ah, *eaten* a part of one of their countrymen . . ." He had a lot of difficulty in saying that.

"Suppose he promised to sick him up again?" Maxim said coldly.

"Bon appetit," Agnes murmured.

Sladen sat up straight as if somebody had pinched his bottom. George looked from Maxim to Agnes, honestly appalled. "Where do people like you two *come* from? I have never heard any two remarks in my *life* . . ."

"You're getting your colour back, duckie," Agnes said.

George sat throbbing and steaming a little.

"Wars are messy things," Maxim said.

"Thank you, Major." Sladen gazed at him as he would at a broken sewer. "If we put out a press release saying that wars are messy things, that should avert any slight agitation our cross-Channel friends might feel. I trust you'll let us quote you?" He stood up. "George, I'd better get back to the pit-head. We'll liaise very soon on this. Give my love to Annette. I can find my own way . . ." his voice faded into the glum twilight as he stalked through to the next room.

"No Cabinet Office Christmas card for *you*, this year," Agnes told Maxim.

George got up slowly, turned on three lights in big simple shades, and pulled the long drapes closed. In the golden light, the room looked a little younger, but not much.

"He's a pompous old fart," George said, "but in this instance . . ." He looked at his watch; it wasn't yet five o'clock. "Does anyone feel like a real drink?" he asked wistfully.

They shook their heads. George hesitated, then went across to a break-front chiffonier in the corner by the fireplace and took out a bottle of The Famous Grouse, a tumbler and a bottle of Malvern water.

"I don't know much about this," Maxim said, "but I don't see who would publish the letter. It can't be proveable unless de Carette admits it, and he's already lied to us about it. So wouldn't they just set a new record for libel damages?"

"Try suing *Pravda* in Moscow," Agnes suggested.

"Try suing *Der Spiegel* in Hamburg, for that matter." George ambled back with his drink and a little coaster to protect the table. "No—but there are underground magazines all over Europe who'd use it, and you can't sue them because they just fade away like smoke and start up again as something else. But that isn't the real question. If Moscow can persuade the French that this *might* be published about the Brit they're negotiating with, then they wouldn't touch Tyler with a ten-foot *gaffe*. They've got voters to think of, as well."

"There is one other little danger." Agnes said quietly. "Publishing this letter would be firing off all your ammunition in one broadside, and Moscow doesn't work like that, not usually. If I were them, I'd use it to put the screws on Tyler. I'd whisper to him, first. So if the letter just might exist and Moscow just might have it, how do we know Tyler isn't already their joe?"

The idea hung over them, like a thunderstorm reluctant to break.

George slumped down, clenching his glass with both hands. "That does it. Luxembourg is off. It has to be."

Maxim waited for Agnes, but she was staring blindly at a picture over the fireplace, a very detailed view of a dead hare and several flowers. He said pleasantly: "You're surrendering rather quickly, aren't you?"

"Harry, in politics, it is better never to have loved at all then to have loved and lost."

"Then Moscow wins without firing a shot. Probably without even knowing they've won, since they most likely haven't got the letter, and won't understand why you've pulled out of the Luxembourg talks."

"You're in deep waters, Harry," Agnes said, without looking at him.

"I'll try and remember to hold my breath." Maxim went on watching George, his face expressionless and his eyes cold. "You're making sure the French would believe anything—anything—Moscow says about Tyler, whether they've got the letter or just dreamed something up on the spot. They could say he was *gay* and Paris would have to believe it, because we've dropped him from the first team.'

Agnes opened her mouth, then shut it again. George grunted, staring at the backs of his hands and finding no encouragement there in the wrinkles and blotches. Some things were irreversible. Life was irreversible. He wished he were Maxim's age.

"Harry—*I* don't take these decisions—"

"You're giving the advice."

"It's for the Headmaster to decide."

"So what can we lose that we aren't throwing away now?"

"Harry, this is a matter of national defence."

"What in the hell do you think Army officers are for?"

"Show-jumping," Agnes said, and as Maxim snapped out of his chair she knew he was going to hit her and possibly kill her. Her training was no use against his training.

Then he stopped, just as abruptly as he'd started.

"I'm sorry, Harry," she mumbled breathlessly. "It was a bloody stupid thing to say. I'm sorry."

George gave a long, long sigh that ended as a groan.

"You weren't called in to advise at these levels, Harry."

Maxim nodded, looking down at his shoes and blinking quickly. "Then as a voter and a taxpayer . . . You must know what Tyler's going to propose at Luxembourg, and he obviously won't go there alone. If Moscow's pulling his strings and he proposes something different, you'll know straight away. And as far as a scandal goes, you have to balance that against the value of an agreement with the French. I dare say it's a risk. But if you don't fight any battles, you won't win any wars."

"That doesn't sound much like the viewpoint of the average taxpayer." He looked up at Agnes. "Since it appears to be the open season, would Little Miss Muffet care to take a shot?"

She frowned and said slowly: "You always have to work with flawed material. There may still be a few saints around—I like to believe there are—but they don't go into politics or nuclear strategy."

For a long time, George turned the heavy cut-glass tumbler in his chubby hands. Then he said simply: "Those are honest points of view. I'll put them to the Headmaster along with whatever else I give him."

◼ 29

George often wondered what the PM would have decided. As it was, two days later, Moscow decided for him.

Professor John White Tyler hadn't slept in college that night. Even so, he would normally have been back in his rooms with plenty of time to make coffee, skim through the morning papers and perhaps hear the radio news headlines before his ten o'clock lecture. But the girl he had woken up with was doing a thesis on Hindu literature, and their farewell was a long and complicated act that Tyler thought he had once seen carved in full frontal colour on a Katmandu temple. He was delighted with a girl of such dedication, but it did mean that he only had time to change his shirt, find the file for that lecture, and hurry out again. He had shaved the evening before. He always did.

"The most carefully conceived and most believable nuclear targetting policy carries with it no guarantee that any government or leader will actually implement it at the moment of decision. You may build the most perfect rifle for hunting dangerous game, precisely fitted to your customer's arm length and the weight of trigger pull he prefers—but you cannot build in any device that will make him aim straight and squeeze the trigger at the moment the tiger charges."

He laid his hands flat on the sides of the lectern and glanced up at the undergraduates stacked in front of him. There were more of them than usual, gazing blankly down from behind their curved stalls made of cheap wood the vivid orange colour of unfried fishcakes. Perhaps somebody else had been recommending this lecture to his own students.

"Nor should you be able to," he said clearly.

"At that point, the hunter has at least four options.

210

He can stand there and be torn apart. He can shoot the tiger. He can fire wild to scare the tiger away—making it back down from a confrontation. Or he can back down himself, metaphorically, by climbing the nearest tree in somewhat of a hurry."

A ripple of laughter went through most of his audience, but not all. There was a pale, unamused group sitting slightly apart from the rest, with a few girls among it, which was odd for a military studies lecture.

"Only two of these four options owe anything to the gunsmith's art, and I think we might agree that it is not his job to decide whether the world would be a better place with or without the tiger concerned. He simply provides his customer with options. The customer decides which one to opt for. In terms of war, which has not yet been downgraded to the status of a sport, where the only objective is to win—"

"Fascist bastard," said one of the girls, but rather quickly and tentatively.

Tyler ignored her. "War remains what it has always been: a continuation of politics by other means. So every option has to be seen as a political one, no matter whether it is offered up by the military, the commercial world, or even the academics—taken together, the gunsmiths."

"Fascist bastard," the girl said again, with more conviction.

"Nazi," one of the boys added.

"Could you make up your minds?" Tyler asked in a polite deep voice. "Either I was in an Italian nationalist movement started in the 1920's or in the National Socialist party in Germany led by Adolf Hitler. I don't think they allowed you to belong to both."

That got a sympathetic laugh from his usual audience. The girl muttered: "Sod you."

At the top of the central aisle, there were double swing doors with big glass port-holes in them—*scuttles*, as the Navy would call them, smugly confusing the landsman—and he had seen faces peeping quickly in. Usually that only happened at the end of the hour, when a new class was gathering for a different lecture.

"But the decision itself remains in the hands of the political leaders, and once a country has a nuclear ar-

211

senal, any decision that touches on the possibility of war becomes a nuclear decision. The decision not to use nuclear weapons is a nuclear decision—"

"Why don't you take a nuclear decision then?" somebody called.

"I'd like to very much, but you're rather too close to me." As he said it, Tyler knew it was a mistake. It got a laugh from his usual audience, but it gave the others just the provocation they had been waiting for.

"Tyler out!" one of them shouted. "Tyler out, out, out!" They got to their feet, moving into the aisle and taking up the chant: "Tyler out, Tyler out . . ."

One of the other undergraduates stood up from across the aisle and was pushed down again. The little crowd moved down on Tyler, and he was suddenly and surprisingly afraid. He wasn't a young soldier any more.

The doors at the top slammed open and a slim figure in a short raincoat danced down the steps and crashed into the crowd. One of the girls flopped aside, sprawled over the top of one of the stalls, one of the men turned to meet the newcomer and then folded suddenly out of sight. The man in the raincoat reached the front and Tyler recognised him.

The spearhead of the crowd was a pale boy with very black curly hair and a black leather jacket. He marched towards Tyler with his right forefinger stabbing at eye-level in time with his chant. "Tyler out, Tyler out . . ."

As Maxim came past he slashed sideways with the edge of his left hand, a blow that moved no more than nine inches. But the pecking arm flopped, and the boy gasped. So did Tyler; he could imagine what such a whack on the biceps felt like. Then Maxim was hustling him off the platform and through the side door.

They waited in the corridor that was supposed to be for faculty only, until George burst through the door behind them, looking rather blown and dishevelled.

"I had to thump somebody," he said, examining his hand. "Haven't hit anybody in years. I'm getting soft. There should be a car . . ."

Inside the lecture room, a full-scale brawl was brewing up as the two groups of undergradutes tangled.

"I should have poked him with my umbrella," George puffed as they scuttled down the corridor. "No, that would have been a gesture of class warfare. Where *is* the bloody woman?"

Dead on cue, Agnes rolled the big anonymous blue Vauxhall up to the outside door. George grunted; they all climbed in.

She drove fast for a quarter of a mile, then relaxed as they blurred into the complication of Cambridge's one-way and no-go systems.

"George," Tyler said, "can you tell me what this is all about?"

"Where have you been all the night? No, you needn't answer that. But we've been ringing you since six this morning, and I'm sure Fleet Street began soon after midnight. Haven't you read any papers today?"

"I haven't had the time, yet."

"Well, Luxembourg's leaked. Leaked?—the dam's broken. Moscow must have put out its own release. It came out in the first edition of the Morning Star: Britain's leading advocate of nuclear warfare going to a secret meeting in Luxembourg with equivalents from France and Western Germany, are they planning a secret nuclear strike force? Provocative behaviour by the old imperialist powers just at a time when America seems to be seeing the light, de-da-de-da-de-da. The real papers had to pick it up, just to cover themselves. Communist sources claim that a secret meeting in Luxembourg . . . and so on. So the cat's in the fire, the bat's in the belfry and the Headmaster would like you to go incommunicado until Luxembourg itself. Can you get a bag packed? We can collect more of your stuff later."

"Where are we going?"

"The FO's lending us one of their hospitality places near Maidenhead. Can we turn right here?"

"No. Take the second left . . ." Tyler leaned forward and gave crisp directions to Agnes. Maxim had never been driven by her before; she was very good, handling what was probably a strange car—it certainly wasn't hers—with a flowing, farsighted confidence.

"There isn't any question of cancelling Luxembourg?" Tyler asked.

George sighed. "No-o. In fact, it rather means it *has* to go ahead, unless one of the others drops out, but that's their affair. Moscow's deliberately challenged us to back down. If we do that, our little Froggie friends aren't going to listen to anything we say for a long time."

"It might even have a unifying effect," Tyler said, mostly to himself.

What nobody said was what they had been discussing on the way down: that this proved Moscow hadn't got the letter and now didn't expect to. "If they're going public in this way," Agnes had pointed out, "it shows they haven't anything more subtle up their balalaikas."

Maxim checked out Tyler's rooms for him, then the three of them paced the court while he packed a bag and ignored the telephone. The snow had melted, but the invading east wind still sprang out of every archway.

"Of course," George said, suddenly moved to look on the gloomy side, "if they're challenging us not to go to Luxembourg, they probably know they're making sure we do go. Perhaps that's what they want."

"We were going anyway," Agnes said.

"That wasn't by any means certain, not after we knew what was in the letter . . ."

"But Moscow didn't know we were having doubts," Agnes said, rather exasperated.

"True, true," George said reluctantly. "At least, I suppose it is."

"You need a drink."

"It is not yet eleven in the morning," George said with dignity.

At that time, in that weather, the big court was almost empty. A porter walked briskly along the far side, a stray out-of-season tourist was peering into the dead fountain, and the lodge cat was showing off its privilege by squatting on the forbidden, and very damp, grass by the gateway. It was the first time Maxim had been inside a Cambridge college. It lacked grandeur, but the uncaring mixture of styles, from the Tudor gateway to the Victorian library, had a comfortable homely look of a dotty professor in odd socks who has never thought about anything as small as grandeur in his life.

He felt a slight twinge of envy at the sort of life that could be lived behind those calm walls, and wondered if Chris would ever get a chance at it.

"What do you think might happen in Luxembourg—now?" he asked.

George glanced the question on to Agnes.

"I don't expect the Centre to do anything sudden," she said. "Now they've taken the initiative in publicising the talks as western warmongering, they'll get the blame if somebody bumps him off. They don't want that; they want a live fascist beast to point at."

"There'll be more of this morning's little rumpusculation," George said.

"I expect so. But Luxembourg's handled top-security meetings before."

"Yes." George paced silently for a while, then said abruptly: "Harry, you'll go too."

"Why Harry?" Agnes asked.

"I want somebody of ours there—just in case—and he'd better know what was in the letter. Either we tell somebody new, or . . ."

Agnes nodded.

"Have you ever been to Luxembourg?" George asked Maxim.

"No."

"Odd-looking place. It gives me vertigo. And be careful not to say the British won the war. They've got General George S. Patton buried there and they're still trying to work out why he didn't rise again on the third day."

In the next three days the weather changed completely and they flew out of Northolt on a hazy blue spring morning, the little twin-jet Dominie rocking and humming in the new west wind. It was too early to be the real spring, but it was a hint, perhaps a promise.

Tyler spent the flight sipping RAF coffee poured from a vacuum flask and letting papers stack up in his lap. He would take one, glance at it, then his gaze would drift back to the little window and the misty patchwork of Belgium, 25,000 feet below.

"That's where it happened," he said in his deep slow voice, "where it's always happened. The Sambre, Ramillies, Mons, Ypres Liège, the Ardennes . . . Belgium's dark and bloody ground. From Caesar to General Patton in about five minutes flying time . . ."

He turned and caught Maxim's eye and smiled across the narrow aisle between the fat VIP seats. He had been talking mostly to himself, but Maxim was the one who would understand.

Tyler added: "I was with Monty's TAC HQ back near St. Trond then. It was quite an interesting Christmas."

"It must have been." That was when Patton had disengaged three divisions from action—tricky enough in itself—then swung them and his whole army with its hundred thousand vehicles through ninety degrees and rammed them north across seventy-five miles of icebound roads straight into the new Battle of the Bulge. All in four short-lit December days. That was what professional soldiers remembered about Patton, not the circus trappings of the two pistols and the bragging.

The Dominie's engine note wound down and they began a gentle slide down the hill of air. Mrs West, the solid quiet-eyed secretary borrowed from Defence, handed Tyler another paper and watched impassively

216

as he let it join the stack in his lap. He was wearing, Maxim noticed, the scarlet thread of the Légion d'honneur in the lapel of his usual hairy dark suit.

The RAF steward came back, stooping in the low cabin, and asked cheerfully: "Would anybody like another cup of coffee? We'll be landing in Luxembourg in approximately fifteen minutes."

They all shook their heads, No Thanks, and the man from the Foreign Office said to Maxim: "Anybody would think the Grand Duchy of Luxembourg had never heard of coffee for itself. Anyway, at four in the afternoon . . ."

He was about Maxim's own age, and his name was Stephen Quinton. He had a round, freshly-washed face, very fine blond hair, and was along, Maxim guessed, to see that an amateur like Tyler didn't make a fool of himself in what were indisputedly Foreign Parts, never mind any Légion d'honneur or nonsense like that.

"Have you ever been in Luxembourg?" Quinton asked.

"No, never."

"It's an odd place, really . . ."

"Does it give you vertigo?"

"No. No, I wouldn't say that." Quinton had a permanently puzzled expression, as if he were always about to ask somebody to say that again but more slowly. "Why do you ask?"

"Just something a friend said."

"Oh. I don't think you'll find *that* . . ." He chattered on, perhaps nervously, as the Dominie slanted downwards.

The little aeroplane stopped less than halfway down the vast runway that was itself a far greater contribution to NATO than Luxembourg's 630-man army. If Der Tag ever dawned, this was one of the 'mobilisation bases', built to take the biggest American transport aircraft that would flock in with reinforcements— unless a Russian missile or air strike had got here first, of course. Meanwhile, it was the tidiest airport Maxim had ever seen: the grass was cropped to the bone and the runway edges trimmed as neatly as any royal garden.

There was a brief unceremonial ceremony behind

the cargo sheds, out of sight of the main terminal, then they were hustled into two hired Mercedes and skimmed off towards the city.

Maxim shared a car with the British ambassador, Tyler and a stolid middle-aged captain with careful eyes who came from the Sûreté Publique.

"Has there been any reaction here, yet?" Maxim asked.

"There was a small demonstration outside the embassy a couple of days ago," the ambassador said. "And I believe today . . ." he nodded at the captain.

A shrug. "A few protestors with notices were at the main gate of the airport. Nothing of importance." Speaking English, he had a dull flat voice like a government document.

"Do they know where the talks will be?"

"They will guess. Senningen is the only place. It is not the Luxembourgeoise to worry about, it is the terrorists from the outside. We have changed the hotels, but . . ." Another shrug.

"Thank you," Tyler said firmly, staring at Maxim.

For real secrecy they should all have arrived in darkness, to hide the national markings on their aircraft; they should have stayed at some easily defended, unexpected, country house; they should have travelled—if at all—using all sorts of decoy cars and helicopters. But as George had said, to try and paint back on all the secrecy that had been stripped off would make the talks seem even more sinister. Whatever Moscow really felt, Washington was showing alarm and despondency. Now they could only hope for security and forget secrecy.

The hotel was elderly and comfortable without trying to be grand. But on the short ride in from the airport, Maxim had guessed that Luxembourg liked things tidy rather than magnificent.

The men shared a suite of three rooms—Mrs West was just down the corridor—a drawing-room bracketed by two bedrooms so that any visitor had to come into the drawing-room first. Tyler took one bedroom, Maxim and Quinton the other, not very enthusiastically. For the moment, the Sûreté captain kept watch.

Quinton got even less enthusiastic when Maxim took off his jacket.

"Great Heavens, man, have you been wearing that thing . . . I mean on the plane and with the *ambassador*?"

"Yes." Maxim wriggled his shoulders inside the wide straps of the shoulder holster. "And I shall be wearing it all the time I'm with Professor Tyler."

"Who told you that you could?"

"Number 10."

That was the Word of Power. "Well, I just hope you know what you're doing. I didn't know you'd got the beastly thing at all."

"You're not supposed to notice. D'you want the bathroom first?"

"No, go ahead . . ." Quinton sat on the edge of his bed, shaking his head in little shivery movements. And he didn't even know he'd missed Maxim shifting the gun to his raincoat pocket so that he could get off the aeroplane with a sensibly buttoned-up coat. Or changing it back in the hotel lift.

It wasn't his fault. You see what you expect to see, and ninety-nine per cent of the world doesn't expect to meet people carrying concealed weapons. The one per cent constitute the problem.

◉ 31

That evening there was a buffet supper, an informal first meetings of the delegations, at another hotel across in the old town, near the station.

Given time to look around, Maxim saw, as they ran out on a long bridge over one of the city's sheer-sided ravines, just what George meant about vertigo. Down there, far down, was a gentle river in formal gardens and flanked by a sprawling village, its lights winking mistily in the blue dusk. But above, the stolid palaces and offices stared at each other across the quarter-mile canyon as if it simply wasn't there, something they would rather not see and certainly not talk about, like a nasty birthmark.

The supper was quiet, restrained. Tyler and the French delegate knew each other, but from what Maxim could hear, they stayed away from the topic of the talks. He spent most of the time talking jigsaw German and English to a Luftwaffe colonel who was dogsbodying the German main delegate. At ten o'clock, the party began to melt away.

They had come in one car—Mrs West had either not been invited or ducked out—and as they reached it, Tyler said: "You go ahead. I'm going to walk for a bit."

"For God's sake," Maxim said.

"I'll be all right."

"I have to make sure of that."

"What's happening?" Quinton demanded. "You can't wander off around here, Professor."

"Just getting a little night air," Tyler said soothingly. He headed off deliberately in the opposite direction to the parked car.

The Sûreté captain and Maxim swapped looks, then Maxim hurried after Tyler.

"You don't have to wet-nurse me day and night, you know, Harry."

"I'm hired to be around."

"Fine. I'll show you some of the sights."

Five minutes later, Maxim saw his first 'sight'. It was a basement in a side road, near the station, and if it wasn't a small room it was too small for the quadrophonic barrage of music battering them from the speakers. Most of the room was dim and vague, lit with candles in wax-dribbled bottles on the small tables. A disc jockey sat at a turntable booth at one side of a tiny stage, lit by a single spot. A few couples danced jerkily in front of him.

They sat down at a table near the back wall, and Maxim stared at Tyler through the gloom. Was this what professors dreamt of behind the Tudor brick walls? It might have seemed exotically wicked to somebody who'd just sailed a yacht single-handed around the world, but to anybody else it was a simple trap for tourists, fleas and fire.

A waiter with LA BOOGIE printed on his T-shirt weaved across, lit their candle and spotted their nationality immediately.

"Good evening, gentlemen," he shouted against the music. "What may I bring you?"

"Harry?" Tyler asked.

"A beer."

"No beer. Sorry." The waiter's voice hardened.

"Scotch, then."

"I don't think so," Tyler said. "Not in here." He smiled at the waiter and then let go a fluent, nicely cadenced speech in French. The waiter stiffened and his eyes glinted wider in the candle-light. After a few seconds he was nodding, then suggesting, finally agreeing happily. He wiggled away again.

"They do quite a nice local wine," Tyler said. "And even in places like this, they're proud enough to serve it properly. I hope all this——" he waved his hand "—— doesn't shock you?"

"Only the price. I've been seventeen years in the Army. Places like this follow you around like flies."

Tyler winced slightly in the dim light. "Of course,

221

but whenever you've had enough, you can always head on home and I'll follow . . ."

"Professor, that's one thing—"

"John."

"*Professor*. I'm supposed to be your security. I *can't* walk out on you. We shouldn't even be here. If you were recognised—"

"I've kept my glasses on," Tyler said mildly. "I've never been photographed in them."

Maxim just stared. The waiter clanged the bucket with the wine in front of them and laid out three glasses.

A girl pulled a chair into the space between them and sat down, looking quickly from one to the other. *"Vous étes Anglais, n'est-ce pas? Merveilleux . . ."* She wore a dark low-cut sweater, that was the first thing anybody would, or was supposed to, notice about her. She also had a narrow, curved face like a puffin, with big wings of blonde hair dragged back over her ears.

The waiter poured them three glasses of wine and hurried away. The music stopped, and the girl clapped loudly. *"Et donc, c'est Pauline."*

A tubby girl danced onto the stage, did a perfunctory striptease to a new record, then stood there managing to make her loose breasts rotate in opposite directions. A handful of customers who had never seen this before squealed with admiration.

In a far corner a single shadowy figure sat down, and stopped the waiter lighting his candle for him.

"Professor," Maxim said.

"Harry, we're paying for it, we may as well watch it." Tyler lit a small fat cigar he had collected at the buffet. The girl beside him gave Maxim a cool look.

Another record, another stripper, this one thin and worn-looking. Halfway through her act she stopped and said something in German that got a laugh, then translated it quickly. "After her, I must look like a couple of aspirins on an ironing board."

The British and American customers howled. Maxim watched the figure in the corner, then Tyler, as he reached for and gripped the girl's hand.

He sipped his wine cautiously, but it was a pleasant

cool Moselle type. The evening was heading for disaster. He could hear George's incredulous voice: 'You let him do *what?*'

The stripper finished, the disc jockey shouted: *"Encore de boogie!"* and started another record. One couple started dancing.

Maxim leaned across the table and said: "Professor, you have got to get out of here. I really mean that."

"Harry, I'm not taking orders from you. I'm sorry, but I'm no longer subject to Queen's Regulations and DCI's, and I'm not breaking any contract or the Official Secrets Acts. I'm a private citizen. You don't have to share my bed."

"Would there be room?"

"I certainly hope not."

They glared at each other through the wavering candlelight. Maxim tried for the last—the next-to-last—time. "Professor, just for the sake of the talks, of Number 10, everything—can't you sleep alone tonight?"

Tyler gazed vaguely upwards, breathing smoke. "I don't think so, thank you, Harry."

The girl was watching Tyler but spitting occasional glances at Maxim. She might not understand English, but she understood a threat to her night's income.

"What are you trying to prove?" Maxim demanded.

"I'm not trying to prove anything."

"Then probably it was just something you ate."

"I beg your pardon?"

"Something you ate. A long time ago."

There was a timeless silence, full only of quadrophonic boogie, the babble of the customers, the clattering of the waiters.

Tyler let go of the girl's hand and started stroking his tie between two long fingers. His glasses were two pale flickering pools of expressionless light.

He is wondering if he can kill me, Maxim thought. And in this town, with its bridges and cliffs, there could be a chance. But perhaps he is also wondering if I am a burning fuse, to be nipped out, or the first crack of light through a door that will never be closed again.

Or maybe he is just realising that even if he lay with

223

every woman in the world, he would still wake with only one memory.

Tyler stood up and started dealing thousand-franc notes onto the table in front of the puzzled girl. The waiter came wiggling across . . .

In the corner, a figure lifted his hand to call his own waiter.

The Avenue de la Gare was wide, bright and empty. An occasional taxi zoomed past, but the rest of the time it was quiet enough for Tyler's footsteps to echo. Maxim wore soft-soled shoes.

"This doesn't seem to be a mugger's city," Tyler said, "and in any case—I do keep forgetting—you are, as our American friends say, 'carrying'. That always has connotations of pregnancy for me. What is it that you carry?"

"A lightweight Charter Arms revolver, five-shot 38." It was in his hand, in his coat pocket. Neither Tyler nor the cloakroom girl had seen that happen.

"May I ask, Major—" the 'Harry' was gone, now, "who else shares your knowledge?"

"George Harbinger, the PM, at least one man from the Cabinet Office and I wouldn't know who else, by now."

Tyler nodded and let out what might have been a sigh of relief. At least he needn't any longer be thinking of pushing Maxim off the bridge ahead.

"Yet they still let me come here?"

"As George said, Moscow rather forced their hands."

It must be a strange feeling when the emperor realises that he actually has no clothes on at all.

Tyler was silent until they reached the long curling bridge at the top of the road. As they paused at the cross-road, Maxim looked back to what might have been a figure stepping into a doorway, and a distant car with only its side lights on, crawling by the kerb.

"I have a feeling that it was you who somehow discovered this . . . *happening,* Major. Can you tell me . . . ?"

Carefully and slowly, ready to be interrupted, Maxim said: "Bob Etheridge wrote a letter when he realised he was dying, that was in Canada, two years or more ago. He got the letter sent to Gerald Jackaman . . ."

"So Bob's dead? What happened to the letter?"

Maxim speeded up. "We don't know. Etheridge died under a new name, but when we found out who he was, I went to see Colonel de Carette."

Tyler stopped dead. "You saw Henri? You can't tell me that Henri told you anything."

"He tried not to. But he didn't know I'd been in the desert as well. He's dying, by the way. Lung cancer."

Tyler gazed down the ravine. A diesel freight clanked and hooted mournfully across the railway arches, black against the stars a quarter of a mile down stream.

"I must go and see him. Major . . . would you say one other name, just for my peace of mind?"

"Soldat de la première classe Gaston Lecat."

"Thank you, Major." Maxim might have been telling him the time. They began walking again.

After a time, Tyler said: "I made a balls of that patrol. But I still can't see what else . . . It went wrong step by step, you never knew where . . . What would you have done, Major?"

"Relied on my seventeen years of soldiering instead of your—what was it?—three, by then?"

Tyler chuckled. "Yes. What else can you say?"

"I might have left Lecat at the village, to be captured."

"Yes, that of course. But I was afraid Henri might walk out on me. I don't now think he would have, but at the time I'd only known him for about a week. And perhaps I just wanted the poor boy along as evidence that we'd actually contacted the French. To salvage something . . . But when we were there in the sand—then what would you have done, Major?"

"I don't know. I'd have stayed out of the sand."

"I suppose so. Shall we try and get a taxi?"

As they climbed in, Maxim thought he saw a figure separate from the darkness of the bridge and move back towards a slow-moving car.

They got out across the square from the hotel, with a

225

wide space of café chairs and tables and a concrete bandstand in between. A few spiky leafless trees stuck up into the cold lamplight. Tyler hesitated, restless and unassuaged, and sat down abruptly on one of the café chairs. His long legs sprawled spiderlike from his short thick coat.

"I suppose I ought to thank you for saving me from that . . . woman tonight. She wasn't really Cleopatra, was she? But Major—how are you going to save me tomorrow? Really the situation hasn't changed. Number 10 isn't going to broadcast my wartime past, no matter what I do." He began to laugh quietly.

"Don't you want these talks to go well?" Maxim hadn't sat down.

"I do, yes. But—"

Maxim swung around, placed his hands on the table, and very nearly lost his temper. "Then stop worrying about Number 10 and start worrying about me, because I know you killed Mrs Jackaman and they don't. Not *yet*."

"I . . . now really, Major, I'd like to see you prove I was in Ireland when—" He stopped suddenly.

Maxim straightened up. "It's all right, that doesn't give you away, her death was in the papers. But you pretended you didn't know about Bob Etheridge dying, and his letter. She'd been trying to sell it to you, she told me that. And I saw her car blow: it wasn't explosive, just petrol. In a funny way, de Carette told me how you did it: the way you booby-trapped the Volkswagen before the village, with the spark-plug in a petrol tin."

Suddenly tired, he sat down across the little table from Tyler, just two men in the whole empty square, where in daytime, in better weather, perhaps men argued about the fate of nations, about life and death.

"You were the only person with a motive for killing her," he said wearily. "Moscow had no reason, whether or not they'd got the letter. They probably think it was me, and I'm not sure George doesn't, either, since I burnt down her houseboat afterwards. Yes, that was me. But she told me she'd turned you down; probably she just wanted you to suffer for her husband's death. So you killed her."

"I would have had to be in Ireland."

"I was in Ireland, the KGB was in Ireland, you can walk in and out of Ireland as free as the wind. The Army wishes you couldn't, but you can. And she'd been in touch with you, so she'd most likely managed to give away where she lived. She was just clever enough to be really stupid. The whole idea of playing footsie with the KGB was stupid."

At the corner of the square a car crept in and stopped, without lights. It was a long way off, too far for a revolver with a five-inch sight radius. Maxim felt awkwardly exposed; the entire situation was one of those dreams of being on the street in your pyjamas.

"I was trying to get you an early night," he said abruptly. "Let's do that."

"She was blackmailing me, Harry," Tyler said softly. So now he was 'Harry' again. "She was blackmailing the whole country. She was going to give that letter to Moscow—"

"Or maybe not. I almost talked her out of it. At least she was coming away with me."

"I couldn't know that."

"You didn't *try* to know. You could have come to us and said you were being blackmailed, that you were vulnerable. *You* were risking the country's position. Back walking into the sand again and hoping for the best and somebody else got killed just to keep your reputation sweet! *Now* get to bed!"

Quietly, Tyler stood up, turned, walked towards the hotel.

"What are you going to do?"

"I understand you're the best weapon we've got, Professor. It's my job to protect you. That's all I'm doing."

"When we first met, you said I—my book—was one of the reasons you joined the Army."

"I don't regret joining the Army."

◙ 32

The Château de Senningen lay just past the airport, down a steep lane off the main road and discreetly tucked away in a park of evergreen trees. Less discreetly, it was now surrounded by a mesh fence on concrete posts, with a barbed-wire topping, but the guard-house was still just a cottage with neat shutters beside the windows and potted geraniums behind them.

Two soldiers with sub-machine guns waved them on through.

"A remarkably consistent country," Quinton said. "Where else would you find a guard-house like that—or a supposedly secret conference centre like this?"

At the end of the drive, *this* was a modestly large but thin country house, two stories high plus little dormer windows with tiled witches' caps poking out from the steep roof. The windows were tall, with white shutters against the pinky-grey pebbledash walls, and the front door was just a set of french windows, held open by another soldier and a uniformed flunkey.

They drank coffee in a reception room just off the hallway. Most of the people there had been at last night's buffet, but Maxim couldn't remember many names. He stayed on the fringe of the gently swirling crowd, watching.

Quinton appeared beside him. "The old man's acting rather subdued this morning. Did he say anything last night?"

Maxim gave a slight shrug. "We talked about the war, about soldiering . . ."

"He's probably just tired. I wish you'd managed to get him into bed earlier, I must say."

"We had this conversation last night." They had, too; Quinton's reaction then had been as if Maxim had borrowed his fifteen-year-old daughter for a tour of down-town Hamburg.

"Well, it really is too bad."

"I expect he'll get an early night tonight," Maxim said soothingly, or as soothingly as he felt like being with Quinton.

At a signal Maxim didn't see, the delegates handed their cups to their juniors and began drifting back to the hallway and the stairs to the first floor, being elaborately polite about letting each other go first.

The conference room was bright and cheerful. The back wall was a long blow-up of a medieval engraving of the old city, there were about fifteen Scandinavian swivel chairs around an oval table under modern chandeliers, wall-to-wall carpeting and curtains. The sort of place where chemical companies met to announce marketing strategies and pin merit badges on themselves for sales performance.

"A modern chancellery of Europe," Tyler said in a heavy whisper. "I sometimes wish I had been in the business before 1914, when they were arguing about the two-power standard and the 15-inch gun was the ultimate weapon." He sat down and Mrs West slid a thin file of papers in front of him. "But I dare say that even then, somebody was complaining that this new-fangled electric lighting made it look like a meeting of *tradesmen*."

Quinton gave a little grunt of relief. Tyler seemed to be perking up.

Their Luxembourg host said a few words in each of the three languages, then went tactfully away, so that there was nobody in the room who wasn't British, French or German. Maxim, like the other bit-part players, sat behind their leaders on armless non-swivelling chairs against the walls. He could spot two others carrying guns.

There was a quick murmur of discussion before they agreed on what they had planned to agree on: that Tyler should speak first.

He moved his papers carefully, waiting until the last noise had drained from the room. *"Ich hoffe, dass wir übereinstimmen und diese Konferenz auf französisch halten."*

The German delegation made a friendly noise and Tyler began again.

"On ne peut plus étre sûr d'une contre-attaque massive Americaine . . ." Maxim tried to follow, but his French was too slow to get all the detail and nuance, although he suspected Tyler was deliberately spinning it out so that the Germans could keep up. He could still pick out the main points.

"If Western Europe cannot any longer threaten the Soviet Union with damage of a quantity sufficient to deter an attack, then it must find a way of inflicting damage of *quality* . . . a short-range policy . . . as the Russian airspace became more and more closed to air strikes, even to missiles, so the Soviet Bloc countries become more and more tempting targets . . . Poland, East Germany, Czechoslovakia, Hungary, Rumania, Bulgaria . . . all these are needed as jumping-off bases or lines of communication . . . and the ranges are short . . . from the Iron Curtain itself, less than 500 miles to Warsaw, 350 to Gdansk, 300 to Posnan, 150 to Budapest, around a hundred miles to Prague, Leipzig, Chemnitz—I apologise, Karl-Mark-Stadt, Dresden . . ."

Maxim saw the German delegate wince, then become impassive and attentive again.

"Moscow might well not believe we could destroy Russia, but Warsaw would certainly believe we could destroy Poland . . . Above all things, we are looking for a targetting policy that will be believed . . . then we have deterrence . . ."

Tyler stopped as the captain from the Sûreté tiptoed into the room, pointing at Maxim and making telephone gestures at his own ear.

"You'd better go, Major," Tyler grunted. He was 'Major' once more.

Maxim had expected George; he got a slightly accented voice.

"Major Maxim?"

"Yes?"

"I wonder if you would take a beer with me. When we last met, we did not seem to have the time."

"Is that Mr Komocsin?"

"Of course." The voice sounded pleased. "There is a

café at the bottom of the hill, the one on the right. A beer, yes?"

"Yes."

Maxim put down the phone and stepped back from the transparent space-helmet fixed to the wall.

The captain, who had politely turned his back, swung around.

"It is all right?"

"I'm going down to the village," Maxim said, "to meet a Russian spy."

The captain just looked at him.

The beer was waiting for him. The café was a single dark room with a floor of tiny mosaic tiles, and its shelves and bar jammed with fancy beer-steins, green-stemmed glasses, calendars, a model of a Luxair Boeing 737 and fleshy rubber plants. At the back of the room a large lady was ironing blouses on one of the tables. At a closer one, a square grainy face with a widow's peak smiled up at Maxim. He sat down and took a sip.

"There was no Guinness," Komocsin/Azarov said.

"It isn't my favourite."

"You looked me up, then."

"The least I could do." Komocsin waited, perhaps to see if Maxim said anything about Azarov, but he didn't.

"How is the meeting going?"

"It marches. And how is your leg?"

"Much better, thank you."

Maxim almost said that he was glad or something just as daft. "This time," Komocsin/Azarov said, "you do not need a knife."

He was looking at Maxim's left armpit—why did they call it a *shoulder* holster?—perhaps because of the way Maxim held his arm, or maybe the leather creaked, or most likely because Komocsin was part of the one per cent.

"But you may need something. There are terrorists from Germany, *your* Germany, in Luxembourg."

Maxim sipped and nodded. A big refrigerator in the corner began to hum loudly, and the woman left her ironing and slapped it a blow that would have left

Maxim spinning. It went on humming, and she went back to her ironing.

The blouses hung over the chair backs.

"Do you have any idea who they are after?"

"No. Your professor is the most famous. Him or the German."

"Is that all?"

"That, and the beer, yes, it was all."

"Thank you. I'll buy it next time."

"I hope so." The voice seemed suddenly tired.

Maxim left his beer half finished and walked out, trying not to hurry.

·

At the château gate half a dozen demonstrators had gathered, holding placards with anti-nuclear symbols and mushroom clouds on them. They booed Maxim as he showed his pass at the gate and strode out along the curving drive.

The session had broken up. The French delegation was already climbing into its black Citröens as he reached the little crowd in front of the building.

He found the Sûreté captain at the edge of the crowd. "I've been told there are terrorists from Germany here—"

"Is that what your Russian spy said?"

"You said *yourself* that was the real risk."

"How can you be sure he really is a Russian spy?"

"Our intelligence people have got him on file . . ." He saw the captain wasn't believing anything he said. The French had gone, the Germans were gliding away, their own hired Mercedes were backing up to the little pavement.

"It went like a dream," Quinton enthused. "You missed the best of it, of course. What *was* that all about? I really do think we may get an agreement. Our man was outstanding, quite first-class."

Maxim was listening, but only to the distance. Nobody had done anything to the French, nobody anything to the Germans. And probably nobody would do anything to Professor Tyler.

"Is there any other route we can take?" he asked the captain.

"We have to go up to the big road. The village is a no-end." He looked at Maxim with bland eyes.

"Harry—" Tyler called, and he slid into the back seat beside him, and the car purred away.

"There's a terrorist threat," he said.

"What can we do about it?" Tyler asked cheerfully. He was basking in the morning's glory.

"I don't know, but . . ." From his seat beside the driver, the captain looked at him sourly. The car leant over as they swung out of the gateway and the crowd of demonstrators waved their placards and shouted something Maxim didn't understand.

The lane led up through steep hairpin bends to the autoroute above, going through clumps of pines where a Boy Scout could have set an ambush. But if it came to that, a Boy Scout could have cut a hole anywhere in Senningen's mesh fence and thrown a grenade through the conference window. He might not have got out alive, but a terrorist who doesn't care about that—and there were plenty—is virtually unstoppable.

Then he saw it.

A small stream came trickling down the hillside so that, at some time, they had wrapped it up to pass quietly under the road instead of flooding it. A simple length of concrete drainage pipe, perhaps eighteen inches diameter. Quite standard.

"Schnell!" he shouted. *"Vite, vite!* Go for Christ's sake GO—" and he dragged Tyler down off the seat as the startled driver rammed down his foot, the automatic gearbox thumped and then wailed and the car shot around the next bend.

Behind them, the road blasted open. Something slammed into their backside, sending the Mercedes staggering across the road with the rear window crazed over. Then they were accelerating uphill, never mind anything coming down, and rocking crazily out into the hooting traffic on the main road.

"That's it," Maxim said. "Slow down. *Moins de vitesse.*" He helped Tyler back onto the seat. The car slowed but began to weave as the driver's shakes caught up with him.

The captain said something sharp, and they straightened out.

"What about the other car?" Tyler looked back at the blind rear window.

"They can't have done worse than run into a hole. Keep going."

"Major," the captain said respectfully, "how did you know?"

"The culvert. Under the road. A standard place for terrorists. They've used it a dozen times in Ireland, and over here . . . Also, I could have been wrong."

"I am glad, Harry, that you took that risk," Tyler said.

By the time they reached the hotel, there was already a small and over-excited group of police around the doorway. Maxim and the captain hustled Tyler into the scrum of uniforms and they charged through the lobby to a waiting lift.

Once inside, everybody seemed to let go a sigh of relief at the same time.

"Who's got the key?" Maxim asked.

Nobody had the key. Everybody thought that somebody else had it.

"Christ!"

"You wait," the captain said as they got out. "I will get it. If the terrorists were there, they will not be here."

They stood around the lift doors as he rode down again. A man came round the far end of the corridor, and everybody turned to meet him, but he was elderly and shambling. In the dim light Maxim didn't recognise him until he said—"Professor Tyler?" then lifted a heavy pistol and fired twice.

Tyler gasped and collapsed against Maxim, knocking him off balance as he snatched for his own gun.

Charles Farthing said: "I will tell you just why—"

Maxim shot him three times. Drawing his own pistol far too late, one of the police went forward and laid a hand against Farthing's neck. He looked back at Maxim with suspicious awe.

"Bon groupement, monsieur."

It was very good grouping. The three holes in Farthing's chest could have been covered by the palm of a small hand.

234

Maxim handed over his revolver, automatically swinging out the cylinder and emptying the chambers so that it couldn't fire by accident.

"Both dead on arrival at the hospital," George said heavily. "We rather forgot about Farthing. Farthing the grenade, Farthing the shotgun, we should have guessed at Farthing the pistol. I suppose he must have read the letter before sending it on to Jackaman."

"He was carrying it around for a month or two," Agnes said. "And it doesn't sound as if he could afford much else to read. Perhaps after a time he started to blame Tyler for Etheridge's death. Fellow Yorkshireman and all that."

George stood up, stretched, and walked slowly to the window. A military band was rehearsing on the Horse Guards and a thin strain of music worked its way in through the heavy glass. "Did you find out what had happened to Farthing in court?"

"He got a fine for the grenade and a suspended sentence for the shotgun."

"We should have had him *shot*," George snapped.

"In the end, we did." She stood beside him, staring blankly down to the trees at the bottom of Number 10's garden, now showing a faint dusting of new green. "And Tyler too. I suppose."

"Harry kept him alive long enough. I think we've got an agreement with the French, they were the ones who mattered, of course, and now if anybody comes up with some silly story about Tyler having *eaten* somebody back in the war—that's just defaming the dead, who can't answer back. Typically crude Soviet propaganda. Not really too unhappy an ending."

"And what about our Harry?" She said it without any trace of fake Cockney.

"The embassy bailed him, and if Luxembourg brings any charges there is going to be one almighty coolness about their security standards. First the bomb and then . . . the only trouble seems to be some local cop claiming that Farthing had already surrendered when Harry shot him. Bloody fool."

"I always said he'd kill somebody. I just didn't expect to be glad. Poor Harry."

"You aren't getting sentimental about him in your old age, are you?" George asked politely.

"Me? No, duckie, not me." She began to laugh quietly, to herself, and then in the middle of it, to cry.

The morning session at Senningen had none of the cheerful babble of the day before. They sat down very quietly, all wearing black armbands and the French delegation with identical black silk ties.

"In honourable memory of our late colleague," the French delegate said, "I suggest that we speak English today." There was a murmur of agreement. It was also a tactful move, since Tyler's replacement—a middle-aged semi-scholar from the International Institute of Strategic Studies—spoke French rather badly.

"Thank you," he said in a clogged voice, then coughed his throat clear. "I will speak from Professor Tyler's notes . . . He says—he believes that we can no longer rely upon an American Armageddon . . ."

Sitting behind him, alongside the British First Secretary who was nominally his warder, Maxim began to pray silently.

Oh God, if there is a God, save my soul, if I have a soul.